PRAISE FOR

DUNGEON LORDS: THE LOST DISCIPLE

"The world-building is rich and meticulously crafted, with each location and moment steeped in history, mystery, and a sense of consequence. The setting feels alive, full of secrets waiting to be unearthed."

"Dungeon Lords is a thought-provoking read for fans of darker, more layered fantasy. It's a storyline that invites you to sit with its themes and characters, and it's likely to linger in your mind long after you turn the last page."

"Dungeon Lords: Fate of Evania is a masterful fusion of storytelling and artistry. J.B. Coleman has raised the bar for a fully immersive world that feels as real as the air we breathe."

DUNGEON LORDS
THE LOST DISCIPLE

FATE OF EVANIA: BOOK ONE

dungeonlords.com

By
J.B. Coleman

ISBN 979-8-9869966-4-6

Book Cover by GetCovers

Edited by Jennifer Coleman & the author.

1st edition

Follow Dungeon Lords

Discord – dungeonlords.com/community/
Bluesky – dungeonlords.com/bsky/
Facebook – dungeonlords.com/fb/

For Extended Lore Content:

dungeonlords.com/foe/

For Pat Offerman, my high school English teacher, who encouraged my dreams of becoming an author from the very start. She read my earliest stories, edited my books, and always pushed me to keep writing. Her guidance and belief in me shaped the writer I am today. Though she's no longer here, her influence lives on in every page.

CONTENTS

Dracarys
Nimbur
Nevareth
Lysira
Mirasor
Caelum Rift
Underoth
Incarta
Morgrid
Umbra's Veil
Zelira
Map of
Evania

PROLOGUE: TWISTED PROPHESIES

The last thing he remembered was death and a flash of bright green light. It was a blinding light and then weightlessness as he hurled down the mountainside.

It had all gone wrong. The war wasn't supposed to end this way. Cosimir the Eternal had ruled over Evania for over three-hundred years. Everyone in the land feared him and his Dark Mage, Eldryn. They had taken the throne from the Evania family by killing every member that bore their name. The only family that history remembered ruling this great country.

Pain. He remembered the pain of smashing into rocks on his way down the mountainside. His vision was blurry. Things were dimming to gray.

The war. The first war had been waged by the kingdoms, rejecting Cosimir's rule. That was until a Scourge was unleashed upon the land and the twelve kingdoms had to dig their way underground to survive. The Scourge thrived in the sun, they'd said. Their once mighty rulers now mockingly deemed "Dungeon Lords" by the new, cruel tyrant Cosimir. All forced to live under the ground like rats.

Darkness. Darkness like the dungeon kingdom he had grown up in. For centuries, his people had been down there. Safer than the surface where Cosimir had ruled. Dark dungeons, lit only by the subfluore crystals of Mt. Fluore, the very mountain where Cosimir kept his rule.

Visions. Visions like the ones flashing before his eyes right now. He couldn't control them. His vision was getting dark. Eli. Eli's visions. Visions given to him by the god of the heavens, Solana. Visions that Cosimir would fall. Visions that Eli himself would be the one to do it.

Betrayal. Eli had betrayed them all. Eli's visions had convinced the kingdoms to provide their princes and princesses to follow Eli and rally the kingdoms. One noble from each kingdom to help lead the rebellion. Armies of brave men and women amassed to take back Evania. Battles. So many battles, all leading to taking Mt. Fluore and killing Cosimir.

Disgust. The conversation that he'd had with Eli on the eve of battle. How he was so scared to sacrifice himself for the kingdom. How he hadn't gotten a choice to be the chosen one that Solana had blessed with the visions of hope. Outright disgust he felt as he watched Eli kill Cosimir with a strange spear, and then take the tyrant's place on the throne.

The magic. Something had hit them all once the spear had pierced the tyrant. He'd felt heavier after he'd picked himself up off the floor and saw the traitor on the throne, with no time to judge what had happened to himself. He just knew he'd been boiling with rage at the betrayal.

Death. Who died? Now, as he stumbled down the mountainside, he couldn't remember. Someone had died. Eli had thought they'd betrayed him. It was ironic because Eli was the real traitor.

The roar. He'd remembered roaring in anger and charging at Eli, ready to rip him limb from limb. Ready to kill him and send the bastard straight down to Baladan where they'd just sent Cosimir.

Falling. Pain. The green light had sent him through the opening of Cosimir's throne room and down the mountainside. The pain of walking was now almost too much for him to bear. Where was he going? He felt like he'd known for a moment, but now the thought was gone.

His hands were heavy. His vision was closing in on him. He lifted his hands to his face as he walked. Hands? Paws? Such an odd curse.

The ground gave way beneath him as his feet slipped on a loose rock that gave way.

Falling. His head smashed hard into the ground as he rolled down the hill, and he remembered no more.

CHAPTER ONE

WHISPERS OF WINDS AND WAR

The burning sun shone down on the sleepy little town of Graeton. It was a mostly unremarkable town as far as size goes, like much of the other surface towns throughout Evania. It was a close-knit town of few neighborhoods, and at its center, the bulk of the town was taken up by the main square.

The main square was a wide cobblestone square, but it was where all the activity of the town took place. A couple of small shops and the tavern owned by a local dwarf named Tobi made up the perimeter. The one thing that commanded attention in Graeton, though, was the church. It towered above the main square, its tall stone column reaching high towards the sky, bringing a feeling of peace to the town, a connection to their god, Solana.

It seemed peculiar that the main square was so large for such a small town, but the amount of commerce that took place within Graeton made it a necessity. For today, like most other days, stalls were set up throughout the large square filled with merchants selling their wares, and those who wished to purchase them. It wasn't only townspeople that would make purchases. Large covered wagons from out of town would come for entire shipments of items to take back to their underground kingdoms and small surface towns. The chatter in the town was loud as merchants worked their magic, trying to unload as much of their product as they could before the afternoon.

The fact was, afternoons were a pretty poor time to do business in Graeton. Just outside of town was a large, lush pine forest, the outlet of a very large valley of trees that ran all the way between the mountain range that rose high in the west. The nearby mountain was so large and ominous that it almost blocked out the entire western hemisphere of the sky, casting the early afternoon of Graeton into deep, chilly shadows until true dark set in. The street lamps powered by rare subfluore crystals helped light the streets after dark, but it still made for a gloomy atmosphere compared to the little daylight they received.

In the little tavern on the main square, Tobi the dwarf walked hurriedly back and forth behind the bar. He knew that there would be a mad rush coming soon as all the potato farmers headed in from their fields (for potatoes were all that would grow well in bulk in their shadowy existence), and the other townsfolk either settled into their houses or headed to the warm, fire-lit tavern to pass the afternoon away. That's why Tobi had known Graeton was a good place to open a tavern: the townsfolk had a lot of downtime. When people were bored, they would drink.

Tobi was a young dwarf. Having lived over a hundred years, he was considered a young adult by any human standard. He had a neatly braided brown beard and a short, stalky build, much like his ancestors who used to mine subfluore crystals up in the mountains. Because he was a dwarf and a bit out of his element when he'd started the tavern, he had a subfloor installed behind the bar that brought him up to the height of everyone else who entered. He would go on and on to patrons about how this was the best way to serve them, but in reality, he just wanted to fit in. It also made it so none of his employees could go behind the bar easily, and that was just fine with him they keep out.

"Aye! Thora!" he yelled across the bar to his bar maid. "Three drinks here for them folks outside!"

Thora, a dark-skinned woman in her mid-twenties, looked up from the table where she was currently serving an ale to a dark stranger. "Catch you later, tall and broody," she said to the hooded man sitting at the table as she made her way over to the bar. Her green skirt billowed around her ankles as she moved, her work smock following the motion of her dress. "I'll get these right out to them, *Andre*." She said to Tobi, using the endearing word that meant 'father' in her native tongue.

Thora started working for Tobi when he found her living on the street as a very young girl. Her family had been killed in a raid by Emperor Cosimir's army, and Tobi brought her into his care after finding her on the streets of a nearby town where he was doing some business. She started by helping him clean the floors and restock the ale, but as she got old enough, she remembered orders and delivered beverages and food to customers with greater ease. Thora made it a habit to work every day of her life against Tobi's suggestions to take some days off. Unfortunately for Thora, she knew nothing else but work.

Grabbing the drinks, Thora set them on her wooden tray and headed out the swinging tavern doors. The bright sun blinded her for a moment before she blinked the sunspots out of her eyes and headed to the tall standing table occupied by the only outside customers. They were three regulars she was used to serving often: Lena, Mathias, and Osric.

She could see they were in the middle of a heated discussion, so approached carefully so as not to disrupt them and began quietly serving the drinks around them as they spoke.

"We had just gotten some new dissertations in on a wagon from Baeville," said Mathias, the town healer. His long, pointy nose and spectacles were unmistakable, making him a familiar sight in town. He often received good-natured jests about a possibility of goblin ancestry from friends. This always seemed to rile him up a bit, because the only goblins he knew of were simple of mind, and he always fancied himself as an intellect.

Dressed in his usual bright-red, intricately detailed tunic, Mathias carried an assortment of herbs and remedies in pouches strapped to his belt, a true symbol of his role. Despite his larger stomach size, he often seemed out of place when standing next to others, his rugged features softened only by his kind eyes and the ever-present satchel on his back, brimming with plants and tools of his trade. "I was hoping to find something that could help me figure out what those strange bumps are that plague that poor little Meeko boy."

Standing next to the man was the tall, slender potato farmer, Osric. He was always in town around lunchtime to refuel for lunch and restock on oil for his torches. Being the owner of a few fields outside of town, he saw it as his duty to work through the shadowy evening and make sure his work for the day got finished. His face and hands covered in dirt, as they always were, he pulled nervously at the collar of his shirt at the sound of what Mathias was telling them. "Nothing like Cosimir's Scourge, I hope?" He bent down a little so he was closer to Mathias' height and whispered, "Knowing that old bastard, he'd love to bring that damn plague back and drive us all underground. Stop all the rebellion once and for all."

Mathias waved his hand. "Nah. Nothing like that. From what I read, it was some kind of dragmar pox. Boy has likely been wandering around the woods too much."

Across the table, the elf, Lena, threw him a dirty look. Her old, wrinkled face wrinkled even more as she glared at him. Mathias withdrew a bit, because she was a formidable form. Standing taller than even Osric, she towered above everyone else in town. She would often come into town to sell her goods that she hunted and gathered from the nearby forest where she lived. Her potions were a hot item, not just in town, but throughout the land. Much like everything in her life, her clothes were handmade, died a light lavender color from some flowers she had gathered in the woods. She was often found taking a break from her stall at the noon hour with Mathias and Osric, her two closest neighbors to the woods.

Glancing back at Lena nervously, Mathias continued. "The boy doesn't know what he's doing out there. You're an expert! Probably stuck his hand right inside a dragmar hole. Dirty little creatures." This seemed to lighten her expression, and she brushed strands of her white hair out of her face and continued to listen.

"Anyways," Mathias kept on, "I was reading in my rooftop study, enjoying the weather, when a crazy light came down from the mountaintop. Seemed to light up the entire sky! It was an eerie green. Never seen anything like it before. Sent a chill right down my spine."

Lena cleared her throat to speak in her slow, rhythmic tone. "The woods were full of a strange wind last night as well. Normally it comes from the valley, but last night it was coming through from the southeast. An icy chill that was not of this season." Mathias nodded at her, indicating he had felt the change in temperature as well.

Osric straightened up to his full height. "The armies were meant to reach Fluore in the coming days. Perhaps they have reached the end of their mission? For better or for worse..." he trailed off.

Thora overheard this as she was walking away from the table, and her ears perked up. The rebel armies of the kingdoms had been waging war to free the land from Cosimir's harsh reign for the last three years. It had finally come where they had freed the kingdoms and were making one final assault on Cosimir's near-impenetrable stronghold of Mt. Floure.

"Could be," said Mathias, cocking his head to the side. "I heard rumors they were still a week out. Hard to tell as they were approaching from Morgrid in the west. If they reached the peak last night, they got blasted to hell by that damn dark mage. That light lit up the whole sky!"

Now Thora turned back around to face them and join in the conversation. "That crazy lightning last night? I didn't see it direct, but it sure lit up the square while I was out here sweepin' the deck. The whole place bathed in green. Never seen anything like it."

Osric shook his head. "So one way or another, it's likely over now. Hard to believe. Feels like it's been thirteen years, not three. The war's been hell on the farm. Cosimir's goons raiding to feed that damn army of Dark Humans. It was a blessed day when Eli and the others drove them out and headed north to free the lumber mills."

"It was a good day indeed," Lena chimed in. "With the trade routes around the mills freed up, the Dungeon Lords were free to make their own decisions on shipments. My moonshade potion exports have been in such high demand, I can't keep up. I keep raising my prices, but the demand just isn't dying down. Guess that happens when you need a lot of healing due to the war."

All of their heads turned as the tavern doors swung open. They all dropped their gaze as Tobi came out to greet them. It was rare that he would exit the tavern and his raised floor. He looked up at all of them and opened his arms. "How are the drinks, my friends? Gossiping about that crazy light last night?

It's all anyone inside can talk about." He turned to Thora. "People in here waiting on some drinks, Thora. I can't keep up all by myself!"

Thora gave a slight curtsy. "Yes, *Andre*. Right away." She headed back inside, and Tobi made his way over to the table that towered over his head.

He stood back so he could see his patrons as he spoke. "Bit of a shady fella in a gray cloak inside. Said he came from the mountains last night. Said he heard all kinds of weird noises after the light hit. Not natural, whatever happened up there. I fear we came out the worst on it."

Mathias held up his hands to calm him. "Don't be so negative, my young friend. Cosimir the Eternal was pretty old and held together by all sorts of dark spells. The light could have simply been the dark magic escaping as Eli blasted him to dust. We'll have to wait for official messengers to be sure."

Tobi nodded, but also said, "You always call me young, Good Healer, but you know I'm twice your age, yeah?"

Mathias narrowed his eyes behind his spectacles to focus in on Tobi closer. "Ahh, I always forget how dwarfs age so much slower than us humans. You're lucky you still look so young, next to an old wrinkled goblin-face like me!"

This sent a laugh across the four of them. It was rare that he would dare mention his goblin characteristics. It was obvious he was elated at the possibility of the war being over. Lena even gave a slight chuckle. "Either way, I always want to think on the positive side of things. Even if Cosimir won, we still have the rest of the army as well as the Dungeon Lords to keep the campaign moving forward. The most that this should affect us is a minor flux in our economy until things get back in order again. Graeton is much too small to matter too much to either side, or to be involved in any serious way," Mathias finished.

As he said this, a swell of birds rose into the sky from the forest a short ways away. They all looked at the trees, seeing an odd rustling.

"The army?" asked Osric, his body stark still, except for his slightly shaking hands.

"Which army?" asked Tobi, wishing he was back at his bar where his axe was strapped to the underside, waiting for trouble.

"Too small of a commotion to be an army," Lena said simply.

"Then what the..." Mathias began, before he was cut off by screams of people on the outer edge of town.

People began running back towards them, away from the stirring in the woods. They turned and watched them fleeing towards the large church that towered over the square, running inside for sanctuary. The four all looked at each other, wondering if they should run, when the cause of the commotion burst out into the town square.

A large beast with a large furry head was charging towards people, anyone it could find. Mathias found it odd that it didn't appear to be trying to attack them. It was walking on two legs, reaching its arms out as if pleading to people. When it was close enough, they could hear it speak in the common tongue. "Help! What happened to me? Help me!"

As everyone cleared the square, the beast stopped its gaze on the four standing at the tall tavern table, the only ones who didn't seem to run away. It charged over towards them. Mathias adjusted his glasses to make sure he was seeing things correctly. It was the large head of a lion set atop a humanesque body. It was wearing a blue tunic and brown pants, all bursting at their seams. The four braced themselves as the creature drew closer.

"What the fuck is that?" Tobi screamed at the others as he pulled a dagger from his boot, bracing for impact.

Chapter Two

A Beast Among Men

Drinks spilled, and the table shook as the lion-man ran into it and slammed his paws down hard on top. The trio at the table were knocked back a few steps, and Osric cowered down and started shaking. This left Tobi the dwarf to square off against the giant lion. You could see the fear in the young dwarf's eyes, but he gritted his teeth and took a step toward the towering beast, swinging his small blade.

"No! Stop!" the beast cried, sticking out his paw and placing it on Tobi's head. His reach was so long he could keep the dwarf at arm's length as he swung the knife. He turned to the others who were regaining their footing. "What am I?" he yelled at them. "I need help!"

Mathias adjusted his spectacles again to get a better look. "What *are* you?" he asked quizzically. "You don't know?"

The lion was still panting from his sprint, his eyes wide in horror. He opened his mouth to speak, but then Tobi changed tactics and drove his knife upward into the lion's forearm. The beast let out the roar of a lion as he screamed in pain and stepped back, holding onto his arm.

Tobi made as if to charge after his foe, but before he could, Lena stepped forward and grabbed him by the collar of his shirt. "What in the hell did you do *that* for?" she asked Tobi angrily, gesturing at the lion, who was now hunched over and staggering around in pain.

"Ain't ever seen anythin' like it!" Tobi yelled, trying to get her to let him go.

Lena sighed. "So we're attacking strangers now?"

"Well... yeah! When the stranger is a fuckin' lion!"

"He's speaking native, you imbecile. Calm down!" Mathias said sharply to Tobi as he stepped forward to calm the lion down enough to look at him. He held up his hands to show he meant no harm. "Friend!" he said, barely audible over the lion's roars. "Friend! I am a healer! Please, let me have a look."

The lion calmed down enough to let Mathias approach. "Ow! Ahh! Youch! Tell me you've got some magic in the dinky little satchel, old man!"

Mathias chuckled. "Not that kind of healer, friend. The magic kind tend to lurk in the dungeon kingdoms in the service of the Dungeon Lords. Especially now with the war going on."

The lion held out his arm for Mathias to look at, still groaning from the pain. "Service of the what?"

Mathias reached into his satchel for some silverbane sap and a bandage to fix up the wound. Though his head was down, he looked up questioningly at the lion-man. "Dungeon Lords. Those in charge of the underground kingdoms. You... you aren't from around here?"

The lion winced as Mathias pulled the sleeve of his tunic back to reveal the wound. "I...uh...I'm not sure," the lion answered half-heartedly.

"Interesting. And what's your name?" Mathias asked as he popped open the vial and dipped out some sap to put on the wound.

The lion let out another roar, and Mathias pushed the sap into the wound. "I... don't seem to know that either," he said, wincing in pain. At this, Tobi calmed down from behind Mathias, and Lena set him down. Osric finally stood from his cowering position, and the three of them listened intently to the exchange happening before them.

A sad look fell over Mathias' face. "Can you bend your head down real quick, friend?" As the lion got down into a kneeling position and leaned forward, Mathias ran his hand through the long, fluffy mane. He felt a clump of matted hair near the back and felt a lump. The lion winced when he touched it. When Mathias pulled his hand away, it was covered in crimson. Mathias heard Osric whimper behind him.

"You've had quite a head injury, friend, which explains the memory loss. Obviously the least of your worries at the moment, being a lion and all," Mathias quipped, half smiling. The lion didn't seem to find this funny. "What should we call you?" he added as he went back to bandaging the lion's forearm.

The lion just looked at him and shrugged, swaying a little from all the pain he was in. Mathias thought it to be a sad look on the creature's face, though he couldn't tell for certain. "Hmm, that's better," he said, finishing the bandage. "No more attacking our friend here!" he snapped, looking back at Tobi. "Our friend... Leo?"

The lion shrugged. "Not very original, but as good as anything else.

"Great!" exclaimed Mathias. "Now, if you would be so kind, my dear Leo, and come back to the office so we can get a look at that head of yours?"

Leo nodded and started to follow Mathias, when a loud yell rang out. There was a loud crash, and Leo collapsed to the ground.

"Ayyaaa!" screamed Thora.

In all the commotion, they hadn't noticed her step back outside carrying a large metal cauldron they used to make soup. Hearing the commotion of people outside, she had glimpsed the creature bounding down on them and grabbed the cauldron to attack.

There was a gasp behind them. Looking back at the door, Thora spoke to the shocked patron in the gray cloak who had followed her out. "What's up, dark and broody? I just saved your life!" The man gave a wide-eyed look towards the lion and glanced at the others standing around him, before bolting off around the corner of the tavern.

"Thora! What the fuck was that?" Tobi yelled at her, gesturing towards the giant, unconscious Leo on the ground. Thora just stood there, looking every part of the daughter who has just been loudly scolded by her father.

"Like daughter, like father," said Lena. "You weren't any better, you big oaf!" Lena stepped forward and bent down to examine Leo. "This poor creature has no memory, Thora, and your father stabbed him in the arm. Doesn't look like his head will get better anytime soon."

"Aye," said Mathias, bending down to check on their new friend. "Now who wants to tell me how we're going to get a large, unconscious lion-man back to my office?"

Some time later, after quickly retrieving the death cart from Mathias' office and struggling to lift Leo up into it, the group snuck him across town. They had worked as quickly as they could to bring him back to the healer's office. The townspeople had come back out from the church with probing eyes wondering what had happened to the beast, so they were glad they had covered the cart with a tarp for the trek back.

After delivering the lion, Tobi had gone back to tending the tavern. Osric had gone back to his farm to catch what was left of the day's good light, and Lena had excused herself to go back to the woods and gather a more moonshade to make more of her famous healing potions; they worked wonders on physical wounds, and their new friend was sporting many. Thora stayed behind to assist Mathias. She had felt guilty for knocking the poor beast out and had volunteered to stay and help with his recovery.

In the office, three cots were spread out on which patients could sit or lie as Mathias ministered to them. A fire was roaring in the fireplace next to a long table full of cabinets and storage boxes where Mathias kept all of his herbs and medicines. Beyond this table was a staircase that led up to

Mathias' loft bedroom, and beyond that a ladder that led up to the rooftop study Mathias always bragged so much about.

Down in the first floor patient area, they had to push two cots together in order to lay Leo down as he was such a wide beast. Mathias directed Thora to tend the fire and get some water boiling so they could clean the lion's wounds.

"Where do you suppose he's from?" asked Thora. "I've seen nothing like him. Beasts are usually much...simpler."

Mathias was bustling about his herb drawers, trying to find a draught that would help wake Leo up so they could find out more about him. "No one has seen anything like him, Thora. Not in this lifetime. Magic like this hasn't existed for centuries. At least not out in the open." The healer glanced sideways at her to see how she reacted to this news. He could see she was looking concerned. "He came down by way of the mountain. No doubt related to that green flash last night. Magic," he said in a serious monotone. "And trouble," he added, shaking his head as if agreeing with himself.

Thora examined Leo closely for the first time as he lay there. He wore a splendid blue tunic with gold embroidery, and a brown fastening ribbon. His fluffy mane overflowed over the top of the tunic. Leather bracers were sported on each arm, and out of the bracers where there should have been paws were furry, beast-like claws that still seemed to function like a human hand. His brown pants led down to what used to be boots. Now they had fur puffing out of the top of the boot, and the claws appeared to have forcefully pushed their way out the toe of the boot. Though he had lion paws for feet, his legs were still straight, like a person.

Leo let out a groan as Mathias pried his mouth open and dumped the draught he had found down his throat.

"Poor thing," Thora said, reaching out and grabbing his paw, stroking the soft fur. "I feel so bad for him."

Mathias chuckled. "You, of all people, should. You're the one who gave him a second lump on the head." She frowned at this, looking sad and guilty. Mathias glanced over at the fire to check on the water. "Thora, the water, dear. Can you grab it?"

Thora turned and grabbed the cauldron of water by the handle and lifted it off the hook, bringing it closer to the bed. Mathias readied his rags as he waited for the water to cool enough to touch and watched as Leo came around. Finally, when the lion opened his eyes to look around, Mathias tested the temperature and could dip the rag into the water without burning himself.

"Stay still, my friend. I need to clean your head wound," Mathias said as he pulled the dripping rag out and walked around to the head of the cots.

"Wha... What happened now?" Leo asked, looking around the room, dazed.

"Well," said Mathias, "our dear Thora over here thought you were a hideous beast and clobbered you upside the head with a cauldron, much like the one she has right over there on the ground. So better be on your best behavior right now." Mathias smiled at his own joke.

"Thought I was a hideous beast?" Leo jested lightly. "Wonder what gave her that idea?"

Thora leaned into Leo's line of sight. "I'm so sorry, Sir. I thought I was protecting my *andre* and his friends. We've never seen anything like you."

"Imagine my panic when I saw myself," Leo said, letting out a half laugh, half slight roar. "What is this place? Ouch!"

Leo winced, and Mathias dug the rag in deeper to clean out the bloody head wound. "My office," Mathias said as he worked. "As I stated before your last unfortunate incident, I am a healer. And by the way, you don't happen to remember your name or where you're from now, do you?"

The lion paused for a second before he answered. "I...uhh... no, nothing."

"Hmm... hoped that second jolt to the head would have at least jogged something, but apparently, brute force isn't the cure for your amnesia," said Mathias.

There was a creaking noise from the stairs and they all turned to look, but nothing was there. "Ahh," said Mathias, "those valley winds have this old place creaking all the time. Nothing new."

Thora nodded in agreement, as the bar always gave off eerie creaking sounds at night when she was closing it down for the day, and she was there all alone. "Mathias says you came from the mountain. Did you see the green light last night? Is that why you're like this?" she felt his mane as she spoke.

Again, Leo took a pause. His head hurt something fierce and trying to think about what he remembered hurt it more. "I... the only thing I remember is waking up next to a tree. There was a rock slide nearby, so I assumed I'd slid down the mountain. Imagine my surprise when I held my hands out and saw these giant claws." He held them up to show them. "I bolted to a nearby creek and looked in the water... the beast was staring back at me... I was staring back at me."

"So you weren't always a beast?" asked Thora. "You remember that?"

"Yeah. I'm definitely supposed to be human, or at least my mind thinks so. Otherwise, it wouldn't have been such a shock, right?" Leo looked as though he was lost, and Thora felt bad for him.

"Almost done here," Mathias interjected, reaching for a bandage for Leo's head wounds. "Thora, dear, a little more water before I stitch him shut, please."

Thora quickly raised the cauldron, and then dropped it in shock as something metal zinged off the side. The cauldron hit the ground with a loud thunk, and water splashed up into the air. They all looked down and saw a dagger laying next to the cauldron on the stone floor. They all looked in the direction it came from and saw a shadowy figure standing on the stairs.

In an instant, the figure jumped over the railing and bolted towards Mathias, another dagger already in hand. Mathias yelped as he dodged too slowly, and the dagger made a cut across his right cheek. Leo made to get out of the bed, but by the time he made a move, the water cauldron went sailing through the air and down on top of the assailant's head. The figure didn't even utter a sound as he dropped to the ground, but his dagger did as it fell from his hand and clattered across the stone floor.

"Assassin!" Mathias hissed, spitting on the man's body, and standing up. He reached up and felt the red, fresh blood pouring down from his cheek. "That dagger was aimed at you, my friend," Mathias said, pointing at Leo with his reddened finger.

Leo sat up on the cot and slowly made his way over to the figure sprawled out on the ground. He didn't recognize who it was, but even if he'd known him in the past, he wouldn't know who he was now either way.

"Oh no," said Thora, setting down the cauldron and examining the man on the ground. "Dark and broody! How could you?" she asked, recognizing the patron in the gray cloak from the bar earlier.

"Apparently our friend Leo here isn't the only newcomer to town," said Mathias. "And you," he said, pointing at Thora. "If we ever find ourselves in a war, dear, remind me to make sure you have a cauldron to fight with."

Chapter Three

THE CHURCH OF SOLANA

The afternoon following the assassination attempt found Leo and Mathias feeling much better from their inflicted wounds. Lena had returned to them shortly after the assassin had been thwarted, an uncharacteristic look of shock on her face. She had almost dropped the Moonshade Potion she was carrying when she opened the door to the healer's parlor.

After the initial shock, she became all business again, administering the potion to Leo and Mathias. The warm sensation of the potion comforted them, and by the next morning their physical wounds started to heal. The seemingly magical properties of the potion sped up the natural healing process within most living species, though for reasons unknown to Lena, it still didn't seem to work on pigs.

By the afternoon, Leo's head wounds were mostly closed shut. His memory hadn't recovered even a bit from the potion, as Lena had warned him it wouldn't. The gash on Mathias' cheek was mostly just a scar, which Lena assured him would mostly fade within the next three days. Impressed by the results of her potion, which he had previously dismissed as snake oil as there was no research to back up the healing properties of the moonshade plant, Mathias agreed to be Lena's regular customer when she had her new stock at market.

With physical wounds on the mend, Mathias released Leo from his care the following afternoon. Though he was free to go, the pair still had some business to tend to. The night of the assassination attempt they had dragged their would-be assassin out to the front of the healer's office where the lawman, Jareth, took him to the Graeton dungeon in the Church of Solana. Now they needed to go and question him.

The towering stone building of the church served many functions for the small town, being the focal point, and the main functioning structure for anything that wasn't a tavern, store, home, or merchant stall. The mayor had an office on the upper floors, the small academy for young students was held within the middle levels, and Jareth had an office near the church dungeon.

Leo was determined to find out why the assassin was after him, and Mathias wanted answers as well, having been attacked in his own home and place of business. The only problem was, the entire town was hunting for a humanoid beast, so Mathias had to go ahead of Leo and do some damage control. The merchants weren't at their stalls today for fear of the beast, and everyone was walking around meekly in the shadows, whispering rumors to each other, ready to dash back inside at a moment's notice.

Going out into the square, Mathias began shouting at anyone that could hear, "People! Citizens! Good people of Graeton! Please gather round!" The people in the square stared at him and slowly gathered in closer. "I would like to address the issue of the lion..."

"Is that what it was?" shouted an old lady from the crowd. "Looked like a damned beast from hell, it did!" Several others around her nodded.

Mathias knew this would not be easy. "No. Not from hell. From the mountain," he said, pointing up at Mt. Fluore behind them in the distance. "We're not sure how, but this beast used to be a man..."

"That what it told you?" screamed another panicked villager, this time a younger man whom Mathias recognized as the mayor's messenger, Idon. "On good terms with this lion then? Best of pals?"

The old healer rubbed at his temples. "I know, the likes of this lion-man have not been seen before, but he is the victim here. A victim of memory loss. And a victim of...” Mathias knew this next part wouldn't go over well, “the victim of an assassination attempt.”

A hushed murmur ran through the crowd as the panic grew. Mathias could hear some whispers as they grew louder, and the common thing his old ears picked up was “...the war...”. He knew he needed to address this.

“We do not know if this has to do with the war,” Mathias yelled out, louder than before, to drive the point home. “We have not seen the brunt of the war here in Graeton. The odd bit of raiding here and there, but compared to the rest of Evania, we've come out on top. All I know, is that Leo, this lion-man, wishes to question his assassin, who is currently being held in the dungeon. We need everyone to remain calm, and give him passage from my office to the dungeon. After he gets his answers, he will be on his way, and we can all get back to our normal lives. This is just a blip in our normal routines, and everything will be back to business as normal within the week.”

Everyone nodded. One person could be heard clapping, and Mathias was surprised to hear the sound coming from the grand church behind him. He turned to see who it was, and was surprised to see Mayor Merrik Thornvale approaching him at a slow gait. His head bobbed up and down as he walked, caused by a hunch in his back, and a limp in his step. No one in town knew what had disfigured the man, but there were rumors that his own mother had thrown him down a well as a child. Given his experience with the man, Mathias didn't blame her. He could see Thornvale's beady little eyes fixed on him, zeroing in on his prey.

Once he reached the spot next to Mathias, he turned to him to whisper so no one else could hear, "I knew you were aiming for my post, you old swindler. Trying to gain the favor of the people? No one addresses them like this but me!"

Mathias chuckled out loud. "I have no want of politics, my good man. I leave that to the people of... diminished morals, such as yourself."

Thornvale shot back a crooked smile and turned to address the crowd. "Yes! Yes, good people. Our *town healer* here is correct." He said the words 'town healer' with a sharp, acidic undertone, as if to drive home the point that was all Mathias would ever be.

"Though close to the stronghold of the Forever King, we are hiding in plain sight, and war will not be upon us." It seemed to calm the people down as Mayor Thornvale spoke these words. "As for our new friend, let us let him pass, shall we?" he asked, throwing his arms out wide and gesturing towards the crowd.

A look of panic came over everyone as they all turned in horror to look. Coming from the direction of Mathias' office,

Leo was walking towards the crowd timidly, looking as though he expected any one of them to attack at any second. The crowd slowly parted to let him through, and he made his way to towards the church where Mathias stood next to the crooked old man.

The hunched mayor stared up in awe as Leo stood next to him. Leo smiled back and stuck out his paw to shake hands with the man in charge of the town. After doing so he realized it was probably a bad move. Something in his brain was telling him he wasn't used to having menacing claws and fur where his hand had been, though he couldn't even remember what his hand had looked like.

The mayor took the paw daintily and gave it a small shake. He leaned in close, his head only coming up to the mid of Leo's chest. He beckoned him to lean closer with a gnarly finger. Leo bent down to listen.

"You go into that dungeon, you talk to that trash, and you leave, understand? We don't need freaks and abnormalities such as yourself here. You're bad for business." Standing tall the mayor gave the crowd a smile and gestured Leo towards the church doors.

Leo gave a look to Mathias, who shrugged and also gestured to the church, suggesting they get out of this situation as soon as possible. They turned and made their way towards the large wooden front doors of the church. Mathias turned to look at the crowd one last time before going inside. He could see Idon, the mayor's messenger, scurrying up to stand beside his boss. The two of them were whispering and glanced towards him and Leo.

Mathias knew their conspiring couldn't mean anything good for them, but also knew he and his new friend had pressing matters they needed to attend to inside the church.

Leo marveled at the inside of the church. From the moment they entered, it was too much to take in all at once. Stepping inside, they were in a small vestibule area. Beyond this small hallway were pillars that held up the main walls of the circular atrium, at the center of which sat an ornate golden alter.

Curious, Leo stepped into the main area and glanced up. From the outside of the church it looked like the height of the church helped support many levels of rooms. Leo could now see that most of the space was, in fact, one large room that appeared to go up forever. Along the endlessly upward ceiling there were paintings of the heavens, and beings that supposedly dwelt there.

At the very top, hanging from the ceiling was a statue. It was impossible to imagine the actual size of the statue if it still appeared so large from such a long way down. The statue was a majestic figure clothed in radiant robes of sunlit gold and sapphire blue. His eyes gleamed with a warm, golden light and his skin glowed with an otherworldly luminescence.

"You remember our God, Solana, yeah?" Mathias threw him an elbow and smiled, knowing the lion remembered little.

"I... no... can't say that I do," Leo stammered back.

"Ahh, well, I'm sure you'll be forgiven. Your state of mind is not your fault after all," said Mathias, only half joking. "This way!" he started walking and waved Leo on.

They walked through the side of the vestibule and down a flight of stone steps. Even though they were going down to the dungeon, everything still seemed very ornate, almost too perfect in its craftsmanship. At the bottom of the stairs they stepped out onto a large landing.

As Leo looked around, he could see that the large landing also served as an office. A wooden desk sat to one side, behind which were many bookshelves loaded with old tomes. Beyond the office was another flight of stairs that went down deep into the dungeons.

Mathias walked right up to the man sitting behind the desk. The lawman Jareth sat there, his face buried in a book. He looked almost annoyed as the old healer approached him. "What can I do for you, Mathias?" he asked. Then he looked past Mathias and his jaw dropped. "And your... friend?" he asked, trying not to sound nervous.

"That's Leo, he's fine," said Mathias, waving off Jareth's shock. "Are we able to go down and talk to the prisoner? We have some questions about why he was trying to kill my friend over there."

"Which prisoner?" Jareth laughed, as if they ever had more than one at a time in the small town. They occasionally had a drunk farmer in that needed to cool off for the night, but as far as big crimes went, Graeton was a pretty dry place. "Yeah, yeah," he continued, catching the glare Mathias gave him. "Head on down."

Mathias nodded his thanks and motioned for Leo to follow him down the stairs. Another intricately carved flight of stairs later and they found themselves in a long stone hallway filled with many sets of iron bars. This dungeon was set up to hold a dozen prisoners, but the place looked spotless, a sign that there was never very much activity down here.

The pair walked past several empty cells before they found the one occupied by the assassin. They approached slowly. They could barely see his face in the dim lighting of the dungeon. He had been stripped of his cloak, and they could now see a head of shocking, long white hair. He pushed his hooked nose out through the bars to greet them.

"You two are lucky to be alive," he said with a smirk. They could hear a bit of laughter in his voice. "Especially you, Faro."

The word hung in the air. Mathias looked at Leo, whose mouth had fallen open, shocked at hearing his real name for the first time since his accident.

CHAPTER FOUR

PIECES OF THE PUZZLE

The air hung thick with the silence that followed. The assassin continued to grin at them through the bars, relishing the fact that he knew things they didn't.

Leo's...or rather Faro's...mind was spinning. The name rang true to him. He couldn't remember much, but somehow he knew the assassin was telling the truth. His name was Faro, and he used to be human. Having two pieces to the puzzle strengthened his resolve to fully restore his memory and figure out the rest of his past. He felt a hole inside himself, knowing that he had a purpose to fulfill here. He just still wasn't sure what it was.

Mathias threw his lion friend a look to see if he was alright. Faro took a step towards the bars and puffed out his big, barrel chest to appear larger and more menacing. "Tell me everything you know, *assassin*," the last word hung in the air, dripping with anger.

"Well," the man said, "one thing for sure was that I was shocked when I saw a damned lion. I thought they were the ones 'lion'," he said, and Faro was confused until he realized the man was telling a joke. The man cackled.

"Enough!" Faro growled. "Who are *they*? Who sent you?"

"Only the elite hire Gnu," the man said. Faro assumed the man was talking about himself. "It was the big man on the mountain, of course!"

Mathias gasped. "Cosimir is still alive? What happened to the invading rebels?"

"Oh, you don't know much yet, do you?" Gnu said, snickering again. He paused, enjoying his momentary upper hand. "Cosimir is dead." This sentence hung between them. Mathias raised his eyes, shocked. Faro searched his thoughts to see if the name rang any bells, but frustratingly it didn't cause any revelation.

"So who is ruling now?" asked Mathias, confused. He had been so consumed with the news of the upcoming battle that he hadn't really thought about who would be in charge once it was all over, much less why they would want Faro dead.

Gnu sneered his smarmy sneer. "Seems to me like I'm giving you a lot of information for free. What's in it for me, old man?"

"Maybe not gettin' eaten by an angry fucking lion!" Faro growled, lunging forward and grabbing the bars with a loud clank. Gnu backed off slightly, but still not out of Faro's reach, showing he wasn't afraid.

"I'm sentenced for death either way, Beast. May as well get it over with," he said.

Mathias put a gentle hand on his friends middle back, the highest he could comfortably reach, and guided him back away from the bars. "I am a good, upstanding citizen here in town," Mathias said. "The town healer. Perhaps I can speak with the mayor on your behalf. Get a reduced sentence. Maybe even an exile to the Outwoods."

Gnu raised his fingers up to his mouth, as if thinking it over. "Shoot for the exile, or I'll escape this place eventually and come after you."

Mathias chuckled. "Solid stone rumored to have been crafted by the greatest artisans in the land. Sure, I'll take my chances. Now tell me, who is the new ruler on the mountain?"

"Some fella named Eli," said Gnu. The name Cosimir meant nothing, but this name, Eli, seemed to gnaw at Faro. Why did that name mean something to him? He looked over at Mathias to see if that name meant anything to him. He could tell that it did by the way the old healer's mouth hung open wide.

"Eli the Prophet?" he asked, dumbfounded. "Was... was that the plan?" he asked, looking at Faro. "Ahh, of course you wouldn't know." He turned back to Gnu. "Eli hired you?"

"Big bastard. Wore a horned helmet," said Gnu, but then looked Faro up and down. "Or maybe he got cursed like this fella and the horns were real, come to think of it. Anyways, yeah, he hired me. Told me he had a rogue that got away. He called in a handful of us. Those not so skilled as me hung around the mountains looking for a trace. Others went west. I saw the broken foliage and headed down to town here."

Mathias looked like he had a headache. His hand was raised up to his head, a finger pressed hard against each temple. "And you were sent to kill Leo...err, Faro?"

"Yeah," said Gnu, shrugging his shoulders. "Didn't think I'd be hunting a fuckin' lion-man, but Eli said we'd know him when we seen him. Said it was a lion. I didn't believe him. Coming out of that bar, I sure knew I'd found my mark. Thought the dwarf was going to do my job for me for a minute!" Gnu sounded excited.

"So, you didn't disappear after seeing him," said Mathias, piecing it together. "You waited in the shadows and watched until Thora knocked him out. Then you followed us back to my office and..."

"Yeah. That rooftop with all the books and parchment had pretty easy access from the trees, Doc. If it wasn't for bad timing from that gal you had with ya, I'd have hit my mark and you all would be dead! That horny bastard on the hill would be paying me pretty right now!" Gnu smiled at the thought, then his face fell, realizing his pay would never come.

Faro's head was spinning as he blankly stared into the dim, torch-lit dungeon. Someone was ruling. Then someone named Eli killed him. He had to have been with them there somehow, because now he was a cursed animal human like the new ruler on the mountain. He now knew for sure that his part in this was pretty big, but he still wasn't sure how he fit into the puzzle.

"What else do you know about me?" Faro asked him sharply.

Gnu thought for a minute. "Not much. Fella said we were hunting a colossal beast of a man that betrayed him. Said he'd pay a pretty fee in gold. Also said he was angry that your body wasn't found dashed on the side of the mountain as you were blasted out of the chamber opening. So that's why he had to call in the professionals. That's about it."

Blasted out? Opening? A flash of green light crept across Faro's memory. Yelling. Cold air. Was it him that had been yelling? Someone died. Who died? What else? Unfortunately nothing else came to his mind.

"Thank you for your cooperation," said Mathias. "And for your terrible timing and aim," he added with a smile.

Gnu waved him off. "Like I said, you're lucky to be alive. Dumb luck. Work on getting me out of that execution, Doc. We have a deal."

"Yes, yes, I'm a man of my word," Mathias waved him off as he turned to leave, motioning for Faro to follow him. "I will head up to see Mayor Thornvale right now."

Faro hesitated for a moment. He wanted to know more. He knew that Gnu likely didn't have anymore information, but he didn't know if he should try to press him for more details. Thinking better of it, he turned and followed Mathias up the perfectly carved stone staircase. He caught up to Mathias halfway up.

"I was there!" he said, exasperated. "And this... this Eli? He isn't meant to be in charge now?"

Mathias took a few more steps and then paused. He slowly turned on the stair to face Faro. Being a few stairs higher than him he was about eye level to the giant lion man. "Not that I'm aware of. Not that I was in on any of the plans, but I tried to stay apprised of the war. Something isn't sitting quite right with me. You all were cursed somehow..."

"And it doesn't surprise you I was with this Eli on the mountain?"

Mathias took his spectacles down from his eyes and polished them with his shirt, apparently stalling for a moment to think.

Finally, when he placed them back on his nose, he said "No, according to the stories you were his closest disciple."

Faro had been dying to know more about what Mathias knew about the war party he was apparently leading with this Eli to the top of the mountain, but Mathias became hushed and distracted. He told him they could sit down later and have a proper talk on the matter, and that he had to go speak with the mayor at once.

Choking down his anger, Faro agreed to meet him at his office that night so they could talk. Not wanting to talk with the greasy mayor again, nor feeling very invited, Faro headed outside to see if there was any sunlight left in the day to enjoy. After the dingy dungeon, he felt the need for light and silent thought to see if he could remember any more details about himself.

Stepping out of the church the light hit him square in the eyes and he threw up his hand to block it until he became used to the change. He could hear hushed whispers and hurried footsteps as people around him dashed off to get some distance away from him.

After his eyes finally adjusted to the light, he saw the dwarf that had attacked him over by the tavern where he had first met Mathias and the other citizens of Graeton who seemed to be okay with his existence. The dwarf was standing on a stool and clearing pints off of a table that had presumably been occupied by the elf and the other human who had been there when he'd arrived. Likely a daily ritual they kept.

"Hello, friend!" Faro called as he approached, not wanting to startle him during his work. The dwarf looked up to see him approaching and threw his rag down on the table.

"Friends, are we, Lion? That's good to know considering I stabbed you and all."

Faro just smiled. "Aye. It wasn't a good start, but I think at this point I need all the friends I can get, Dwarf."

He smiled back from atop his stool. "Please, Leo, call me Tobi."

Faro cocked his head a bit. "And you can call me Faro. According to my would-be-assassin, that's my real name."

Tobi smiled at this new information and nodded his head slightly. "Well then, Faro, not sure what a lion drinks, but how about one on the house?" Tobi said, climbing down from his stool.

"I'm not even sure how a lion drinks," Faro answered. So far he'd just lapped water awkwardly from his paws with his tongue. They both burst out in laughter at this. The laughter was short-lived, however, as screams from people at the edge of the town rang out. Both of them looked that way, alarmed.

"Not another giant lion-man, I hope," said Tobi, only half joking. He wasn't sure what to expect anymore.

They both made their way into the center of the square, looking at the commotion that was coming from the trees that sprung from the mountain valley, the same place where Faro had burst into town the day before.

They soon wished it was just another lost beast-creature looking for help. Instead, what came out of the woods was a marching nightmare. The sun had just dipped back behind the mountain, and the town was cast in shadow. A group of creatures the likes of which neither of them had ever seen walked in a steady pace directly towards the center of town. They couldn't quite make out what they were, but they could see their grayish, scaly skin and horrible, gaunt eyes as they approached.

The sight of the hideous, large creatures made them almost miss the short creature that was leading them. It was a creature almost as short as Tobi himself, and from what Tobi could tell looked like a tiny wolverine-man that had been afflicted with the same curse that had beset Faro.

Tobi nudged Faro's leg. "I think I should just pop inside the tavern and grab my axe," he said.

Faro didn't take his eyes off the approaching group. "Yeah, that's not a bad idea. Grab me something if you've got it."

"Aye," said Tobi as he slipped off into his tavern with as much haste as his legs would allow.

The town square had cleared out as Faro braced himself. He squared his shoulders to show them he wasn't afraid of what was to come. The wolverine creature and his crew stopped on the other end of the square, just within shouting distance. The creature spoke.

"Faro Envato!" the creature hissed. His silky voice echoed across the empty square.

Envato? Faro felt like he was slowly finding pieces to the riddle of his identity that were drawing a picture that would eventually, hopefully, come into focus once he had the right piece of the puzzle.

"Obviously," he roared back.

The creature had a look of pure malice on his face. "The High Ruler has put a price on your head. He's sent us to complete the task that others could not. Come forward now, and we won't tear this town to shreds after we finish you."

Faro glanced towards the tavern door. It was completely still. What he wouldn't give just to have even the dwarf's dagger that he'd been stabbed in the arm with, or even the barmaid's cauldron. Anything to defend himself, as it looked like there was no way out of this fight.

CHAPTER FIVE

THE BATTLE OF GRAETON

Faro stared hard into the waning light to see what he was up against as the moment before attack hung in the air. The tiny wolverine man stood at the front of the pack. He was wearing a small leather outfit with fur shoulder pads. His extremely fluffy head and pointy ears would almost be cute if not for the glowing yellow eyes narrowed in such malice, along with the insanely long claws that were braced for attack, his lips curled back in a terrifying snarl.

Surrounding the wolverine were at least a dozen of the most horrific beasts Faro ever remembered seeing, though that wasn't saying much. Their faces appeared to be ribbed skulls, with beady blue inset eyes and a gapping hole with razer sharp teeth where a mouth should be. Their bodies almost appeared to be made of stone, save their razer sharp claws that rivaled that of their wolverine leader. They had huge spikes protruding from their back, and Faro noted it would be hard to get his hands - paws - around them to toss them out of his way.

The wolverine's sneer turned into a slight smile, and in a snap he lurched forward to get down on all fours and close the gap in short order, running at full speed towards Faro. The lion had just enough time to glance at the tavern one more time to see that help wouldn't arrive in time before the wolverine lunged forward, its claws spread out, aiming for his throat.

Faro swiped his paw wide, trying to catch the little creature in the air and knock him out of the way before he reached him. Instead, all he managed was to knock his aim off slightly, and the claws sank into his left shoulder instead of his neck. Faro let out a roar of pain. The wolverine was fast. Faster than Faro could combat. Being barely the size of his torso, Faro was having a hard time pulling the raging animal off of him.

The creature was clawing his way around him and all Faro could do was scramble to use his own claws to catch the assailant. The wolverine paused for a second and drew his head back to sink his sharp teeth into Faro's neck, but before he could a long wooden stick came out from below and knocked the creature back.

Faro glanced down to see Tobi had arrived and had used the handle of his axe to butt the creature away from him, apparently fearing the sharp end might catch Faro if someone moved too suddenly. Faro nodded his thanks and glanced at the other object in the dwarf's hands. It looked similar to a battle hammer, one blunt end for smashing, the other end sharp for piercing. The only thing was, that it was more sized for a dwarf, and when Faro grabbed it from his new friend, it looked more like a club hammer than a full war hammer.

Still grateful for the weapon, he gave it a quick swing to test its weight, and something in his brain told him he'd used a hammer before. It felt so familiar.

Bracing himself, he squared off against the strange creatures that were about to clash with them. With all the strength his new, bulky lion body could muster, Faro gave the hammer a huge swing, and it came crashing hard into the tall creature's chest.

A tingle of reverberation shot up Faro's hand as hitting the creature felt like he had smashed his hammer into a solid mountainside. The tingle ran up to his shoulder, and he took a step back to recover from the shock. He looked at the beast and could see a decent sized crack in the thing's chest where his hammer had landed. Other than the crack, the creature seemed unfazed and quickly advanced again.

Next to Faro, Tobi had his axe swinging at the wolverine who had gotten angry at the dwarf for getting between him and his target. The axe clinked against to cobblestone of the town square with each swing as Tobi missed the quick Wolverine. Whenever the creature would move it to attack, Tobi would bunt him away with the axe handle to keep him at bay, and then move to strike him with the blade when there was an opening. The similarity in size made the foe a little easier to handle for Tobi than for Faro.

The rock creatures were almost surrounding them now, and Faro's smashing attacks didn't seem to deter them as he only smashed little bits of them away. Though they were overwhelming him, Faro felt like he was in some kind of gear he didn't know he had, yet still seemed familiar, like he was used to fighting. He was taking on three at once now and holding his own, but could feel the others pushing in. He heard one creature roar from behind him as it went in for the kill, and before he could turn he heard a quick swishing sound through the air.

Thhht... Faro turned to face his new foe, only to see an arrow sticking out of the creature's beady eye hole. The other blue eye flickered in and out for a second, and then the light of the eye went out completely and the creature fell to its knees before doing a face plant right next to the lion. The thud of stone on stone echoed through the town square.

Glancing up Faro followed the arrow's only possible trajectory and saw the elf lady, Lena, standing atop Tobi's bar, her bow and arrow in hand. Realizing the eye was the weak point, Faro flipped the mini war hammer quickly around in his paw and drove the point directly into the eye socket of the next approaching creature. It too dropped to the ground, the light in its eyes put out.

"Go for the eyes!" he yelled to Tobi. Tobi grunted in understanding, but was too occupied with the swift little wolverine to care about the big rock monsters. The wolverine, however, turned to look at Faro and saw now that a few of his creatures were on the ground. Malice returned to his face, his eyes went wide, and a hiss like nothing they had ever heard before left his mouth.

The wolverine, hate still filling his eyes, stopped pursuing Tobi and started swirling his arms through the air, speaking in a foreign tongue so loudly that it could be heard over the ongoing fight. Black flames surrounded the wolverine. Tobi lunged forward with his axe blade, but was too late. With one last scream, the wolverine cast a deep black fireball into the nearest structure, which was the Graeton General Store. The magic quickly caught the building on fire, and it went up in flames at an astonishing rate.

"No! Thora!" Tobi screamed. The store was right next to his tavern, and they could see Lena struggling to find a way off before that building, too, was consumed. Tobi quickly bolted towards his tavern as fast as his legs would carry, leaving Faro alone.

The wolverine howled with laughter. "Vorath Shadruul!" He screamed into the fray. "Surround him! Kill him!"

Faro turned from the scene and smashed the tip of his war hammer into another rock creature, the thing the wolverine had just addressed as a Vorath, killing it, and creating an opening that he could retreat from. Lena and Tobi spilled out of the tavern as Faro ran past. The building was now being overtaken by the magic, black flames. Between the pair they were dragging Thora out with them. The young girl had obviously been told to stay inside by Tobi, which Faro now knew had caused the delay in getting the weapons.

"To the church!" Lena yelled at them, pushing Thora away from the advancing Vorath. They all took off in a dead sprint towards the towering structure. Faro's long stride got him there first, and he yanked open the large wooden doors, ushering the other three in past him. The Vorath were hot on their tail, but he stepped inside and slam the door shut before they thudded into the other side. He dropped the lock bar across the door, locking them out, at least for the moment.

Being as strong as they were, Faro knew it wouldn't be long before they reduced the door to splinters and overtook their position in the church. They didn't have much time.

As they all entered, hurried steps came from the nearby stairs, and Mathias came barreling down. Seeing the party of familiar faces, he waved his arms frantically at them. "We've been betrayed!" he screamed at them. "The mayor sold us out! The people who sent the assassin know Faro is here!"

"You think?" asked Faro raising a furry brow, pointing to the door that was shaking from the impact of the stone creatures on the other side.

"Faro?" asked Lena and Thora at the same time.

Faro threw his hands up and stared pointedly at them, as if asking if this was the proper time to question his name change.

"Right," said Lena, snapping out of it. "Everyone get into the auditorium!" she yelled over the clanging of the door, gesturing to the ornately decorated nave. They all rushed in, but Faro was unsure how the open, circular room would be of any strategical advantage to them. To him it just seemed like they could be easily surrounded. Taking the stairs and narrowing their formation seemed to be the better strategy. That would allow them to take them on one-by-one. That he could do. Still, he trusted the resolve in the elf's voice and did what she said.

They all moved to the center. Mathias was shaking with rage. "In front of his own granddaughter! That son-of-a-bitch Thornvale sat there in his office, right in front of his little granddaughter, smuggest fucking smile on his face, and told me he'd sent his little messenger to sell us out to Eli. Said he was getting a pretty payment and protection under the new regime!"

"We don't have time to dwell on that," said Lena. "Everyone get to the side furthest from the door. Stay here in the center chamber so we can lure them in. Don't go out the other side until I say!"

Faro looked at Lena, the spindly looking, aged elf standing before him. Sure she could shoot a bow, but she seemed to think she could take on the remaining Vorath, and the feisty little wolverine, by herself.

"With all due respect..." Faro started, but he was quickly cut off.

"Do as I say! Now!" the old elf barked back with the ferocity of an elf half her age.

Faro, seeing her resolve, nodded and used his wide arm span to herd the rest of the group to the side of the chamber furthest from the front door. No sooner had they taken position then the doors burst open, splinters of wood flying. What was left of the doors was now swinging inward, weak on their hinges.

The Vorath ran into the circular center chamber where Lena stood in front of the others. They formed two ranks of four in a semi-circle, standing as tall as Faro; nearly immovable walls. One remained by the door to prevent any chance of a simple escape. The wolverine came up to the archway of the main chamber and assessed the situation.

"You cannot protect the lion, *Elf*," this last word seemed to hold some disdain as he spoke. "Give us Faro, and we'll be on our way. The High King still needs subjects to serve him. No sense in more bloodshed here today."

Lena put one leg behind her and raised her arms. He hands were empty as she had strung her bow back across her back. She held them up in a fighting stance, as if she was going to knock the wolverine and the rock creatures out with her fists.

The wolverine just smiled. "You just met this... *thing*," he said, gesturing behind her towards Faro. "You would give your life for him?"

Lena narrowed her eyes as she stared back at him through her clenched fists. "I will always give my life to do the right thing," she said tartly at him. "Move! Now!" she screamed. Faro pushed Thora, Tobi, and Mathias back out of the nave as Lena began waving her arms and speaking in tongues similar to what the wolverine was spouting out in the square.

The party watched as their friend's hands started glowing bright white. They watched until they couldn't anymore for how bright the light was. They heard the wolverine yelling "Attack! Kill her!" as the Vorath sprung forward to tear her apart.

The building shook, and a glow from the ceiling caught Faro's eyes. He glanced up and saw the radiant, golden eyes of the god, Solana, come to life in a brilliant bright light that matched that of Lena's hands. The light built until it shot downwards and filled the circular chamber. They could hear sizzling and falling rock as the light burnt through their adversaries and reduced them to rubble.

When the light finally subsided, smoke filled the room. Piles of rock surrounded the center of the chamber, where Lena still stood, unscathed. Out by the entrance stood the wolverine, his jaw agape. Before he could say anything, a shriek rang out over by the stairs. Everyone turned to look and saw a small, blonde girl standing in the stairway. She had obviously been roused from her grandfather's office by the shaking of the building and had rushed to evacuate with him. She was screaming in shock at the site of the wolverine and the one remaining Shadruul that blocked her and her grandfather's path outside. Mayor Thornvale could be heard whimpering and cowering behind her.

"Seize the girl and kill the man!" the wolverine snarled at his one remaining soldier. The Vorath Shadruul lunged for the stairs and grabbed the girl with one arm, smashing a rock fist into Thornvale's head, sending him crumpling to the ground on the stairs.

No one in the party dared move for fear they would cause the monster to hurt the little girl. The wolverine snarled at them. "Meet me at Umbra's Veil, Faro. Alone. Or the girl dies."

With one last demonic hiss, the wolverine and the Vorath ran out of the church, their captive in tow, through the splintered door. Lena made a move to run after them, but Faro had come up behind her and grabbed her by her cloak.

"Don't," he growled. "That thing will squeeze her to death if we pursue now."

She nodded, and he loosened his grip. Mathias, Tobi, and Thora all moved to the center of the room, looking around themselves in amazement.

Finally, Mathias was the one to speak. "How, in the Maker's Realm, did you know it could do that?" he asked egregiously, pointing up at the hanging statue that still looked as beautiful and pristine as ever.

Lena took a moment to straighten her cloak that Faro had wrinkled when he grabbed it. "How do I know? I should know! I built the damn thing."

Mathias' mouth dropped open. "What? How?"

Lena opened her mouth to answer, but a noise from the doorway cut her off. They all turned to look. The sound came again, a faint whimper echoing through the church. Faro nodded at Lena, signaling to move. Together, they rushed to the broken doorway.

As they stepped outside, Thora let out a cry. Lying in the town square was their farmer friend, Osric, blood seeping through his fingers as he clutched his chest. They hurried over, and Mathias dropped to his knees beside his old friend.

"Tried... tried to stop... them," Osric wheezed, his voice barely a whisper.

A tear rolled down Mathias' cheek. He looked up at Lena with desperation in his eyes. "Do something!" he shouted.

Lena's expression faltered, her hands trembling as she shook her head slowly. "I can't... I'm sorry."

Chapter Six

An Unlikely Party

The desperate moment hung in time as they all stared down at Osric. He was clutching the part of his chest where the wolverine or Shadruul had sliced him through with their sharp claws. The surrounding ground was soaked in crimson.

On the ground next to Osric, Mathias' fists shook with rage. "What in the hell do you mean you can't help him, Lena? We just saw you turn rock monsters into piles of dust! You've obviously been hiding magic!" he yelled as he glared daggers at her.

The old elf just simply shook her head. "The injury is too severe, Mathias," she said solemnly. "My magic is too depleted at the moment to take on a mortal wound. I used everything I had to save us from those demons just now." She was panting and looked tired, two things Mathias had never seen her be in all the time he'd known her. Then he saw another thing he'd never seen before: a tear rolling down the stern elf's face.

Mathias was shaking as he turned back to Osric and ran his hand across his dying friend's brow. His forehead was burning and dripping with sweat. Mathias' voice cracked as he spoke, his words barely a whisper. "You'll find peace in Solana's Light, my friend."

A small smile cracked Osric's face. "I can see, him, Mathias. I..." Osric's face froze, and the party knew that their friend was gone.

Thora let out a cry, and she bent down to bury her face in Tobi's shoulder for comfort. Faro knelt down next to Mathias and placed a paw on his shoulder, his voice soft. "There was nothing more you could've done."

The healer was still shaking, but instead of grief, he now looked angry. "I could have. I've always been so against magical healing, Faro. I've hated magic ever since I was a young boy. A healing spell went wrong and killed a dear childhood friend, but that's stopped me from pursuing the education in magic that could have just now saved a good man's life. I just... I don't... I can't..."

Lena knelt beside them, her eyes downcast. "Advanced magic is a hard life, my friend. I'm sorry I kept my abilities from you, but I knew your feelings on the subject. It takes years of study, endless practice, and a will stronger than most can imagine. Even then, it doesn't always bend to your will. It's unpredictable. It flows like a river. Sometimes it shifts, and it's dangerous, and sometimes...in the case of your childhood friend...deadly."

Mathias looked at her, his eyes full of sorrow and frustration. "Why? Why does it have to be so difficult to master?"

Lena met his gaze, her expression solemn. "Because magic isn't just knowledge. It's understanding the forces of the world—forces that don't want to be controlled. Magic can give, but it can also take away just as quickly. Every spell has a price, and the stronger the magic, the greater the cost. Few can wield it without losing a part of themselves."

She paused, her voice softening. "That's why so many fear it, why it's so rare to find a true master of the craft. The deeper you go, the more it takes from you, and sometimes, what you lose can never be regained."

Mathias clenched his fists, the weight of Lena's words sinking in. "I won't make the same mistake again," he muttered. "I'll learn... whatever it takes."

Lena placed a hand on his arm. "Just remember, Mathias. Magic can heal, but it can also harm. Don't lose yourself in it, or you may find there's no turning back."

Behind them, Tobi and Thora had shuffled away to stare at the smoldering rubble that was their tavern. It had been their livelihood and contained almost everything they owned in the world, as they lived in a small room at the top.

"It's gone!" Tobi roared as he pushed away from Thora. She moved to put a hand on his shoulder and calm him down, but he took another step away from her.

"It will be okay, *Andre*. We can rebuild. We can make it whole again," she said timidly, not wanting him to lash out at her.

The dwarf let out another roar and grabbed his axe from his back. With all the strength he could muster he brought it overhead and down hard into the ground in front of himself with a mighty force. The blade cracked the cobblestones and stuck there.

"With what, Thora?" he said a little more angrily than he had meant to. He took a breath to calm himself down. Thora looked him in the eye and could almost swear she saw them glistening as if the thick-skinned warrior were about to cry. "A good man is dead. Everything we own is up in smoke. We've got nothing left but the clothes on our back, and my axe," he said, gesturing at the weapon buried in the ground in front of him.

Thora nodded slowly. "Yes, but we still have each other, Tobi."

At this, a small tear fell down his cheek, and Thora's eyes widened in shock. Sadness was not something that had ever crossed the dwarf's face, in all the seventeen years Thora had known the man that had raised her as a father. He was always gruff and haughty, but sometimes happy when the right conversation or drink crossed his path. But sadness was always something he had never shown, or at least had hidden from her all these years.

The other's left Osric and came to comfort the pair and stare in awe at the wispy black smoke that rose from where the building stood not minutes before.

"That magic," said Faro. "I don't remember much of magic, but should that fire have taken that building down so quickly?" he asked, in awe of what he might be up against.

Standing next to him, Mathias shook his head. "No. That was no normal magic. At least not magic much of the land has seen in centuries. That was some sort of twisted, dark magic. Powerful..."

"Virmorphia," Lena cut in. "Not seen outside of Cosimir's use in millennia. It is forbidden magic that Solana has kept the world protected from." All eyes were on her as she spoke. "If this dark magic has found it's way to other beings, that means that the death of Cosimir has allowed it to spread. In that case, the world has just gotten a lot more dangerous."

All of this was too much for Faro. From barely knowing who he was, and hearing all of this new information about the evil that was coming into the world, it was almost too much for him to bear. That thought reminded him of the conversation he and Mathias were having down in the dungeon earlier, and he had a sudden urge to know more about his past.

"Mathias," he said. "Earlier you said I was a disciple of this Eli. What does that mean? Why are all these beasts after me?"

Mathias was silent for a moment until he collected his thoughts. "A man is dead, Faro. Let us bury him and talk about it another time." The older man was solemn as he walked away from the group, saying something about going to talk with the town undertaker.

There was silence until he was gone, and then Faro turned to the others. "And what of this wolverine fellow and the little girl. How do I find the place where they went?"

Faro didn't get an answer as there was a bustling over by the church. Through the shattered doors stumbled a hunched figure, frantically scurrying towards them. It was Mayor Thornvale. He was holding onto a huge crimson spot on his head where the rock monster had smashed him before stealing his granddaughter. A guttural moan was coming from his throat, a ghastly wail that sent a chill down Faro's spine.

"Gone!" he finally managed to cry. "Veronica's gone! That... that thing! Took her!" he stumbled into the party and grabbed two fistfuls of Faro's blue tunic.

"And you sold us out, you son-of-a-bitch!" yelled Tobi from beside Faro. "Tell me why I shouldn't take this axe and bury it in your skull!" With one mighty heave Tobi freed his prized axe from the cobblestone and brandished it before the mayor.

"I didn't!" he yelled in agony. At this Faro picked the tiny man up by the scruff and held him up to his pointed muzzle. He let out a fierce, bellowing lion roar right in the old man's face. The vibration from the sound shook the man to his core.

"Okay! I did! I tried! I sent my messenger to sell you out! But it's impossible that he made it to the high mountain in time to deliver my message. Those beasts were already on their way here! My messenger... he... he hasn't returned."

Faro narrowed his eyes at him, and then let him fall to the ground. "The intent was still there, old man."

"Yes!" Mayor Thornvale spat up at him. "I do not need a damned lion monstrosity and that do-well-do-gooder Mathias running around my town stirring people up. You are an abomination, *sir*, but that doesn't mean that you should let an innocent girl be whisked off to her death!" He got up to his knees and clasped his hands together. "Please...please..."

Faro paused a moment, relishing the begging of the crooked old mayor. "I was never going to let them. As soon as we bury the farmer, Osric, I will be on my way to find that wolverine and put an end to this."

At that, Lena perked up. "You cannot go alone," she said simply. "You have no memories, you don't know the way, and trust me, the way is perilous."

"Point me in a direction and I will get there," said Faro, sure that his instincts would kick in and he would find the place that he needed to go to save the little girl and get his revenge on the wolverine.

"No," she said, holding up her hand. "You don't understand. Umbra's Veil is a week's journey from here on foot. Less if we can arrange some sort of animal transport, a horse or a duwala. Not only that, but in order to get to the forbidden city you have to cross Mournfall Lake. You will not get through without a proper guide and a bit of magic to ward off the spirits of the fallen. After the lake is a barren wasteland. The light doesn't even dare to shine there, so it is hard to navigate, night or day. Not to mention the perils of the forbidden city itself. Unless you catch that little bastard before he gets there, you will need help to get to where you seek to go."

Faro looked disappointed at this news. "The *little bastard* said I had to come alone or he would kill the girl. Plus, you all have already done enough. I cannot ask for any more help in cleaning up whatever mess I seem to have created by surviving my fall."

Thora went to stand by Lena and square off against the mighty lion. "You are not the only one who has a debt to square with that *little bastard*," she said, relishing in their enemies new nickname. "He took the life that my *andre* and I built and burnt it to the ground without a thought. We have nothing left here. But what we can do is come with you and help to save that poor little girl's life."

"What?" said Tobi sharply to her, finally taking his eyes off Thornvale to give a stern look to his daughter.

Thora's sharp gaze back at him matched his intensity and then some. Her eyes narrowed, and she stared at him until his face softened. He let his axe head clink to the ground. "Alright. Fine. We'll go." Thora smiled at him. "Veronica used to come and bring fresh flowers to the bar every day of spring. Told me it made the place look friendlier," Tobi said, smiling. "But we're doing this for her, not *you*, you crooked old fool!" he added, pointing at the mayor.

Thornvale gave a slight smile underneath his hand that was still holding his wound. "As long as you get her back, *Dwarf*," he said in an 'or else' type of tone.

Faro sighed. Extra people tagging along was going to get Veronica killed. He was supposed to go alone. After a moment's deliberation, he decided they could be his guides, and he would lose them somewhere close to Umbra's Veil. He didn't want to risk startling the wolverine into doing something stupid.

"Okay. Fine. The four of us will go," conceded Faro with a sigh.

"You will also need a healer and a master of antidotes!" came a voice from behind him. Mathias had returned. Faro looked over at the body of Osric and saw another man hunched over the poor farmer, stooping to lift his body onto a death cart.

Faro turned and looked down at Mathias. "You? You want to go on a perilous journey to save this girl? Mathias, you don't seem to be the adventuring type!"

Mathias smiled. "I'm all books now, my friend, but you've no idea what adventures I've had in my youth! I think it's time I got out to see Evania again. Clear my head and... get away from all this for a while," he said, glancing at his fallen friend who had now been lifted into the cart by the undertaker. "I've got a score to settle, just like any of you!"

The lion stood and stared at the small party of four people who stood by him, looking intent on joining him on a dangerous journey that could lead to the death of any one of them. An old elf, a tavern maid, a bar owner, and a quirky medicine man. He had not known them at all the previous morning, and here they were, ready to lay their lives down for a little girl, the granddaughter of a man they all despised. Not only for her, but to help a wild lion-man in his quest to find out why he was being hunted.

Faro threw his arms out wide into the air, as if to welcome and embrace their heroism and company. "Thank you, my new friends. Our unlikely party will leave with haste tomorrow after the funeral." Four smiles beamed back at him.

CHAPTER SEVEN

THE WAKE OF THE FALLEN EMPEROR

The purple light faded as the spell ended, and the body hit the hard, stone floor. Idon, Mayor Thornvale's messenger, lay crumpled on the ground, his eyes wide open in shock. Above him towered a beast of a man. Almost as wide as he was tall, the hulking figure sighed, wondering what had become of his life. Almost reflexively he touched the horn that grew out of his head, as he had done countless times in the last few days, and flinched.

Decisions. Choices. As Eli Ashford stood over the dead body of the messenger he had just killed, he again wondered if he'd made the right one. He could feel the power coursing through his veins, right down to his bones. The power to do so much, accomplish so much, but also the power to do wrong. The urge to do terrible things. Things like killing an innocent messenger who was in the wrong place at the wrong time.

"He overheard us," came a cool, chilling voice from behind the throne that sat on a raised platform towards the back of the room. "You had no other choice, Master."

Eli turned and frowned. It was the silver-tongued, raven-haired elf-mage who had led him to make the choices he had, speaking his sly words from the shadows. Eldryn always spoke softly, kindly, as if he had your best interests at heart, but Eli could sense the undertones of malintent.

"Yeah," said Eli, in his low, booming voice. "Seems like there was another way we could have dealt with him..." he said, trailing off as a voice sounded in his head. *No! The messenger knew what we were after in Umbra's Veil. He HAD to die!*

He put a hand up to his head. The voice had come again. The same voice that told him to kill the messenger to begin with, even though every fiber of his being was begging him not to enact such a terrible deed. When the voice first appeared, on that night when it told him to command the dark mage Eldryn to blast his friend Faro into oblivion, he had thought it was the same dark mage who was casting voices into his mind. But the next day Eldryn had accompanied Jarl the Wolverine into the woods to give him instruction on his mission, and the voices continued to haunt him, even with the dark presence of the elf far away. Wherever it was coming from was inside Eli, and he wasn't sure how to rid himself of it.

"Absolutely not," said Eldryn, conferring with the strange voice in Eli's head. "He heard us discussing the next phase. He absolutely had to be killed. I mean, I can bring him back if you wish?" Eldryn asked, smiling slyly.

Eli grimaced. The dark elf dabbled in necromancy. Eli had found this out immediately after taking the throne. After he had killed Cosimir and took his place, a traitor in his midst was revealed to him as a rat, a literal rat-man made from the twisted dark magic that overtook them all. Eli's dark inner voice had ordered him to kill the rat, and Eli obeyed. After Faro was dealt with, Eldryn had approached the traitor, Renn, and risen him from the dead. The man was no longer Renn, disciple of Eli and traitor. He was now Renn the obedient rat.

"No, I think we're all good with that," said Eli, a chill running down his spine. "What we really need to focus on is getting messages out to the forces we have throughout Evania. I may be strong as an ox now, but I cannot take on the armies of the people all by myself." It was true. Eli had been a big hulk of a man before, being a large, burly blacksmith from the depths of the mines of Incarta, but once the magical transformation took hold, his muscles bulged with animalistic strength. Not only was he large still, but now he was stronger than any person he had ever encountered. "We can try to send out an emissary first to show our good faith, but if we're to restore Evania to its former glory and restore the above-ground kingdoms, we will need to make sure supply lines are secure and resources are divided where properly needed. We can't do that amidst a war."

Eldryn paused as if collecting his thoughts. "You know what that means, Master. As I've said before, we have to raise more Shadruul. The Dark Humans simply won't suffice, and Cosimir could only raise the one small batch of Shadruul that we sent with the dwarf down the mountain."

Eli shuddered at the thought of the rock monsters they had sent down the mountain with Jarl in search of Faro. They had received a crow from the dwarf-turned-wolverine that he had failed to kill Faro, but had plans to trap him at Umbra's Veil as he completed his other mission.

"I know you've sent my other disciples into the mountain villages to gather the people for the sacrifice, but I cannot..." Eli's eye started twitching. His head cocked slightly to the side. The voice. The voice was back. *No! They are necessary sacrifice! Build the army!*

To Eli's surprise, he had said this last line of thought out loud. Eldryn just gave him a small, sly smile. "I agree, Master. We must build the army and secure Evania, no matter the cost." The mage spoke while leaning on the high throne, giving an air as if he owned the place. He just stood there smirking in his black cloak, one hand holding his scepter that Eli assumed enhanced his magical abilities, the other hand gently stroking a black onyx gem at the top.

After a long, almost menacing pause, Eldryn tossed his scepter from one had to the other, coolly catching it, and strolled down the five steps below the high throne to be on the same level with Eli. "You know..." he said slowly, with a long pause on the end, "...the army could use a solid leader. One who has experienced leading before. Someone of *much*... tenure..."

The dark elf turned to look behind Eli, and the new High King closed his eyes, knowing exactly what he was referring to. Behind Eli on a raised dais lay the crumpled body of an old man. He wore a gray flowing robe that draped over the side of the dais, much like his long, silver, flowing hair. No one had bothered to fix him up much since Eli had pierced him with a spear, and crimson stained his flowing robes. The blood still appeared bright red and fresh. Eldryn had cast a preservation spell over Cosimir and laid him on the Dais of Dead Kings. Eli felt the tyrant didn't deserve such honor, but Eldryn had convinced him it helped his image as a more compassionate ruler flourish once word got out that he showed respect to the previous regime, no matter how vile he was.

"You can't possibly be thinking about bringing him back," Eli snorted. "Not after everything he's done to this land.

Everything that we now have to work to rebuild." He turned to look at the site of Cosimir laying on the slab, the same way he had looked when placed there a few days prior. "He's a tyrant. A menace."

"He's a skilled military leader," said Eldryn, coolly. "Even after the Scourge sent everyone underground, he still squashed countless rebellions from the Dungeon Lords. It wasn't until *you* came along that they all got organized. And honestly you only defeated him with *my* help!"

Eli knew that to be true, but the voice inside his head sparked with rage. *What the fuck did he just say?* Eli could feel his eye twitching again as he held his head to steady himself. He wasn't sure what part of the dark magic this cursed voice was, but he knew he had to rid himself of it so he could think straight and make the best decisions for his new rule. As it was, the voice seemed to take over his mind, and he couldn't help but wonder what dark demon or spirit Eldryn had placed in him during the transformation.

"Yes, and I'm still wondering if listening to you was the right thing," Eli said dryly.

"You're still alive, Master. Count your blessings," said the dark elf with an air. "And with the Virmorphia magic you now possess, along with your touch of Solana, you can raise an army the likes of which Cosimir could only dream of! You are the chosen one, and restoring this land to it's former glory is your calling. Rebuild it, but rebuild it in your image, how you know it was meant to be. It is your dominion to rule. I just gave you the power to not have to die for it."

Eli sighed. "Solana chose me to lead the rebellion, not Evania. My mission was to set the people free, not become this beast with dark magic."

Eldryn's face fell flat as he stroked his black goatee. "Now, now, Young King," he said, his voice dripping with fake concern. "If not you, then who? I am hardly a grand ruler in my current state, and the Dungeon Kingdoms would hear nothing of me being in charge. Not after all I've done. But you are their champion, and even in your... *unusual state*, they will follow you, Master. Especially if you are helping them to build back what was taken from them."

This was answered with a snort from Eli. "Yeah, my unusual state. You failed to mention any of this would happen to me in the process of killing the most evil man in Evania," he said dryly, gesturing a thumb over at the fallen Cosimir on the dais.

"Virmorphia magic is *most* unpredictable, Master," Eldryn said. "While I had planned for it to turn your disciples into animals that you could rule, and expose your...*rat problem*...I had no idea that you would turn beast as well." He paused and examined the onyx gem on his scepter again. "Although it seems a small price to pay to become ruler of the great

Evania," he said, gesturing out the window and out to the grand landscape of Evania below them.

Eli looked out into the expanse. The mountainside had been cut out and glassmiths had created intricate windows for the ruler of Evania to look out almost a hundred miles upon their kingdom. A vast mountain range, and flat grasslands in the distance. Eli had spent much of his time since the transformation taking in the view, and wondering if he had done the right thing. One thing he knew that was absolutely wrong though, was allowing Eldryn to get what he wanted with the old emperor.

"Even so, we cannot bring him back. Even if you think you can control him, Elf, I feel as though the dark magic will consume him again. I don't want any chance that he gets his own faculties back about him and tries to rule from the undead," said Eli, knowing he still didn't understand the dark magic that had consumed Cosimir, the same magic that now consumed him. "But this new army, though. You think we need to go to such lengths? I'm not even sure what's involved, but it sounds like we'd be hurting a lot of innocent people."

Eldryn sighed. He looked annoyed that his new master had some morals bubbling near the surface. "You said it yourself, Master. We need to secure the supply lines, or there will be all-out war between the kingdoms. Once they know their champion is in charge, they will want to pop back up to the surface and restore their former glory. There will be nothing stopping one kingdom from waging war on another to rebuild their lives above ground." The dark elf took a step forward and looked down at his former master. "Cosimir barely had any good in him, so he was unable to raise more than a small pack of Shadruul. He had to turn his magic to driving regular humans insane, torturing them until they turned dark and did his bidding."

"The Dark Humans," said Eli nodding. "But they won't answer to me?"

"They've been set free from Cosimir's magic, Master," Eldryn said. "I cannot say as to whether we will still have enough hold to get them to do what we need. Shadruul, on the other hand, are beasts of the earth. If you combine the persuasion of dark magic with the life force and elements of light magic and nature, you get a beast that is completely obedient, and a mighty force."

Eli thought about it. He didn't like the idea of sacrificing the people of the mountains for the greater good of the rest of Evania. There had to be another way. *But there isn't.* It was that voice again. *The people of the mountains are savages. Humble tribes that didn't want to conform to the rest of the kingdoms. They live in the mountains like animals.*

Shaking his head, Eli found the voice speaking for him out loud again. "Yes, whatever it takes to secure the new Evania."

Eldryn shook his head, pleased. "Glad you agree, Master. And we should also bring Cosimir back to life. He will be completely loyal to us. The undead have no choice but to be loyal to the necromancer who brought them back. They act upon my will."

Eli wasn't sure if he was more afraid of Cosimir regaining self-direction, or of him being completely at the will of the dark elf. He couldn't let either option happen. With the flick of his wrist, his new magic produced a dark black fireball in his palm, a look of determination on his face.

Eldryn slowly glanced down at the fire in Eli's hand. "What do you think you're doing with that?" he said, his always-calm voice not breaking its cool stride.

What are you doing? Echoed the voice in Eli's head. *Don't do anything foolish.*

"Cosimir can't come back. He's done enough damage to Evania," said Eli, determined to shake the voice and burn Cosimir the Eternal beyond magical revival. He hoped beyond hope that dark magic would prevent dark magic from reanimating the old emperor.

"He can control the Shadruul and lead the army," said Eldryn, uncharacteristic haste in his voice now.

Eli paused, the flame flickering in his hand, but not burning him. This magic was weird. Unnatural. Just like raising people back from the dead. He lifted his hand high.

"Don't!" Eldryn yelled, the first time Eli had heard him raise his voice barely above a whisper. The fire flew from Eli's hand to the dais, and Cosimir the Eternal's body erupted in black flames.

Eldryn stared in shock at what his new Master had just done. At the same time the voice was yelling in Eli's head, deafeningly loud. So loud the Eli winced from how high the scream was coming from within his head. *Fool! Don't burn me!*

Chapter Eight

IN THE PRESENCE OF THE PRINCE

All heads were bowed as the Geusto of Solana, a sort of preacher of the church, sang his lamentation over Osric. Given all the destruction caused by the wolverine and his stone minions, it was a miracle that no one else had been killed in the fray. While this helped console some, for many it was still a very solemn occasion.

The Geusto reached a high note towards the end. Faro wasn't sure what the words were in the song. It was an odd language that sounded like what he'd heard Lena and the wolverine speaking when they cast their magic. Despite not knowing the meaning of the words, he could definitely hear the sad emotion in the notes and could see the song moving some of his new friends to tears.

Of the unlikely party, only Tobi still had dry eyes. Faro imagined it was largely because of the type of dwarf he was, usually serious and stone-faced. He also bet that part of it was annoyance from the tall, spindly old lady that was standing next to Tobi the whole funeral chattering away.

"You know, you weren't the only one to lose everything," she had whispered to him when the song began. "My store went down first, Tobi. All my wares, gone!" She threw her hands in the air in dramatic flare, and Tobi rolled his eyes.

"No one is saying you didn't suffer a loss too, Karen," the dwarf cut in, trying to defend himself. "All I said was that I am now *homeless* because we *lived* above the tavern!"

This sentiment didn't seem to faze her a bit. "Yeah? Well, my cat. I haven't seen him since the incident. Have you seen my poor cat, Tobi?" Karen prodded him, bending down and getting right in his face.

Tobi shut his eyes. "I've already told you. I haven't seen your cat, Karen. This isn't a contest either. We've both had losses..."

"Yeah?" she cut in. "Well, my back room was full of priceless family heirlooms that..." Faro had tried to tune the old woman out but she just kept talking through the entire song. Now, as the song was winding down, Karen was still raving mad, talking about how her great-great-grandfather had spent his last dollar to buy the general store at an auction from the mayor of Graeton, and how he was probably looking down on her now from Solana's Plain in shame.

The dwarf just stood next her, one hand burying his fingers deep into his eyes, the other gently caressing the handle of his axe. Faro could only guess what the dwarf was thinking about doing, but he was pretty sure he had the right idea.

The lament ended, and there was silence. Even Karen cut off abruptly as she didn't want to be heard as the only one talking, lest people peg her as a disrespectful complainer. The Geusto, dressed head to toe in white, including the expressionless mask he wore over his face, said a few parting words, and the friends went up to say their last goodbyes to their farmer friend Osric.

They had all agreed that they would leave immediately after the funeral, and Faro was itching to go. Sure he was sad that a man had died trying to save a little girl's life, but he had barely known Osric, and time was of the essence if they were to save Veronica. The fact that it was already two days after she and the wolverine had left Graeton made Faro's anxiety spike. He had wanted to leave the day before, but the party insisted on staying for the funeral, and Mathias had told him they needed time to gather the proper weapons and supplies for the mission.

Tobi had his axe, and Lena her bow and two swords. They had found a nice-sized mace for Thora, as the young barmaid seemed to be pretty good with blunt objects. Mathias didn't come off as much of a fighter, but had agreed to carry a short sword and several daggers for the trouble they may find on the road. As for Faro, he had tucked the small war hammer into his belt, and now had a larger version as his main weapon. Lena had brought it from her cottage in the woods, along with the food supplies they would need, and leather satchels to carry it all in.

All the horses in town were being used in the fields, or by merchants who would need them to travel back out of town. All the duwalas, giant swine-like creatures, were nowhere to be found. This unfortunate bit of news meant they would have to set out on foot, making their journey much longer. Mathias had assured him they were likely to find someone willing to sell their horses on the way to Umbra's Veil, but Faro wasn't so sure they would. Either way, they brought a good amount of treads with them in case they ran across an opportunity to make a purchase.

They left without a word to Thornvale. This mission wasn't about him. It was about saving an innocent child. When they were ready, the party gathered their weapons and their packs of supplies and headed out of town.

Just past the main square there were a few streets of houses, but after that it quickly broke off into potato fields filled with the short, green stocky tops of the plants. The sun beat down on them and there wasn't a cloud in the sky. Only a soft breeze greeted them along the way, pushing them off on their adventure.

As they made their way carefully through the rows, Faro could hear Mathias grilling Lena about something that had been bugging him, but had been put off since they were busy prepping for the journey.

"So, magic," Mathias said, nudging Lena with his elbow. "You built that entire temple?"

Lena kept looking straight, her face as serious as ever. "Yes, Mathias. I built it when I arrived in Graeton."

"That's a really old temple," said Mathias impressed. "Hundreds of years old!"

Lena cracked a small smile. "I am not a young elf," she said simply. "The light was leaving Zelira, and it was my job to establish a new presence for Solana." At this she shrugged, as if building the perfect structure and its magnificent hanging statue were no big deal to her. She went very quiet after this and didn't elaborate further.

The healer shook his head. "Zelira," he said, almost perplexed. "Read all about it, but never been!"

Faro wasn't surprised he knew nothing of Zelira, given his condition, but he figured it best that he begin to relearn things and see if anything would jog his memory. "Zelira? What's that?" he asked.

Lena was still silent and staring at the ground, so Mathias spoke up. "It's the great Elven kingdom by the sea. I've read that it used to be quite the place of renaissance and refinement back in the day. Unfortunately, the rumor is that the once eloquent Queen Zelira has become something of a recluse. She won't come out of the seaside caves they built during the Scourge. Won't let anyone in. Won't let anyone out. Even setting foot onto their land is a death sentence."

Faro thought about that for a moment. "Did a lot of the rulers become isolated during the Scourge? Everyone was driven underground, right?"

This time Lena answered. "When the Scourge spread, all the kingdoms were forced to dig underground. They had to build new kingdoms for the few survivors their kingdoms had. The surface was choked with bodies. Cosimir kept the kingdoms under his thumb by boosting the price of the subfluore crystals up to insane heights."

The lion felt a crunch and looked down. He was having a hard time making his way through the fields without stepping on the green plants sprouting up from the ground. The others were managing fine, but they also had much smaller feet than him. Ignoring the plants, and hoping that he wasn't killing too many, he stroked his mane in thought.

"I think you all have mentioned those crystals before. What makes them so special?"

At this, Thora sped up to walk in stride beside them. "Subfluore are elemental crystals. This particular type generates energy very efficiently. The kingdoms used them to provide light and power for their underground civilizations during the Scourge. You probably saw some being used for street lights back in Graeton. My family used to manipulate them into new and wonderful inventions... before Cosimir raided our town and killed my parents."

Thora looked at the ground, a sad look on her face. Faro had wondered what had happened that made her come under the care of a dwarf, and now it was starting to make sense. "I'm sorry to hear that," he said to her. "At least Tobi found you."

At this, her face brightened. "Yep! Tobi has been the best *Andre* an orphan girl like me could ask for," she said as she reached down and clapped Tobi on the back. Faro couldn't quite tell because of the beard, but it looked like Tobi was blushing a bit.

"Aye?" he said, trying to play it cool. "I mean, you offered to shine my shoes while I was there on business. Made me look right professional in front of the merchant I went to buy from. He even threw in some free steins because he thought I looked like a dwarf who meant business." Thora giggled, being taken back to the little girl she was when Tobi found her.

They all walked in silence for a bit after this, heading for a cluster of trees behind a small border wall in the distance.

Lena assured them it wasn't a very big cluster, and that they would be back on open ground after that until they reached Mournfall Lake.

Faro adjusted the pack strung across his back and let Lena, Tobi, and Thora walk ahead a bit. Mathias had dropped to the back of the pack to check out some herbs that were growing amongst the potato plants in the field.

"Always on the lookout for new herbs, eh?" Faro asked.

Mathias held one of the white flowers he'd picked up to his nose and sniffed. He flinched a bit and then offered it to Faro to take a whiff. Upon smelling the flower, Faro flinched too. It was a spicy, musky smell.

"Yah!," he said, coughing a bit from the overwhelm of the smell. "What is that?"

Mathias smiled and placed a handful of the herbs into his pack. "It's yarrow," he said simply. "It's great to reduce inflammation of wounds, and just healing in general." He paused, looking down at another clump of it sticking out of the ground. His face fell. "Osric used to bring it in from the fields and sell it to me."

Faro nodded, realizing Osric's death was still on Mathias' mind, and wondered if it was the right time to broach the subject of Eli. He decided it was as good of a time as any.

"I know you told me it wasn't the right time the other day..." he started, but Mathias cut him off.

"Yes, yes, Friend," Mathias said, holding up his hand to stop Faro from talking further. "I know I owe you an explanation of what I know." The healer paused as if wondering where to begin.

He took a deep breath and started explaining, "I'll start by saying, I haven't been outside of Graeton in years, so this is all hearsay from patients, traveling merchants, and what I've read in my studies. The entire rebellion, at least this most recent one, started when Solana spoke to a blacksmith from Incarta and told him he was destined to be the spark that triggered the new rebellion that would take Cosimir the Eternal down."

"Eli?" Faro ventured a guess.

"Yes," said Mathias, nodding. "Eli received a vision from the Great God himself. Of course no one believed him, and no one dared to raise an army against Cosimir without solid proof they had Solana backing them." Mathias straightened his glasses. "That's when Eli got another vision. A vision that told him the waters of Morgrid would run again."

Faro looked down at Mathias, confused. "Morgrid? A river?"

Mathias smiled. "Of sorts. Morgrid is a kingdom that water flows into from the Great Ocean. Once it passes under Morgrid, the waters turn into two flowing rivers that move North through Evania."

"You mean South," said Faro. He may have some kind of amnesia, but he still knew how basic principles of nature worked.

Mathias raised a finger into the air. "Ah! One would think. But they say these rivers flow through Morgrid to be blessed by Solana, and the magic power of the god gives them the strength to defy logic and flow north. Although, to be fair, the land slopes downward from the mountain to far North Evania. Gravity is really at work, but whatever the reason you choose to believe, the rivers had run dry since the reign of Cosimir began. Some say it was Solana's protest to dark magic ruling over his land."

"Whatever the reason, the rivers were dry," Mathias continued. "That was until after Eli received this second vision. As he told everyone of what he saw, no one again believed him. After all, the rivers had been dry for almost three-hundred years! It was unheard of that they would flow again. Funny thing was, within the week, the water ran from Morgrid again. And not just a trickle, mind. They came pouring out with such substantial force they flooded the plains around Incarta. The message that Eli was trying to tell the people was... let's just say they knew to listen after that."

Faro tried to connect the dots, but he was still missing something. "And what does all of this have to do with me?" he asked the healer.

"Well..." Mathias started slowly, cocking his head as if leading into something big. "The leaders of Incarta believed Eli should travel to the other kingdoms and spread this message to help rally an army to take on Cosimir. To show the support of each kingdom and give more weight to his message, the king of Incarta believed each kingdom should send someone of great importance to accompany Eli and help rally the troops. The king of Incarta sent his only son... Faro."

The lion raised his eyebrows at the little man. "I'm...I can't be a..."

"Prince of Incarta!" Mathias said, joyously clapping his hands together. The other three turned to stare at the odd pair, and Thora tilted her head in interest. "You accompanied Eli to the other kingdoms and grew close to him as a friend and disciple," Mathias continued. "I don't know what went on at Mt. Fluore, or why Eli has taken Cosimir's place as ruler, but some dark magic has overtaken you, and turned you into this." Mathias gestured at all of him. "Despite being a lion, you are the sole Prince of Incarta none-the-less."

They all began walking normal pace again towards the border wall in the distance, the three in front whispering quietly among themselves, Faro and Mathias walking quietly behind as Faro tried to process all of this new information. They finally stepped out of the fields and up to a wall that marked the end of Graeton's farmland. It was a ten-foot-tall wooden wall with no gaps to see through and with no gate in sight.

"We must climb," said Lena, unshouldering her pack and pulling out some rope. "The gates are several miles to the north and south. Over is our quickest path. Faro and I will climb over since we're the tallest, and pull the rest of you over with the rope."

Faro agreed and easily scaled the wall with Lena. He tossed the rope back down to the others, glad to be of service, but silently wondering if the members of his party now saw him differently knowing he was a prince.

Thora climbed up first while Faro held the rope, and Lena grabbed her hand to help her over. Tobi climbed next, and he and Thora used another rope to climb down the other side. Mathias was last, and slowest to make his way up. He got about halfway when they heard Tobi scream from the other side.

Faro and Lena looked down and saw Tobi. He was trying to fight off the grip of what appeared to be a cloaked human. Thora was still by the wall, brandishing her mace at three other similarly clad figures, daring them to come any closer.

The man holding Tobi looked up to the top of the fence and gasped. "A fucking lion-man! Benny! Look up there!"

The group of people looked up. Next to Faro, Lena let out a sigh. "I knew I forgot something," she said. "I made you a magical cloak that would hide your... this..." she said gesturing at him. "It's stuffed somewhere down in my pack."

"A little late now," he said, assessing the situation below them. There were three men advancing on Thora, one holding Tobi, and five more hanging back in case they were needed. Two of these men in the back had bows drawn, aimed right at him.

Faro, currently crouching down on the wall, slowly transferred the rope from his hand and put his weight on it with his foot and stood up, hands in the air to show he held no weapon. He felt the rope slip a little, but it held firm with Mathias hanging onto the other side.

The man holding Tobi spoke again. "Climb down nice and easy like, lion-man. We don't want anything to happen to your little friend here, *tsssk*" he said, holding his dagger to Tobi's throat.

"Dark Humans," Lena whispered to Faro. "We have to be careful."

CHAPTER NINE

LIGHT THROUGH DARK MADNESS

"I said, come down now, or the dwarf gets it, *ttsstsk!*" the Dark Human screamed up at Faro and Lena on the wall.

Faro looked down at the grizzly man. He wore a dark green cloak like the rest of them. This man had a long, mangy black beard, and appeared to be getting on in years. His skin appeared dark purplish-gray, though Faro wasn't sure if that was his skin-tone or some weird lighting from the hood of the cloak.

The oddest thing though, was the twitch. The man's hand remained steady, but his head kept twitching violently to the side as he made strange, guttural noises. Noises as though he was trying to scare away a stray cat that wasn't there. A quick scan of the others told him they all had this weird, similar affliction.

Faro didn't know what to make of it. He looked sideways at Lena for a second and she nodded down at the rope under his feet. He glanced down, and then nodded back to her as if he understood. At that, he slowly put his hands down and spoke to the crazed man down below.

"Let's not be hasty here, okay fella? I'm going to grab this rope and use it to come down, okay?" Faro said, gesturing to the rope beneath his foot.

"Yeah, yeah, get on with it then! Tssstk!" The man said, ending his sentence with the weird noise again. The others jerked and jumped at this noise and followed with their own weird noises. Faro slowly squatted back down and grabbed the rope, slowly pulling his weight off of it. He could still feel the weight on the rope, meaning that Mathias was still hanging on the other end. He hoped that the old healer was ready for what was about to happen.

In one swift movement Faro grabbed the rope with both hands and jumped off the wall. Instead of trying to catch his feet on the other side to repel down, he let all of his weight pull the rope down as fast and as hard as he could. His heavier weight pulled the little healer easy enough, and Mathias came flying over the wall.

To Faro's delight, Mathias already had his short sword drawn and was ready for action as he came down on the other side. Faro judged his landing place and turned, hunching a bit, giving his friend an easier place to land than the solid ground. Mathias' feet landed squarely on Faro's shoulders, and the lion shifted his weight forward towards the crazed man holding Tobi. The momentum from this movement sent Mathias lunging forward at break-neck speed.

The Dark Human that was holding Tobi let out a yelp and took a step back, loosening his grip. Judging by his poor reaction, Faro could tell that they weren't aware that Mathias had been hanging on the other side of the wall. Tobi used the moment to slip away just in time, as the healer took his short sword and stabbed the man right square in the chest. The man gasped in surprise and pain; the air rushing out of his body.

Faro loosened his full-sized war hammer from its holster on his belt and stood up straight just in time to see an arrow sink into the neck of one archer in the group of five, courtesy of Lena working her bow from atop the wall.

Thora saw her cue and went to work with her mace. Faro just stared in awe, not really sure if he would be of any help in her fight. On her own, she had already taken the spiked mace to one man's head, and the hip of another. The third man that had surrounded her hung back a bit, determined to kill her, but also now weary to come within swinging distance of the wild woman. He could see the red eyes of war in her, and looked as if he were about to run when Tobi ran up behind him and butted him in the back with the handle of his axe. The man stumbled forward towards Thora's waiting swing and was down in an instant, blood flying from his face where the mace's spikes made contact.

Faro looked up and saw that Lena had dropped three more in the group that was hanging back from the fight, leaving just one Dark Human left. Faro wasn't sure what came over him, but he dropped the hammer and lunged forward like an animal, pouncing forward on all fours and grabbing the last one before they could escape, or before Lena shot them down.

With a huge, lionesque roar he wrapped his paw-hands around the Dark Human and slammed them into the ground. He quickly ripped back the hood and saw that it was an older woman.

Lena landed behind him with a thump, and the entire party circled in around Faro and the woman, weapons drawn. Faro could see the woman's entire face contorting, her left eye twitching, her mouth uttering gibberish. Faro roared again and then spoke.

"Were you sent by Eli?" he roared at her. "Did he send you to kill us?"

After a moment of sheer panic, the woman calmed down enough to talk. "Eli? No, no, no. We don't... we answer to no one now. No one. Tsst. We can't... we won't be answering to anyone else. We just want... tssstk... we are trying to get our lives back!"

Faro didn't understand what she meant, but Lena apparently did as she sprung into action, shouldering her bow and bending down next to the old woman. The elf held up her hand and began speaking in tongues again. The same tongues that the Geusto sang in his song at Osric's funeral.

White light built in Lena's hand as it had back at the Church of Solana, but this time it seemed calmer, less intense. Faro tried to look at it to see where it was coming from, but all he could see was light and particles swirling in an orb within her palm. As she kept speaking words she moved her hand closer to the old woman and slowly opened her fingers, as if releasing the light directly into the lady's face.

The old woman squirmed in Faro's grasp, let out a shriek as though she were dying, and then a calm came over her. Faro gasped as he watched the woman's purple-gray skin turn back to a normal light brown tone. She lay there for a moment, as if completely at peace with the world, almost as if she were sleeping, and then slowly opened her eyes.

"The colors!" she said. Faro thought that was an odd thing to say. Lena told him to let the woman go, so Faro let her sit up. She was blinking really slowly and staring around in amazement.

"The colors of the world are so vibrant now. It was so gray and gloomy in there," she said, but Faro wasn't sure where *there* was.

Lena nodded as if she did. "Yes. The Virmorphia no longer has a hold on you. Can you tell us where you were going?"

The woman thought for a second and then recalled. "We were going to see the new ruler on the mountain." She saw the looks of concern on the party's faces. "Not to join him," she added. "We hoped we could be freed from the dark magic prison we were kept in. Madness..." she trailed off.

Thora knelt down beside Lena, a strong look of concern on her face. "The magic drives you mad?" she asked the old woman.

The lady nodded, "Yes. Raving mad. The world is dark. You hear voices. Voices making you say and do things you don't want to. Sometimes you can fight it. Other times... I've done things. Things I can never forget, and probably can't forgive myself for. I've killed...killed children of kings and merchants. Killed people who were bringing supplies to a kingdom that was under siege for non-payment to Cosimir. Terrible... all terrible..."

Lena grabbed the woman's hand in her own and patted the top, showing her sympathy. "We're sorry about the rest of your party. We were under attack."

"No," the woman waved her off, but a tear still rolled down her face. She looked around glumly at all the men that were with her. Their skin had turned back to various shades of brown and peach. "I get it, and they are free now, too. Many wanted to kill us over the years, because we were so unpredictable and violent. I'm just glad they will rest easy."

"What's your name, friend?" Thora asked her.

"Maggie," said the woman. "It used to be Maggie. Back when I lived in the mountains. Back before..." she stopped and shuttered.

"It's okay," said Lena, urging her to continue. "Talking about it can often be helpful."

The woman continued, "...back before Cosimir brought us all up to the top of the mountain for the ritual. I was so young then. We were all drowned. Drowned in the dark pool. Literally held under until we could no longer breath and only saw blackness. When we came back up it was like we were reborn, but in great darkness."

Silence followed this grim recollection. After a long pause Maggie finally stood up from the ground and brushed herself off. Looking around at the party her gaze settled on Faro. "And you're..."

"A lion, yeah," he said, still not used to the fact himself.

"Beings as you're a crazy animal man and you're heading this way, I assume you must be looking for that crazed wolverine man, Jarl?"

Jarl? The name sounded familiar to Faro, but he couldn't quite place it. They hadn't picked up on the thing's name during their fight in Graeton, but it was still good news that he had been seen coming this way.

"Yes," said Faro. "How long ago did you see him?"

The lady stroked a few white wispy hairs that were growing from her chin. "Yesterday. Other side of those trees," she said pointing at the grove not too far away. "Him, that girl, and that weird rock man."

"The girl?" asked Mathias. "Was she still alright?"

"Seemed to be. Just scared out of her wits. I mean, no wonder, given her traveling companions," Maggie said. "That little wolverine introduced himself and offered to buy our horses. When we refused they killed two of our group and stole the two horses. Had the nerve to ask for directions to Umbra's Veil after that, too."

"Horses!" exclaimed Tobi. "How are we going to catch them now? It will take us three times longer to get there than them," he swung his axe and buried it into the ground in frustration. Faro sensed a pattern in what the dwarf did to quell his temper. "There will be no catching them by surprise now," Tobi growled.

Thora put a hand on his shoulder, trying to calm him. The dwarf seemed to calm down and take deep breaths as she spoke. "If they get to Umbra's Veil, it will be harder to save Veronica. No one's alive that's went into that place. It's just a shroud of mystery and death."

Faro saw everyone nodding, except for Lena who was oddly still. He thought that weird, but then again the elf rarely showed much emotion, so it could have been that she wasn't afraid of the gloomy place they were headed. Still, her demeanor seemed to tense a bit at the mention of Umbra's Veil. Faro didn't want to pry now, but thought about asking her what she knew before they got there.

"So this Jarl and his companion took horses?" asked Mathias. "Maggie, did your group have more horses? We're on our way to save the little girl that was with those monsters." Faro gave him a dirty look, and Mathias added, "Not like you, Faro. You have good intentions." Turning back to Maggie he said, "We need to catch them before they get to Umbra's Veil, or our chances of success go down greatly."

Maggie nodded and pointed to the grove of trees. "We left the horses there when we went out scouting for food this morning. That's when we saw you. I can get you to the horses if that's what you need. Just need to leave me one so I can go back to my home in the mountains and see if there's anything left." Another tear rolled down the old woman's cheek. "It will be nice to do something good for once, helping you save that poor girl, I mean."

Faro felt himself smile at the sentiment. There was some good in the world, even if they had to be the ones to drive the evil out to find it. Finding out that he was a prince had also given him a renewed sense of duty to those in need. Rescuing Veronica felt much more personal to him now. He wasn't sure how close Incarta was to Graeton, but people were people, and he was going to do everything he could to set things right. Also, if he could find out a bit more about himself from Jarl, that would be a win too.

Thora rummaged through her pack and found a loaf of bread she had rolled up with the food provisions. She handed it to the woman who took it without question and started eating it ravenously, as though she hadn't eaten anything real in years. Faro didn't want to venture a guess at what Dark Humans normally ate. The way they had attacked the party without question, he was pretty sure he had some idea.

After scarfing down the entire loaf of bread, Maggie looked around at the five of them and gestured her hand off towards the grove of trees. "Let's get moving before the horses get picked off by a raiding party, shall we?"

They all adjusted their packs and slung and holstered their weapons. Maggie took off at a decent pace for an old woman, and the five of them followed her off towards the woods.

CHAPTER TEN

VEIL OF ILLUSIONS

Jarl snarled and shook his head. It had been like this for days now. Once the little girl had gotten used to her captivity, she had gone from scared and silent to loud and jarring. The wolverine had barely had any good sleep in the last few days as the girl's questioning grew more insistent.

"Do you really need this rope?" Veronica asked him, pulling at the rope that was tied around her waist and held by the Shadruul.

"We wouldn't if you hadn't tried to escape three times already!" he barked at her. He was irritated from the questions and from the amount of walking they were doing. The horses they had stolen from a group of Dark Humans had been spooked by a leopard snake briefly after they had entered the dark lands. They had bucked off their riders and run off, leaving them to trek the rest of the way to the castle on foot. Having never even been to Umbra's Veil himself, Jarl wasn't sure how much farther they had to go. At the time he was just happy that the horses had given them a good head start ahead of Faro so he could complete his mission before the lion arrived. Now he was regretting not going back after the horses. They had been very helpful to get them swiftly around Mournfall Lake and through Zeliran land unnoticed. They would have helped whisk them to Umbra's Veil now, but he had decided forward was better than backwards.

"Not like I have anywhere to go now!" Veronica shouted back at him, her tone deep with sass. "Like, what? I'm going to run and hide behind that rock spire over there? Or that one there? Or that..."

"Please! Just stop talking!" he snarled at her. "Can we just...please... walk in silence?"

The silence that followed lasted maybe fifteen seconds before she spoke again. "So, you're not going to tell me where we're going?"

Jarl hung his head. He wished he didn't need the girl to attract Faro to Umbra's Veil. But if there was one thing he knew about Faro in his travels with him as a disciple under Eli, it was that the insufferable do-gooder couldn't resist rescuing someone in need. And a tiny wolverine taking down a giant lion of a man in open combat just wasn't an option. Their last fight had proved that. He needed Faro to follow him into unknown territory where he could lay a trap for him.

"I've told you, child, we're going to the land of Dark Elves. We're going to Umbra's Veil."

"Yeah? But like, why?" she asked, either unaware how annoying she was, or keenly aware and dead set on annoying him to death.

"That is for me to know, and you to never find out," he said for what felt like the hundredth time in their journey. He didn't know how someone had the capacity to talk so much. Even his own children didn't talk this much. Thinking of them now made him wish that he was home with them, instead of on this mission.

The truth was that after Eli had turned on them all, and the dark magic had turned him from dwarf to wolverine, he had been scared and ready to run away. Instead, when Eli had commanded them all the stand at attention, Jarl couldn't refuse. He didn't know what dark magic was bound to him, but he was no longer of his own volition when it came to Eli. His mind grew cloudy and dark when the new ruler spoke, and he found himself obeying against his will.

The will of Eli had been for him to hunt down Faro and kill him, and then go to Umbra's Veil and try to recruit more dark magic users to their cause, or steal any secrets he could from Umbra. Of course the existence of Umbra's Veil was all hearsay. No one alive was known to have left the Veil. Some didn't even believe that it existed.

The rumors in Jarl's home kingdom, Underoth, had been that the great king, Umbra of Zelira, had gone mad on his quest for dark power and just simply blew up the entire region of the dark lands where the Academy of Solana's Light had been. Rumor was that he was now just a hermit living in a tent or a shack, holding onto the facade of running a dark kingdom. This had created a lot of myth and legend about what lay within the dark abyss.

Unfortunately for Jarl, the Dark Mage Eldryn and the new High King believed Umbra was still alive, and they wanted him recruited to their cause. Jarl hoped that if the evil elf king was still alive, he would simply kill Faro for him upon arrival. Given his luck in killing the lion so far, something told Jarl he wouldn't get off that easy. Still, Eldryn had given him instructions to find the dark secrets of Umbra's Veil, no matter the cost.

"You know, my grandfather is a powerful mayor. He'll be sending an entire army after me. He'll be so upset that you are taking me away from my studies of Solana," she stated this as if it were simply a fact, and that studying was the most important thing right now.

Jarl just chuckled at her. "You think the mayor of a ramshackle little town like that has command of an army? That's hilarious, child."

Veronica didn't appear to like the sound of this, and folded her arms and hung her head to pout. Jarl didn't care if he'd upset her. She was just a means to an end. Plus, if it meant that she stopped talking for at least five minutes, he would keep insulting her intelligence all day long.

"Boss." The statement came from the Shadruul that accompanied them. There were no more words that accompanied the simple phrase, just a long, sharp claw pointing out into the distance. Jarl followed the line of the Shadruul's finger and saw it. The mist that covered the dark lands, and seemed to cast them in eternal night, was covering some kind of formation, and Jarl could just make it out through the mist.

"I'll be damned," he said. "There really is a castle here."

Through the mist, Jarl could just make out the outline of a dark spire rising into the gray mist. As they took a few more steps, other towers' silhouettes came into view. The wolverine smiled. Even if he couldn't control himself around his new High King, being on his good side and completing his mission would sure make his new life easier.

"Good eye, Rotung," he said, still feeling weird using the thing's name. Commanding and traveling with the Shadruul had taken some getting used to. He had never seen anything like them before, and he wasn't sure he wanted to know where they came from. It was just all a part of the world that he was forced to live in now.

Jarl flinched when he heard the voice. "Great. We've found an old, creepy castle. You know they probably don't even live there, right? We'll have to find the dungeon they dug during the Scourge," Veronica said in her adamant, matter-of-fact way.

The wolverine felt his eye twitch. "Double-time until we get there. Come on!" He sped up, knowing that the sooner they got there the sooner he could get Umbra to lock this annoying child in the dungeon and get some silent time away from her.

Rotung pulled on Veronica's string, and the mismatched trio quickened their pace towards the shadowy kingdom in the distance.

Many hours later they were getting close to the castle. As they got closer and could see more clearly through the mist, they could see that the castle was in ruins. The mist made the entire structure look brown and dirty. Large pieces could be seen missing from the towers, and rubble littered the ground around the base of the structure.

"What a dump," Veronica said, to no surprise of Jarl. "I told you this place isn't habitable. They are all either underground, or dead!"

"Fine," Jarl snapped back at her. "I told you we will either see them in the castle, or you will start digging to find them!" He turned to glare at the little girl, who stared him right back in the eyes, unfazed.

"We don't have a shovel," she shot back, her mouth curling into a half smile.

Jarl smiled back at her. "You have hands. You can dig."

Her mouth fell open at the audacity of the thought of this, and when she closed it, Jarl hoped that the shock would keep it closed for good - or at least for the next ten minutes.

The trio kept walking, examining the ruins as they plodded their way closer. Jarl wasn't sure what to expect when they got there, but it sure wasn't what happened next.

They all walked side-by-side, and approached a tall, wide rock formation. It was an old border wall of some sort. Not that he was tall, but Jarl couldn't even attempt to scale the wall. He had to have Rotung lift him up to the top. The Shadruul then pulled Veronica up. Atop the wall, Jarl expected to cross over and quickly jump down, but when he took a step, he got a jolt that sent shock waves through his body. It was as if gale force winds were trying to push him back.

Instinctively, he clung to the Shadruul, using the bulk of the rock monster to anchor him down. Veronica quickly did the same. They closed their eyes against the wind, and Rotung used all of his strength to pull the trio forward until they made it to the edge of the wall. With a mighty grunt and a leap, they jumped the distance back down to the earth. Jarl felt the jolt of the ground through his legs, but it was much more padded than he had expected.

Surprised, he looked down and saw grass. Green grass, as far as his beady little eyes could see. He rubbed his eyes with both paws and looked again. The meadow of grass and white flowers wasn't the only thing that had changed. Tilting his head back, he looked up in awe. Where there had been ruins of a once-magnificent castle, now stood the magnificent castle, fully intact. The mist was gone completely, and the sun penetrated the scene. The shining white stones were almost too bright to look at after all the darkness they had just waded through.

"What the fuck?" Veronica exclaimed.

Jarl turned to her quickly and snapped, "You watch your mouth, girl!" The sentence had left his mouth before he could stop it, and a moment of sadness hit him. He was speaking to her like his own children back in Underoth. It was a momentary lapse of strength that showed weakness, and he ensured himself he would not make that mistake again. Veronica just stared at him in shock, not sure what to make of the parental snapback her captor had just made at her. "It's obviously some sort of spell," he said, trying to push past the comment and move the conversation along. "The true veil is the illusion of the destruction, I suppose. Keeps people out."

They moved their way through the grass. Veronica bent down and felt it with her hand, chuckling a little under her breath, and picking a small white flower as they passed it. Rotung gave her rope an extra yank and sent her sprawling forward, almost falling.

As they neared the castle, there was a drawbridge over a moat. It was made of strong, wooden planks, its chains running up through the castle wall where a crank could reel the bridge up if needed.

They paused at the head of the bridge, unsure whether it was safe to cross. On the other side of the bridge, they could see that they were no longer alone. Two elves wielding spears and clad in green were standing on either side of the entryway. Jarl tried to size them up and see if they would be welcomed, or if he should brace for a fight. He decided that their posture seemed a little lax for warriors who were looking for a fight.

Waving the other two along, Jarl led the way across the bridge. As they approached, the elves didn't change their positions. When they got within calling distance, Jarl decided it was best to introduce themselves and their business.

"Ho there friends! We seek council with the great King Umbra. Would it be possible to gain an audience with him?"

The elf on their right relaxed his spear grip and broke out into a slow smile as they approached.

"The great King Umbra welcomes all honored guests, my friend. Welcome to Mireholm!"

The name surprised them. To the rest of the world, this was known as Umbra's Veil. They obviously had the right place because they said Umbra was here. Jarl exchanged a quick glance with Rotung. Shrugging, Jarl took the first step forward and through the gateway into the kingdom of Mireholm.

CHAPTER ELEVEN

A KING'S WELCOME

J arl nodded his head at each elf guard as they walked by them. They didn't say anything else as they passed, but just kept smiling. Veronica cheerily waved at them as they passed, finally happy to see someone besides her captors and Dark Humans.

"Hi!" she exclaimed cheerily, giving them a wave.

When the elves remained silent, Jarl realized that he finally needed to break the silence and get further directions. "Say, friends. We've never been here before. Not really sure where King Umbra is, or how to gain an audience with him. Any chance you'd be so kind as to help us out?"

The elf nodded, never breaking his friendly smile. "Of course! Just follow the main road up East that way, and when you hit a row of houses, take a right. He'll be up in the keep. You can't miss it!"

Easy enough to get there. "But what about getting into the keep? He just accepts any and all visitors?" Jarl asked.

The elf nodded vigorously. "Of course! King Umbra is a kind and gracious king. He welcomes all honored guests who come to Mireholm."

Jarl nodded. As he did so, he felt the ears wiggle on the top of his head. He hated the feeling and just wanted to have his normal tangle of dwarf hair back. He sure hoped Umbra was as kind as they said. Maybe he could help turn him back into a dwarf. He noticed Veronica lift her rope and look pointedly at one elf, who just smiled back at her, same as before.

"Perfect!" said the wolverine, awkwardly trying to cut the moment short. "We'll just be right on our way then!"

Rotung and Veronica followed him onto the cobbled street. It was fairly deserted for it being so bright and sunny out. Before they'd passed the outer wall of the kingdom, Jarl hadn't even been sure what time of day it was. The mist had blocked the sun and with it any indication of whether it was night or day. Upon entering the kingdom it was clearly day, but it was weird that there were so few people about.

"Child on a rope!" Veronica yelled. "Child on a rope is completely normal here, apparently? What type of society thinks child on a rope is normal!"

"Quiet!" Jarl hissed at her, though he saw her point. The guards were obviously too enthralled with their guard duties to do anything about it, but he knew it looked odd leading her around on a rope. He had been expecting a place full of dark sorcerers who wouldn't care. Instead, he got the sunshine kingdom and friendly faces. "Fine," he conceded, stopping to untie the rope from around her waist, "but if you run, Rotung takes one step to your four. He *will* catch you."

She just waved her hand at him, "Yeah, yeah, got it. Not sure I want to get lost in the land where they think children on ropes is normal anyways."

Jarl looped the rope and threw it over one shoulder across his chest, saving it just in case he needed it to keep her tethered again. At that, they all headed down the street again. They were greeted with shops, taverns, and blacksmith forges on both sides. They could see some elves through the windows of some of them, hard at work with whatever task they were doing, paying no attention to the strangers that walked their streets. The more Jarl thought about it, the more it made sense. The kingdom appeared to be in ruins from the outside. No outside trade, and the people of the kingdom hard at work. There really wouldn't be that many people out and about.

At the end of the empty road, true to the guard's words, they came to a row of very fancy dwellings. The stonework was decorated with intricate carvings of foliage and Jarl could see some animals carved into the red stone as well. No, the stone was brown. Gray? Jarl blinked again and tried to clear his vision. He could have sworn he'd seen the color shift, but now it just appeared as solid red colored stone. He decided that being in the sun after all that dark was playing tricks on his mind.

Trying to clear his thoughts, he turned to look up at the keep. It was down a much shorter stretch than the main road was. Towering above the rest of the surrounding town, it seemed to hold a lot of the same intricate carvings. Where Jarl came from, the military stronghold of Underoth, everything was very plain, bland, and serious. The elves seemed to take a different approach, making things more aesthetically pleasing and beautiful, thinking beyond just the functional.

Another bridge greeted them, the only path over to the stronghold where the king held residence. As they crossed the bridge, Jarl did a double-take as a familiar sight greeted them. It was two elves with spears standing on either side of the bridge. Jarl had to squint his eyes and lean in. They looked almost exactly like the elves that had been guarding the front gates to the kingdom.

"What in the world?" he asked out loud, wondering if he was just unfamiliar with elf culture and how much they must all look the same.

"Spooky," said Veronica, apparently noticing the same thing. "You think they teleported over here to greet us again?"

Jarl smacked his forehead. "Don't be ridiculous. We're just not used to their culture, so they look a little bit the same to us. They are different elves," but even as he said it he was still doubting himself.

As they got close enough, he greeted them as he had done with the first guards.

"Ho there friends! Guard at the gate said we could get a meeting with the great King Umbra!"

The elves again followed the same motions as the ones at the gate, but Jarl wrote it off as protocol. They both relaxed their grips on their spears and adopted the same, over-friendly smile. "The great King Umbra welcomes all honored guests, my friend! Go on through!"

A chill ran down Jarl's spine, but he smiled and nodded politely as they walked through. They hadn't questioned the child on the rope. They hadn't questioned their business, or that he was a talking animal-man. Something wasn't sitting right with him, but he knew that his mission was to talk to Umbra, so he took it as a win that it was so easy to gain an audience with the ruler of a kingdom.

They stepped into a lavish courtyard. Grass covered most of the area, with stone paths going around the perimeter, leading to different entry points of the keep. Fixed in the center of the courtyard was a giant water fountain. Jarl gaped at it. It wasn't some demonic figure as one might expect given all the dark rumors surrounding Umbra's Veil. It wasn't even a statue of Umbra that stood in the middle. It was a giant statue of Solana. One of his hands was raised high in the air as if he were creating the heavens, and water shot out of his palm and rained down onto his body and down into the fountain below.

The wolverine's ears perked up. Why would a statue of the heavenly god be in a place of dark magic? Why would a place of dark magic look so bright and cheery? He was wondering if Eli and Eldryn had Umbra pegged correctly as a mage of the dark arts. Maybe he was simply just a hermit who hid himself away from the world to avoid its drama and wars.

The trio skirted their way around the fountain and followed the path directly through the courtyard to a set of huge oak doors that were the path to the court of King Umbra.

Before they could quite reach the doors however, they flew open, and a figure stood before them. He appeared to be a much older elf, though Jarl wasn't entirely sure how elves aged, so he couldn't determine how old he was. Even so, he was cloaked in extravagant, golden robes. As the elf spread his arms wide in greeting, the sleeves hung way down towards the ground, the extra cloth showing just how elegant the attire was.

"Greetings, my honored guests!" boomed the elf. He had the same friendly smile as the others they'd seen so far. "I am King Umbra, of Mireholm."

Jarl cocked his head a bit at the man. "Were... were we expected? Or do you just let everyone waltz right up to your front door?" he asked.

"Both!" chimed Umbra, simply. "As one who can see the future, it is no surprise as to who is about to knock on my door, Jarl. Foresight is both a blessing and a curse, as one would imagine."

At this, Jarl nodded, unfazed by the use of his name by a man who could tell the future. He could see Umbra moving his eyes around and surveying all of them. When his gaze fell on Veronica, she spoke.

"So, your kingdom is above ground? All the other kingdoms are still hiding. How did you manage that?"

Umbra raised one eye at her and smiled at the girl's spunk. "I was tired of being a *Dungeon Lord* to that insufferable oaf on the mountain. I simply used my power to rebuild my kingdom and cloaked it in ruin and despair to hide the fact it was above ground again. Now if you don't mind, please do come in. I feel like we have some matters to discuss before the others arrive!"

"Others?" Jarl snapped. "What others? If you're talking about that fool lion who is following me, he's at least three days out."

"Is he?" said Umbra with a smile, and then he turned and waved them all to follow.

Jarl glanced at Veronica and Rotung, and shrugged, gesturing for them to follow the odd elf king inside the keep. As they stepped through the doors, the sight that greeted them was as awe-inspiring as stepping from the wasteland into the lush green pastures when they had entered Mireholm.

The entry hall they stepped into appeared to be made of solid gold. Everything from the two staircases that curved up to the upper levels, to the chandeliers that hung from the ceiling, illuminating the room with what appeared to be dozens of subfluore crystals per fixture. Even the rug they now stepped on shined gold, as though gold fibers had been spun into a cloth that was simply meant to be walked on.

Veronica's mouth was agape the entire time in awe. The Church of Solana in Graeton was the nicest place she had ever been exposed to before this. Even Rotung seemed to stare around in awe, though Jarl couldn't see much change in expression on the Shadruul's rock face. He himself felt his fingers twitch. This much gold and subfluore would fund five dwarven lifetimes of munitions and living expenses for the entire kingdom of Underoth. And here it was just sitting in the middle of a wasteland with the happy elf clan watching over it.

They followed the flowing gold robe of King Umbra across the carpet and through the double doors that sat between the two curved staircases. Immediately they knew they were in the throne room. It was even more magnificent than the previous room, however that was possible. The throne was huge, golden, and inset with dark red gems, all shining so bright in the room's sunlight that the trio had to avert their eyes until they adjusted to the change in lighting. Windows were set into the top of the walls around the entire room, letting in the natural, bright sunlight from the outside, making the room sparkle and shine. Behind the throne was a giant statue of a magnificent, yet curious, white marble stag. It was just the front half of the horse's body, but it was reared up, hooves hanging over the top of the throne, its head kicked back and facing the heavens.

Umbra took three steps up to the dais and took his place on his throne. He stared down at them with a wide, beaming smile. "Please, friends, state your business here."

Jarl blinked his eyes again so he could see Umbra against the brightness. "I bring you a message from the new high ruler on the mountain, Eli Ashford. He would like to work on a truce with you, and establish an open exchange of knowledge."

Umbra just smiled. "Is that so? New king you say? It was my understanding that Eli was meant to free us from such tyranny. What happened there?"

The wolverine was taken aback that King Umbra didn't know something, and also admittedly, Jarl wasn't really sure what had happened. They had followed Eli around Evania, rallying kingdoms to overthrow Cosimir, and fighting battles against his hoards. The thing was, Eli wasn't supposed to be in charge now. "I believe that many of us didn't understand the prophecy, Your Highness. Either that or the whole thing was corrupted by the Dark Mage Eldryn."

Umbra raised his eyebrows as Jarl spoke the name. "Eldryn, you say? He's still alive then?"

Jarl nodded. "Yes, Your Highness. He's kept his place alongside the new Evanian ruler during the... transfer of power."

"I see," said Umbra, looking concerned for the first time. The elf king thought for a long moment. What was almost a look of sadness came over him. "We will need to talk more about this truce that Eli wishes to establish, my dear Jarl. But we can talk about all that in due time. For right now," Umbra pointed one of his long, slender fingers at Veronica, "I do not allow people to have prisoners in my kingdom."

Jarl felt his face go flush. "I only needed her to..."

"Yes, I know," Umbra waved him off. "You wanted to lure the lion here so you could beat him with an unfair advantage. And no," he added, "I will not kill him for you."

The wolverine's body went rigid. This elf knew all of his thoughts and intentions. He wasn't sure how he would get any advantage on him if he didn't want a truce. How could he complete his mission then? It was likely that he knew exactly the means he was told to pursue to get what he needed for Eli and Eldryn.

Umbra turned and smiled at Veronica. "You are free to go, Dear." He waved his hand and an elf maid appeared from behind his throne, as if from nowhere. "Elia here will take care of you during your stay. Please make sure that she gets cleaned up and a good set of clothes, my dear."

The elf maid nodded and walked forward, taking Veronica by the hand and leading her away from the other two. Jarl felt like a child in trouble, but Umbra didn't pay him any further attention at the moment. Instead, he turned towards Rotung. "And you, my poor soul. Roland here will take you down to the lower dungeons. We will see what we can do to free you from your prison."

This time a male elf emerged at Umbra's beckoning and led a confused-looking Rotung away. Now it was just Jarl alone with Umbra, though he wasn't sure how many more servant elves were stashed behind that golden throne. It was the first time Jarl had been alone since his transformation. He had lived life being shorter than most, as he was naturally a dwarf, but now, standing alone before the huge throne of the mighty king, he felt smaller and less significant than he ever had in his life.

Umbra looked quizzically at his small guest. "Can you tell me, what has caused you to turn into a creature such as this?"

Jarl was surprised at the question. "Did your visions not show you the battle inside the mountain?"

Tapping his fingers on the arm of the throne, Umbra thought for a moment. "No. Mt. Fluore has always been shrouded in a fog my visions cannot penetrate, at least since Cosimir began his reign. All I have seen is the lion and you coming down from the mountain after going up as men. And you have informed me that Eli now rules, and Eldryn still holds power."

"Yes, Your Highness," said Jarl. "I believe it was something Eldryn did during the transfer of power. Some spell he put on the weapon that killed Cosimir. Everyone in the room but him was transformed into an animal. Even Eli looks like some sort of beastly ram now."

"Interesting," said Umbra, deep in thought. "You and I have much more to talk about, Dear Friend, but I'm afraid I will have to cut it short for now. We need to greet our new guests."

Jarl's blood ran cold. "Guests? What guests?"

Umbra looked at him pointedly. "Your lion friend and his party of course."

Jarl just shook his head, not willing to accept it, not wanting a confrontation with Faro without more time to prepare.

"That's impossible! We've only been here an hour tops. They were at least three or four days behind us!"

"Yet, here they are!" said Umbra, smiling again. "Let's go greet them at the gates! I've been waiting a long time for this reunion!"

CHAPTER TWELVE

THE THREADS OF FATE

FOUR DAYS EARLIER...

The party from Graeton, along with Maggie, took stock of the grove just twenty yards in front of them. From their vantage point they could see the tall, green trees reaching up for the sky. Each leafy tree was adorned with red apples, and the floor of the grove was carpeted with them as well. A quick scan didn't show any sign of movement within the grove, but Maggie assured them that not only did raiders frequent the area for supplies, namely fresh fruit and whatever their unsuspecting victims were carrying, but there was also a magical nymph that lived in the forest and liked to cause mischief to travelers and raiders both.

"Well," said Faro, satisfied with their survey and wanting to get a move on to catch Jarl, "I'm not seeing any sign that we will be bothered. And honestly, we will never be one-hundred percent sure until we go in for the horses."

"I agree," said Mathias as he walked back up to the group. He had taken a chance to get a closer look at the grove and reported that nothing seemed to be out of place there. "I also suggest we pull out our weapons in case we're ambushed," he said a little nervously, drawing his sword. Though he had done well in the fight against the Dark Humans, Mathias was still a little leery of battle. He was a healer, not a fighter. Thora pulled out her mace eagerly, and Tobi grabbed his axe with his usual fierce determination. Calm as ever, Lena knocked an arrow on her bow. Maggie only had a dagger on her now, but she held it so tightly in her grasp that her knuckles were stark white.

Faro nodded at all of them, and they started forward. When they were mere feet from the first apple tree, they could make out the horses within the grove. They were several rows of trees in, each tied up to their own tree. They could be seen ducking down and picking up apples with their mouths and chomping them down.

"Aye! A snack does sound good!" said Tobi. He took the butt of his axe and drove it into the nearest tree. A dozen apples rained down on them and he quickly identified the fresh-fallen fruit amongst those already spoiled on the ground, and distributed them to the party. Maggie politely declined, still full from the loaf of bread she had wolfed down an hour earlier.

The air filled with crunching as they ate and made their way further into the grove. Faro smiled as they approached the horses. Now they'd be able to get to Umbra's Veil at a much quicker pace and make up all the time they'd lost.

The only problem was, when they got up to the horses, they vanished right before their eyes.

Faro reacted by waving his war hammer into the air, stepping carefully side to side and surveying the area. The illusion of horses meant a sorcerer was about, likely the wood nymph Maggie had mentioned, though he thought she had been joking. Glancing back, Faro could see the others waving their weapons around, confused as well. Then, just as suddenly, they weren't there either. The blackness pressed in around him, and then there was nothing.

Lena blinked and found herself in a familiar scene. Familiar, but so long ago. Her parents were laughing at the head table of the great hall of Zelira. Around them their guests danced merrily, most of them likely having partaken in too much wine during the festivities.

She watched her parents from the side of the room, leaning against the wall and taking in the scene. It was her parents' wedding anniversary, the last time they would be happy together during such an occasion. So much darkness was soon to take them over. So much darkness had already crept in, and Lena felt herself torn between staying loyal to her father and his kingdom, and following her training and staying in Solana's Light.

The sight of them up there, being happy, was too much for her. She turned to leave but was instead greeted by a stranger she had never seen before. He was a tall, slender man. A human. He was bald, but sported a full beard and mustache, mostly obscuring his friendly smile. The bridge of his nose had a big gash in it, as if he'd been in battle and narrowly missed having his head cut clean in half.

"Funny time to be having a party!" he exclaimed, and Lena just stared at him.

"I mean, it's their wedding anniversary," Lena shot back, but it was clear that's not what he meant.

"Dark times ahead. I know it. Your father knows it. Given your studies of The Light, I'd wager you know it, too." She studied the man as he spoke. He didn't seem to mean her any harm, she just wasn't sure why he was here stopping her from leaving.

"I don't know what I know anymore," she admitted. "I know The Light is the way, but my father, he feels we need more to stop the darkness."

At this, the man laughed. "Funny way to stop the darkness," he mused. "More darkness? When has the dark ever stopped the dark? No. When it comes right down to it, it's only the light that can stop the dark. It's the only thing that makes sense."

Lena smiled at the man. "Yeah, that does make sense, actually. Thank you," she said, smiling at the man. With that she turned towards the door and walked out, no longer wishing to speak about her father, nor the darkness ahead.

Before she was out of earshot, she heard the man call after her, "Only The Light will save the heir."

The words sounded odd to her. Heir? Heir of what? As she turned to ask him, she saw he was no longer there. He was gone as suddenly as he'd appeared.

She never saw the man again.

Little Thora padded across her parents' shop. The room shone bright orange as it always did, lit by the inordinate amount of subfluore crystals that always occupied the space. Her parents worked with the precious crystals to help develop weapons and machines of wonder for the Evania family and other kingdoms, as her family had done for generations.

The little nine-year-old girl loved the warm glow the crystals provided, and seeing her brilliant parents' inventions come to life always left her in awe. She was an only child, so her parents often had the time to show her what they were working on, and they would introduce her to the patrons that would come into the shop to buy inventions of lesser importance, like street lamps and lighting for their dwellings.

Now and then they would even get royalty through their doors, which was always a special treat. Just a few days prior the king of Incarta, James Envato, and his son Faro had been in to purchase a large load of special lighting brackets that were going to be hung around their mining facilities, along with a subfluore-powered grinding machine that her mother had invented that would help them refine iron ore at an astonishing rate.

Today her mother and father were in the back, and she was tending the front of the store in their absence. And by tending, her parents had told her, that meant to call them immediately when someone came in. She found it annoying when they did this. She knew she was big enough to handle a customer, they just didn't want to admit their little girl was growing up.

As she waited for the next customer, she tossed around a crystal like a ball. It was funny, because she had read there used to be wars over this stuff, but here it was, sitting around the shop like bread on display at a bakery.

During one particularly high throw, the bell to the front door dinged and distracted her. The crystal dropped into a vase of flowers her father had gotten her mother the day prior, and the vase fell to the ground and shattered.

"Oh no!" she cried, forgetting the customer, and getting the broom instead of her parents. She had to get it cleaned before they came back. She was sweeping the second half of the broken vase up when the customer engaged her.

"Hey there, little miss. Looks like you've got a bit of a mess there!" said a man's voice.

Startled, Thora glanced up and saw a tall, slender, bald man staring down at her, smiling through a bushy beard and mustache.

"Ugh, yeah I know. The ding of the door made me miss my throw." Looking up at his face, Thora noticed something odd. "What happened to your nose there, mister?" she asked, showing no tact as is typical of children.

The man just chuckled at her. "Someone tried to take my head off. Let's just say I'm good at dodging," he said, flicking his finger off the gash on his nose playfully. "Now," he continued, "I hear this is the best subfluore shop in all of Evania. I'm in the market for a weapon with a little extra kick."

"To stop people from chopping your head off?" she asked without pause.

"Yes," he chuckled again. "Exactly."

"Well, I'll go get my parents and they can help. They're in the shop out back," she said, finally remembering her protocol.

"Well, I have a feeling you can help me," he said, kneeling down beside her. "I want a sword that delivers an energy jolt to make sure the bad guys stay down when they're hit."

She thought for a moment and then started showing him various swords they had for sale. He sure was a picky customer, as nothing she showed him seemed to fit the bill.

While she showed him a particularly gnarly, curved scabbard with a subfluore embed in the hilt, they heard a loud bang from outside. Thora felt she should go and check, but the man insisted that the customer comes first, and that she continue to help him out. She agreed and kept showing him the weapons.

After what felt like an hour of showing him around, he finally settled on a longsword with a double subfluore embed. As he was paying, he tossed her an extra coin. She caught it and was struck by its odd nature. One side had a crown that looked like the royal seal of Evania. The other had strange markings that she couldn't decipher. She looked back up to thank the man, but he and the sword were gone.

She pocketed the strange coin and headed out back to tell her parents about the sale she had just made. Only they weren't there, and there were signs of a struggle. Later she had found out the Cosimir had sent his Dark Humans to kill her parents and steal their war machines from the shop in the back. This was the start of a dark six months where she had to survive by herself on the streets.

Tobi stood behind his bar on his raised sub floor, polishing a glass. He had sent his daughter Thora next door to the general store to see if she could make a deal on their next month's ration of food for their dwelling upstairs. The general store was run by a woman named Karen who was always wound up tight, which was funny because she had a particular liking for his special brew, and would often give them discounted food for a special supply of the vodka. Tobi always thought that would loosen her up more, but she was still wound tight every time he saw her.

As Tobi set the clean glass down and made to pick up another, a man walked into the tavern. Tobi sized him up. He was a tall, slender man with a balding head. Strapped across his back was a big, menacing looking sword with two subfluore crystals embedded in the hilt. Tobi instinctively felt under the bar for his axe, but the man simply strode up to the bar and took a seat.

"Two please!" he said cheerily.

Tobi laughed. "But there's only *one* of you, Sir!"

The man smiled at him. "Seems like a good day for a drink, so it seems like it will be an even better day if I have two!"

Tobi couldn't argue with the man's logic, and so got him his drinks. He pulled out a stein he'd bought in Baltha, where he'd found his daughter Thora living on the streets, and poured his special vodka mix in it. After repeating the same action to make another, he slid both over to the man.

"Quite the sword you got there!" Tobi chimed in, trying to keep his customer happy and engaged.

"You think so?" asked the man. "It's done me some huge favors in battle."

"Apparently not enough favors," Tobi quipped, pointing at his own nose, indicating the scar across the man's own nose.

"Oh yeah? What if I was to tell you that without this sword I wouldn't even have a head!" Both men burst out laughing, and the man happily slurped down his drink. Tobi was impressed at how the man downed his alcohol. Vodka usually had a burning feeling, but it didn't seem to bother this man. They made small talk, and the man downed his other drink, ordering two more. Tobi was sure he was going to be cleaning the man off the floor by the end of the night.

The man started to slur his speech. "Cutest... cutest... cue... little girl... she sold me this sword. Ten years back or so. You know that? Sweetest little girl in the world."

Tobi smiled, thinking of his own little girl next door still haggling with Karen. "Glad I met my cute little girl. She's trying to haggle with the hag next door for our food for the next month!" Tobi boomed proudly. "Sweetest thing she is. Gave me this," he said, yanking his axe from below the bar, "when she first met me!"

The man drew back a bit. "She ga...gave you an axe! I thought you... heh... thought you said she was sweet!" The man bust out laughing, his mouth hanging open wide as he did in his loud guffaw.

Tobi laughed just as hard back. "No, no, no!" Tobi yelled over the man's laughter. "This!" He pointed at a coin that was forged into the joint of the axe where the head met the handle. The man stared intently at it. It had the crown of Evania on the side that was facing out, surely the more decorative side if the dwarf had chosen that side to be outward facing.

"Quite the coin," the man said, and Tobi was taken aback by the sudden clearness of his voice. "Crest of the Evanian family. A sure sign that the heir will return."

Tobi's eyes grew wide. "Who are you, friend?" Tobi asked in awe.

"Just a traveler," said the man, getting up to leave. "Thank you so much for the drinks," he said, flipping him three gold coins, way more than the drinks were worth. "Stick by your little girl, and you can't go wrong, Tobi," said the man. Tobi was bending over to hook his axe back under the bar when the man said this.

"I never told you my name," the dwarf said, standing back up to face the man, but he was gone. Not even the tavern doors were swinging.

Mathias shivered as he sat atop the peak of the mountain. He could see the taller, snow-covered peak of Mt. Fluore in the distance, and was thankful that he didn't have to trek up that far. In fact no one did, as the ruthless Emperor Cosimir hardly allowed anyone up to his summit.

Instead, Mathias was here to help with the Darmarkan people, the primitive tribes that had settled the mountains around Mt. Fluore after the Evania family and their armies had freed them from harsh slavery in the country of Darmark to the south.

Mathias was a traveling healer, and he had heard that a grave illness had befallen the tribes of the mountains. Being the caring man that he was, he had rushed to their aid. He not only wanted to see if he could cure them, but he had also heard rumor that the symptoms were that of the once-dreaded Scourge that Cosimir and his Dark Mage Eldryn had cast upon the land to control the kingdoms. He had to see for himself if it was as many had feared was coming for years: the Scourge had returned.

Now as he sat on a rock in a hut, tending to a young, fair-skinned child, he was fairly certain what had struck the village was a case of awful food poisoning from a village celebration they'd had a few days prior. Not knowing the cause, they had continued to eat the tainted food for days until Mathias had arrived. There wasn't much he could do for them except make them all some ginger and peppermint tea to help with the symptoms and wait it out.

Leaving the hut and looking for a campfire to start the brew, Mathias heaved a sigh of relief. The Scourge wasn't back. No one really knew why it had subsided to begin with, but no one really cared, as long as it didn't come back.

It was night on the mountaintop, so locating the nearest fire was easy. It had burned low, as there weren't many well enough to be out tending to it. Mathias stoked the fire and then set up his camp stove from his supply pack and began preparing the peppermint and ginger plants to add to the water when a man's voice cut the night air.

"The simple remedies are always the best, are they not?" asked the voice.

Mathias set down his knife and looked towards the voice. Before him stood not a villager, but a tall, slender man with a balding head. In the flickering of the campfire, Mathias noticed that the man had a noticeable chunk of his nose missing, but he had enough tact not to mention such a deformity.

Curious as to why someone else who wasn't a villager was here, Mathias asked as much. "What brings you to these parts, Friend? Severe case of food poisoning here, so I hope you brought your own rations!"

The man smiled and pulled out his pack of rations from his side satchel. "Everywhere I go!" he said.

"Excellent," Mathias said back, going back to chopping up his ingredients. "And yes, a simple tea is about all I can do here. That and time to let this pass for them." The man nodded.

Mathias glanced at the stranger again and noticed the large, glaring weapon he carried. A longsword with two subfluore crystals embedded in the hilt. "Brave man," said Mathias. "Come to the mountains with a loaded weapon such as that, and the Dark Humans, maybe even Cosimir himself, would likely hunt you down and kill you for it."

The man just patted the sword. "That man's not the true king. He can come try and take it if he wants it. I can't interfere, but I can sure defend."

Mathias raised his eyebrows, impressed. "Not many are willing to speak so openly about such things, nor to make threats to the emperor on his own mountains."

The man pulled a cloth out and unwrapped it, revealing dried meat. He offered a piece to Mathias who took it happily and munched on it between brewing the tea.

The man took a piece for himself and chewed on it. "This land still has so much blood to shed before the true heir rises," he told Mathias simply.

The healer wasn't really sure what to make of that. "An heir you say? To the Evanian throne? An honorary heir at best, no doubt. The Evania line was stamped out when Cosimir slaughtered them all."

"Were they?" the man asked calmly. "They may yet be wiped out," he continued. "That's what the forces of evil seek to do. Evania will need a man who can heal both flesh and spirit if the heir is to take their rightful place on the mountaintop."

Mathias wasn't sure what to make of this man. "You're speaking in riddles, Friend," he said, hoping the man would elaborate more. He didn't.

"You are a kind and caring soul," said the man, pulling out another piece of dried meat. "But traveling as a healer must be hard on you as you're getting on in age."

"A little," Mathias agreed. He was here shivering on the mountaintop, sore from the rough climb to the top the day before. "But healing is my calling. Has been since I was a child."

The man shook his head. "There's a little town I was at, not too long back. You'd think it was a quiet, cozy little town, but it's actually bustling with life. Town called Graeton, just to the east of the mountain range through the valley. A lot of trade goes on there. More than almost any place in Evania since it's so close to the mountains, but not quite. I have a feeling they could use a talented healer there."

Mathias bent to taste test a ladle full of the tea, and then sat back up to ask the man why he thought it was such a good place for a healer, but the man was gone. Even a man of science like Mathias was baffled at the man's silent departure.

Faro held the shield tightly in his grip, waiting for the impact. When it came, it was not as hard as he had expected. It was true that he was a big, burly man, but he was still expecting a harder hit from the bigger, burlier man he was training. "Come on,

Eli! Is that all you've got?" Faro yelled at his opponent. "My old gran can swing a hammer harder than that!"

Eli brushed his long black hair from his face and struck again. Faro just laughed at him. Eli became frustrated. "I don't understand why I have to train to fight!" he yelled in frustration. "I thought my job was to deliver Solana's message to the kingdoms and be done. We've done that, now it's time the real fighters take over!"

Faro clicked his tongue at the man. "Tsk. Tsk. Eli, you are the face of the rebellion. You hold the hope of the entire country of Evania on your words. That also means that you drive its fate with your hands. Now strike like you mean it!"

This time Eli summoned up all his pent up frustration at being called to something he wanted no part of and swung the hammer hard into Faro's shield. Faro felt the strike reverberate through his entire arm and took a step back to absorb the recoil of the force. "Excellent! There's that blacksmith swing! Just pretend your enemy is an anvil, you will do just fine!"

Eli's face broke into a smile. "I'm glad you've been there for me through all of this, you know," he said to Faro. "I didn't ask for these visions. I'm a nobody. I don't deserve all this grandeur."

Faro shrugged at his friend. "Solana chose you, my friend. Out of everybody in Evania, He chose the blacksmith from Incarta. Doesn't sound like a nobody to me."

This didn't make Eli look any happier. Rather, he looked like he might throw up. Instead of continuing the topic, he changed the subject. "Do you think the Dungeon Lord Council has decided on a proper successor if we're to succeed in the war?" Eli asked him.

Faro thought for a minute. It was an impossible decision for the kingdoms' rulers to make. Who among them had the right to sit atop Mt. Fluore and rule all the others, when they had all been made equally low for so long? That was the decision that the rulers had come to Evania to make, and the debate had lasted days. There were rumors they were close to a consensus, but Faro could also see it dragging on a while longer. Either way, once the decision was made, that king or queen would become the acting High King or High Queen, and take their place atop the mountain when the war was won.

"First of all," said Faro, "I don't think they like being called 'Dungeon Lords anymore. That was Cosimir slang that just stuck. It's demeaning."

Eli nodded. "Yeah, I get it, force of habit."

"If they're smart," Faro continued, "they'll pick someone who isn't a standing king. Someone who can be impartial and have the best interest of all kingdoms at heart."

Eli's face went pale. "Oh, Solana. I hope that's not me," he said, knowing it was a small possibility given his prominent stance in the rebellion.

"You are the most timid savior I've ever heard of," Faro laughed. "It's like a thousand to one shot it's you, but if it is, you'll do just fine. And," he added, "you already got your right-hand man!" Faro said, pointing two thumbs at himself.

"Hah! Absolutely," said Eli. After a beat he said, "Enough sparring for one day. The thought of all this is making me sick to my stomach. I need to get back down home and get something to eat," he said, referring to his home with his mother down in the lower dungeon levels of Incarta.

"Yeah, for sure. I need some chow too," said Faro, waving at his friend and heading off to the upper level mess where people of higher standings always had food waiting for them.

The corridors he walked through were all stone, hewn out from the existing stone beneath what used to be the grand kingdom of Incarta. Once Cosimir took over and the Scourge drove everyone underground, the dungeons were made below the surface by mages and masonry workers. They provided a safe haven for people to keep clear of the Scourge, which needed the sun's power to make its magic thrive. Down here it was dank and dark, with only the provided subfluore crystals to help provide any light to their dark existence.

Faro saw the door to the mess and was about to excitedly rip it open when he heard voices. Two men were talking down the hall by his father's council room. The same room where the meeting was taking place to decide the fate of their world.

Being as sneaky as he could for a larger fellow, Faro made his way down the corridor and hid behind a pillar. Now he could hear every word the guards were saying. One man, a tall, slender, balding man, was talking quickly in a hushed tone to the other.

"It's done! They've decided!"

The other, a short, stocky man answered excitedly back. "You heard what they said?"

"Yeah, yeah, yeah. They weren't very quiet about it in there. James Envato is the new High King!"

Faro's heart sank. Of all the people in the room, his father was one of the last he would have expected, or at least hoped, got the vote. After all, Cosimir himself was from Incarta, so Faro assumed that would have put some sort of stigma on choosing another Incartan ruler. Besides, what did that make him now? Was Faro the King of Incarta now in his father's stead? He had to be. There was no other heir, and with his father moving up in the world, that made Faro next in line to be king. He swallowed hard. Was he even ready for that?

The shorter man answered excitedly, "Good at eavesdropping, eh?" This statement made Faro's heart drop, until he realized he was talking to the other guard still, and not him. "Must be how you got that huge gash in your nose!" Both men laughed before the short man continued. "Think we'll get a ticket to ride along with the king up to the top of the 'ol summit?"

The tall man smiled. "You might, maybe. I think my job here is done. I'm likely off to something else here soon. I just hope there's a peaceful transfer of power."

"Peaceful?" yelled the short man. "No way old dust bones up there is giving up his throne without a fight."

"No, no, no," said the tall man. I mean when the true heir of Evania returns. I hope the Envato family graciously bows out to the rightful heir."

The short man scoffed. "An old wives' tale for sure," he said. "The whole Evania family was wiped out when Cosimir slaughtered them all."

"I don't believe that for a second," said the tall man. "The heir is hidden and safe somewhere far away. The fate of Evania hinges on the strength or weakness of that heir."

The short man laughed. "You keep to your wives' tales then, friend. Seems like we're done here. Let's make another round and come back."

Faro could hear the footsteps of the men walking away. He dared a peak out from around the corner of the column, but what he saw made him raise his eyebrows. Only the short, stocky man could be seen walking away.

CHAPTER THIRTEEN

LAKE MOURNFALL

The first thing Faro saw when he awoke was treetops and the sky. He blinked his eyes and slowly tried to move. He felt like he'd been hit in the face with a blacksmith hammer. Slowly, groggily, he sat up. The next thing he saw was Maggie, the former Dark Human, a short distance away, bending down over Thora.

From the looks of it, everyone had passed out like he had except for Maggie. This seemed suspicious to him, except for the fact that it looked like Maggie was now kindly helping Thora to her feet and brushing her off. Getting tenderly to his own feet, he slowly worked his way over to help up Lena who was closest to him.

"What...what happened to us?" Faro asked, reaching a paw down, which the old elf gladly took, using the leverage to pull herself up to her feet. "Why was *that one* not knocked out?" he asked, pointing his nose towards Maggie.

Lena rubbed her head, looking like Faro felt. "Well," she said weakly, "we all passed out, and Maggie didn't. She didn't eat from the trees, so I assume there was some sort of curse on the fruit."

Faro's eyes narrowed at Maggie. He raised his voice in anger, "Maggie! Did you and the Dark Humans curse the fruit before you left to attack us earlier?"

Maggie was helping Mathias up, and just waved him off. "I told you, there's a wood nymph here that causes mischief. You all were only out about five minutes, though."

Mathias grabbed Maggie's hand to help himself up, but now looked shocked. "Five minutes?" he asked. "It felt like much longer than that. I had time to relive a memory I'd all but forgotten."

"Weird," Tobi chimed in, helping himself up from the ground. "I had some kind of vision, too. I was in my tavern, and there was a man that looked like he'd had a narrow miss with an axe on the battlefield right..."

"...across his nose," Thora finished.

Tobi stared at her, flabbergasted. "How did you know that, child? Did you have the same vision?"

"No," said Thora sadly. "Mine was about the day my parents died. I showed that man weapons. Sold him one eventually.

I always wondered if he was there to distract me from saving my parents, or somehow knew the attack was coming, and distracted me to save my life. He gave me this weird coin…"

"This coin?" Tobi cut her off, pointing at the coin embedded in his axe.

"Yes, Andre. My most valued possession that I gave to you when you took me in. But this man, he was an odd fellow. Talked about the heir of the Evanian line."

Now Lena cut in, her face stern. "There are many who believe that the line of the Evania family is still intact, and that an heir was hidden away during Cosimir's attack. Many believe that somehow through that escape, the line has continued all this time, hidden away in a secret location, preparing to take back their throne and free Evania from the darkness."

Mathias adjusted his glasses on his hooked nose and chimed in. "I've heard much the same, but in all my studies there has been absolutely no record that anyone escaped the slaughter. It is weird that this man was in all our visions though. I saw him while I was tending to the natives on the mountain. He had said something about all the blood that will be shed, and someone will be needed to heal body and spirit if the heir is to return. I thought he was just a madman wandering through. But you all actually saw him? Like in real life, you remember him?"

They all looked at each other, nodding. After a moment's pause, Lena turned to Faro. Her face looked intense. "What did the man say to you?"

Faro was still reeling from the vision, and was still trying to gather his thoughts on what he'd seen. It was odd to have such a vivid memory returned to him after not knowing anything about his past since the accident. It was even weirder that they'd all met the same man, as though this wasn't a random gathering of people, but fate bringing together a band of people that were meant to do something important.

"It was on the day that the Dungeon Lord Council was meeting to decide the successor to the throne if we were to be successful in defeating Cosimir. Apparently I had overheard two guards who had eavesdropped on the meeting. The bald man with the gashed nose was one of the guards. Apparently he'd heard that my father was chosen to rule on the mountain," he said, a look of worry on his face.

Thora's mouth fell open. "That means that you're the rightful King of Incarta and heir to the throne of Evania?" she asked, perplexed.

"No," Faro shot back sharply. "King of Incarta, maybe, but ruling Evania is not my destiny."

"And how would you know?" Tobi chimed in. "You don't remember a whole chunk of your life. Maybe you were more determined to hold a good and honest rule back before your injury. How do you know what your intentions were then?"

Faro furrowed his hairy brow. He didn't like the question. What did he really know about himself other than the glimpses of information he'd gotten from this vision? It was infuriating not knowing what he was like before. Did he even have the same personality now? Had he always been willing to go gallivanting off on quests to save little girls he didn't even know? Or was he a selfish, spoiled prince looking for power? Judging by the hesitation he felt as he'd lived out the vision, he believed he was much the same as he was now.

After a beat, he spoke again. "Eli is obviously not meant to be the ruler on the mountain, but I do not feel that the fate of Evania rests in me ruling over it. I will if I must, but when all of this is over we will need to hold a new council and decide who is best fit." He chuckled, "Especially if I'm still a lion. No one wants a hairy beast ruling over the land. We're not exactly gaining ourselves a good reputation, me and the others." They all broke out into smiles.

Their belongings had been scattered around the ground when they had passed out from the visions, so they gathered their packs and weapons so they could continue on their way.

"How do we know this wood nymph isn't just waiting to cast more magic on us out there?" Tobi asked leerily as they all stared into the trees.

"We don't," said Maggie. "But the horses are right here. Let's get them untied and we can part ways."

They all agreed and moved towards the horses. Faro was unsure as he approached the horse. When he saw them the first time they had seemed to disappear into thin air, but now he realized that was just the magic vision taking over his mind and sight. This time when he reached out to touch the horse, his paw landed on the soft fur and leather of the saddle. He was surprised that the horse was so calm at his touch; him being a beast himself. The fact that he talked and acted human seemed to set the horse at ease.

Carefully, he made to mount the horse, and was pleasantly surprised that the horse let him. He looked around and saw Mathias and Tobi mount the smaller horses as they were shorter and a better fit for the smaller men. Lena and Thora easily mounted their horses, and Maggie mounted her own horse that had been waiting for her here.

They all smiled at her and thanked her for her help. "Good luck on your trip home!" Thora said, cheerily waving to her.

Maggie sighed. "I'm not hopeful much is left there. The new ruler is probably worse than the last."

This made Faro think back to his vision. Big, hulking, and yet oddly hesitant Eli, barely able to swing a hammer in a fight. He didn't know what had happened between that point and the time of his rule, but there's one thing he knew for sure.

Eli had once been hesitant to hold any position as important as the Ruler of Evania. It was hard to imagine that his friend from the vision had become a dark and evil ruler.

Faro let this thought go and simply nodded to Maggie. "You should always hold out hope for the best," he said to her.

Maggie nodded in agreement, gave them all one last smile, and took off back the way they just came from. The party was a party of five again, and they all took off through the grove at a quick trot. When they came out the other side, Faro's skin crawled. He couldn't shake the feeling they were being watched.

Glancing over his shoulders back at the trees behind them, expecting to see Maggie, he gasped. Staring at them from up in an apple tree appeared to be a man's face. The leaves obscured most of the head, but he could see eyes peering out at them, and a nose with a gash across it.

Faro blinked quickly to clear his vision and get a better look, but when he opened his eyes, the face was gone, and the trees were absolutely still.

Late the next day the party found themselves up on a high hill, looking down at a beautiful lake scene. Trees were spotted around much of the perimeter of the lake, though they were full of browning leaves, which was odd because it wasn't the time of year for trees to change. Despite this oddity, the lake sprawled out as far as they could see to the left and right, and the cool, greenish water was quite a sight after just seeing flat land for the past day.

"Lake doesn't look too bad," said Tobi as he hopped down from his small horse. They had all decided to rest on the hill and take in some rations before heading to the lake.

Thora was already down and digging in her pack for some of the dried meat, bread, and berries they'd packed for the trip. Mathias, ever the healer, was eyeing the ground to see what types of plants and herbs he could forage for his pack.

Lena was petting her horse when she spoke to answer Tobi. "Mournfall Lake is not a force to take lightly," she said. "I've not been here in hundreds of years, but there are rumors of a great darkness that surrounds the lake. We must be careful as we find our way across." After discussing the best way to approach the lake, under the cover of night seemed to be the consensus. That way they would be less likely to be seen by bandits.

Faro eyed the lake as he bit into a piece of bread. When he finished chewing, he said, "If it's so dangerous, would it not be better to go around?"

Lena shook her head. "No. It will take extra time to find our way around it either way. The northern route would take an extra four days. Going south will take two and would lead us through Zelira. We can cross the lake in a few hours if we're lucky."

Tobi thought for a moment, nibbling on a piece of grass and stroking his beard. "Deadly lake or friendly elf kingdom. Even if it's a little longer, seems we hedge our bets and go south, aye?"

For the first time since he met her, Faro saw Lena's face go flush. "I may... or may not be banned from Zelira, punishable by death." Faro remembered Mathias mentioning the queen was a bit of a recluse that didn't allow anyone on her land, but this confirmed it.

Everyone stopped what they were doing and stared at her. Lena seemed so by the book and perfect at everything she did, it was a shock to hear that she had such a harsh penalty set against her.

Lena looked at the ground, kicking at the dust, as they all stared at her. "Well, I was banned when my father ruled there at least," she said. "He's since moved his rule...elsewhere."

They all thought about this for a moment, but it was Thora who got it. "Umbra?" she asked, aghast. "Umbra is your father?" Lena nodded. "Then that makes you..."

"A princess of Zelira," Lena said, looking ashamed, "and also Umbra's Veil, if you look at it that way."

The silence that followed was palpable. No one spoke until Lena was ready to continue. "I don't know when he left Zelira. I don't know how he found the Veil, or what's there. I don't even know how Mournfall Lake was created. It used to be called Lake Carana; lush and green. The bluest water. All I know about Umbra... my father... is that he was becoming darker and darker in his knowledge and magic by the day, and as a student of Solana's Light, we had a falling out where he exiled me from Zelira."

Faro wasn't sure what to make of it. On the one hand, the elf had surely saved his life several times already. On the other, having her here was making the mission harder. Not to mention Jarl had told him to come alone, and here he was with four extra people.

He decided it was more important to honor his new friend's loyalty than the demands of a mad wolverine. "We're with you through to the end of this," he said to her. He looked around at the others for support and got nods all around. Faro wasn't entirely sure what had happened in her past, but it must have been traumatic because a single tear fell from the usually-stern elf's eyes.

After they fueled up on their rations, they made their way timidly down to the lake. While it was a beautiful scene from a distance, the closer they got, the gloomier it looked. The waning light made it look especially glum up close.

Faro had thought the water was green from algae that had settled on top, but as they approached, the water was simply glowing green, despite the dark purple sky above. Aside from that oddity, the browning tree leaves looked more sparse up close, and the trunks of the trees were blackened like death. There was no sign of life anywhere around the lake, so much that even the grass stopped at a certain point and just simply turned to blackened soil.

The oddity that stuck out to Faro was a raft by the edge of the water. Not just a small raft for a few people, but a big, wide raft with a rope attached that ran down into the water. He estimated the raft was big enough for three of their horses and them, which meant they'd have to leave a few horses behind. Before he could ask about the raft, Tobi asked the question that was on his mind.

"Why is there a raft here waiting for us? Is this a trap?" he asked, stroking his beard quizzically.

Lena opened her mouth to answer, as she always seemed to have an answer for everything, but it was Mathias who cut her off and spoke. "I've never ventured this far East before, but I've read that a ferry used to take people across the lake. The ferryman would bring people back and forth to the open-air church of Solana that lay in the pastures beyond the river. It was the biggest shrine to our God in all of Evania. A hundred miles square of lush green fields. Grass and gardenias as far as the eye could see. And in the center of this massive sanctuary was a giant statue of Solana, reaching up to the heavens, though not as impressive as the one Lena built in Graeton," he finished, eyeing her suspiciously.

Lena stared back at him pointedly, knowing he was still searching for an explanation of why she built the temple. Instead, she built on his point. "The Academy of Solana's Light was where Umbra's Veil is now. My father, myself, and one of my brothers all studied there. I have no idea what dark and twisted evil he has turned the place into. I spent several decades learning there. And now..." she trailed off, looking sad.

Thora patted her on the back to comfort her. After a moment, she pointed out into the lake. "Do you think this is safe to cross, Lena?"

The elf stared at the raft, and then at the lake. "I honestly do not know. We'll have to board the raft and find out." At that she looked at the party, the five horses, and then the raft, sizing them up. "I do know that we'll have to let loose two of the horses and double up riding on the other side. No way we'll fit on the ferry otherwise."

They all agreed and set two of the horses loose, the smaller ones that Tobi and Mathias had been riding. After the horses trotted back the way they came and out of sight, they walked the other three horses onto the ferry. Faro, being the biggest and strongest among them, grabbed the rope up from the water, and started pulling on it with all his might. The wet rope was heavy, full of the slimy lake water. They had seen the post in the ground that used to hold the rope high above the water, keeping it dry, but it had been knocked sideways, much lower to the ground, causing the rope to sink down into the water.

The ferry broke loose from the bank with a loud snap, and off they went across the murky green lake. Faro was being taxed already by the extra weight of the wet rope, but was thankful that the tension was still enough on the other side of the lake that they could pull themselves along on the rope. As Faro pulled, the rest of the party stared out into the lake. The water was unsettling, neither reflecting like normal water, nor letting them see down into its murky depths.

As they made it about thirty yards out from the shore, the raft came to a sudden, jerking stop. Afraid they'd struck something that would sink their raft, they all looked around frantically for the obstruction to see if they could free themselves. And then Faro noticed that the water in front of them was rippling. Something was rising out of the depths.

They all stared in shock and horror as a corporeal form arose from the lake water, floating in the air, its hand outstretched and bathed in purple light. Faro realized this being was using magic to stop the raft.

The form of the person gave off a dull, greenish light. It was clothed in sopping wet rags that looked like they used to be a fine cloak embroidered with all manner of plant and wildlife patterns. The face was gaunt, not quite a skeleton, but with very thin skin stretched over the bone. The eyes were deep and gaunt. Faro noticed the pointed ears and long flowing hair, and saw that this had once been an elf.

A chill ran down the big lion's spine as the thing opened its ghastly mouth and spoke.

"I am Amazadan, keeper of the lake. You will join us in the depths."

Chapter Fourteen

The Keeper of Mournfall Lake

The long, grizzled finger bathed in the purple light still pointed at them, stopping them in their tracks. Faro didn't even have time to think about his next move when an arrow came whizzing over his shoulder. The whooshing sound cut through the air, and was so close to him he felt the air from the arrow's path on his big, furry ear.

Lena's arrow found its mark and hit Amazadan in the forearm, making him draw his arm back momentarily. The magical light disappeared, and Faro took that as his cue to pull as hard as he could on the rope. A few pulls further didn't get them very far before bony, green hands began reaching up from beneath the water and trying to pull their owners onto the raft. As night fully set in around them, the eerie green glow from the undead elves clamoring up was all the light they had.

"Circle up! Take a side!" Lena yelled above the din of groans that filled the air as countless undead elves tried to heave their way up to overtake them and pull them down into the depths.

Lena, Thora, Mathias, and Tobi each took a side of the raft, and as they began knocking back the hands and slashing into the faces that emerged, Faro pulled with all of his might to get them closer to the other side of the lake. He wasn't sure that forward was the best option for them to go, but they still had a mission, and he hoped forward would yield fewer undead to face than this spot.

Amazadan pulled the arrow from his arm and began flying around them in the air. Lena was now distracted by the undead coming from the water, so the sorcerer elf could use his magic unchecked. Faro caught a glimpse of him and saw that he now looked angry. The scowl on his face showed wrath as he ignited his hands in purple and raised them both into the air, fingers up as if grasping something.

This motion caused undead elves to rise straight up from the water and into the air. With a flick of his hands, Amazadan sent these elves flying down to land in the center of the raft. When the animated corpses landed they spooked the horses, sending them barreling over the side of the raft. Thora had to quickly skirt around one of them, almost falling in herself from the big beast careening into the green water.

They could hear the horses high, panicked whinnies as they were pulled down into the depths by the undead creatures lurking there. Now it was just the five of them on the raft with five undead elves right in the middle, and more coming up over the side.

Faro thought the fight in Graeton had put them in a tight spot, but now they were utterly surrounded by these ghastly creatures trying to pull them down into the depths below. Outnumbered, he dropped the rope and pulled out his war hammer. "Keep the perimeter!" he yelled to his friends, charging into the elves that had taken the middle of the raft.

Luckily for them, the quick move by Faro brought all of their attention to the lion, and they moved to attack him. Faro swung the hammer with all of his might, dropping two elves in one quick move. The other three moved in on him. Each had a long, Elven blade. Their weapons appeared to all be decorated with the same ornate designs that their clothes were. Faro wondered why, as he dropped the other three, these intricately dressed and armed elves had suffered such a fate.

Amazadan was busy pulling up more undead elves and hurling them onto the raft. Faro made it a point to bash them and kick them over the side before they gained their footing. He could see Thora flailing her mace as she lost some ground and a few elves climbed up over the sides. The other three seemed to keep their attackers at bay well enough. Faro thought they were doing pretty well for how outnumbered they were, but they were sitting dead in the water with no end to the onslaught in sight. He wished that he had some kind of ranged weapon to take Amazadan down. If he could just get the sorcerer elf down, they could move the raft out of this mess.

Faro swung his hammer into another elf, and stepped in closer to Thora, kicking one of her assailants overboard and smashing his hammer into the chest of another.

"Thanks!" she yelled to him as she focused her attention back on the edge where they were trying to board the raft.

Another set of elves landed in the middle of the raft and Faro charged at them, but instead of hitting them, he grabbed one and rolled off his back, using the momentum to launch himself over closer to Lena.

"I've got this side!" he yelled to her over the groans and the clashing of metal on metal. "Clear out the middle, and then take down that sorcerer!"

She nodded and got to work, unsheathing her two trusty Elven blades, not too unlike those blades they were up against. She went low and sliced out the legs from a pair at once, dropping them down to the floor of the wooden raft. In the same swift move she brought both swords up crossed the blades, taking off the head of the last elf standing between her and a moment's reprieve to make her next move.

From there, Lena quickly sheathed her swords at her hips and snagged the bow from her back. An arrow quickly found her hand, and she was aiming at Amazadan a split second later.

Catching on to their new tactic, Amazadan crossed his arms and brought the new set of undead elves straight from the water to float right in front of him, making a shield between himself and the raft. Lena quickly loosed an arrow and dropped the center elf blocking the sorcerer. With another arrow quickly knocked she aimed at Amazadan's face, but the arrow was blocked by a quick move from Amazadan, sending another undead elf to take the arrow for him. After this happened two more times, Lena knew she needed a new tactic, and she could feel her quiver was down to one arrow.

"Faro!" she screamed. "Hammer! Up top!"

Faro turned and saw her point at the meat shields their enemy had deployed against them and then remembered his little hammer he had fought the Shadruul with in Graeton. He pulled the smaller weapon from his waist and, taking aim, slung the hammer as hard as he could through the air at the three elves blocking their target. The hammer only caught one of them in the leg, but the sudden, unexpected weapon flying at him had caused Amazadan to move a little too high behind his blockade.

Lena's arrow found its mark in the undead sorcerer's neck. The three meat shields dropped into the lake with a splash, and Amazadan let out a high-pitched shriek. The sound pierced the air causing everyone in the party to flinch. They all turned to watch as the elf faltered. He careened through the air in a swirling spiral until he caught himself just above the water and floated back up a bit.

The shriek stopped, his face a picture of wrath, and he started quickly chanting in tongues. It was the magic language that Faro didn't know, coming out as almost a gurgle because of the arrow lodged in his neck. Despite the injury, words could be discerned from his mouth none-the-less.

Lena reached instinctively for another arrow in her quiver to find that she was empty. "Dammit!" she yelled, re-slinging her bow and pulling her two swords again. The onslaught of undead elves seemed to have stopped their attempt to board the raft and moved away as the water below Amazadan started bubbling.

The party stared in horror, wondering what was about to come out and attack them. Then, quicker than any of them could register, something shot up straight out of the water and into the air.

It was a giant black serpent as thick around as an old redwood tree. In one swift move it launched itself ten feet out of the water, mouth open wide, and snatched up Amazadan whole.

"Oh, shit!" Tobi yelled in shock, dropping his axe head down to the raft while still holding onto the handle. The tail of the serpent's body was still in the water, even though its head was ten feet in the air.

With a tremendous splash that sent a wave of the foul-smelling green water over all of them, the serpent plunged back down into the depths, and the water became still, save for the ripples where the serpent reentered. They all slowly made their way over to the edge of the raft and tried to look down into the depths, but saw nothing.

"Maybe he didn't say it right?" asked Thora, perplexed at their turn of good fortune. Tobi burst out laughing at the thought.

"That's what magic will get you," said Mathias from behind them all. He had pulled a rag from his side pouch and was wiping a green slimy substance from the undead elves off of his blade.

"I thought you vowed to learn magic?" Lena asked him pointedly.

Mathias sighed. "Okay, fine. For Osric. I guess that's what *dark* magic will get you. I know I said..."

"Shhh!" shushed Thora sharply. "What's that sound?"

They all drew quiet and listened. At first, there just seemed to be silence. But then Faro heard it too. There was a dull hum that was slowly growing louder.

"Where is that coming from?" Tobi asked. Faro pointed down into the water.

Where they couldn't see past the murky green water before, they now saw a faint purple light. Tiny ripples moved through the water again and grew bigger as the light got brighter. The light appeared to be moving towards them at a frightening speed. As it got closer to the surface, Faro could see hundreds of undead elf bodies waiting for them just below the surface, but they were quickly making a path for a large form that was blasting past them.

"We've got to move!" Faro yelled, dropping his hammer and grabbing for the rope. He pulled as hard as he could and the raft moved out of the way just as the snake came shooting back out of the water behind them, creating a wave that sent them lurching forward. Looking back over his shoulder, Faro could see that its whole slick, scaly body was emanating the same purple light that Amazadan had been commanding just moments before.

The serpent didn't go back down into the water this time. Instead, it hovered over them, its slitted eyes staring them down, its body arched as if ready to strike. The party stared up in awe at the magnificent and terrifying beast.

"Hydralisk," Lena whispered.

"What do we do?" asked Faro, feeling very inferior and small for the first time since he became a lion.

"Pick up your hammer, and start praying to Solana," she said, taking an attack stance with both of her swords. The snake swayed overhead, dominating their entire field of vision, sizing them up and deciding where to strike. Faro wasn't sure how much good his war hammer would do against such a beast, but he supposed it was better than using his fists.

They all got into attack positions, expecting a strike; instead the snake opened its mouth and spoke words. It was the same language that Amazadan had been speaking before.

"Oh, fuck no!" exclaimed Tobi as the water stirred around them. Hands clamored back onto the raft, as the undead elves of the depths made their attack again.

Faro was now thinking that Amazadan hadn't made a mistake with his words. Instead of going down to a watery, final grave, he had called this creature to consume him, to become him. The thought sent a shiver down Faro's spine, but he shook it off and brought his attention back to the situation at hand. Their odds didn't look so good.

Without prompting, Mathias and Thora stepped to the edges of the raft and fought off the elves that were trying to board them. That left Lena, Faro, and Tobi staring down the snake, who hadn't taken its eyes off of them.

The water serpent opened up its jaws, exposing its massive fangs, ready to come down hard on them. Its tongue shot out of its mouth and the creature let out a massive, guttural hiss that shook the air around them.

Faro was expecting it to strike down on them, but instead the snake sent out a torrent of purple light straight from its mouth, aiming to blast them into oblivion. Lena quickly dropped her swords and threw up her hands. In an instant her yellow, blinding light magic pierced the air in a sphere around them, blocking the purple jet of magic from hitting them, and keeping the undead elves at bay. The old elf was already grunting from the effort it took to shield them.

Her magic seemed to set the snake into a rage. It cut off the stream of magic and struck at the shield with its fangs, its mouth opening wide as if trying to eat the force field that was protecting them. Faro stared in terror from inside the shield as the snakes large, curved fangs attempted to pierce the shield and kill them. He could see the dark abyss of the inside of the snake as it struck down on them with its mouth open wide.

After several attempts to destroy the shield, the serpent let out a hiss in frustration, and it dipped back below the water. The scene went quiet and still again, and Faro felt a huge sense of unease. Should he pull the rope and try to move them further, or stand ready to fight?

Before he could even decide to go for the rope, the serpent's head bobbed out of the water, slow and methodical, pulsing in the purple glow of the dark magic. It was staring down at them with its cold, purple eyes, making circles around the raft, coiling up into a sharp circle around them up into the air.

It took a moment, but then Faro heard the cracking and he knew what the serpent was trying to do. It was trying to crush the raft by constricting around them. Looking at Lena, Faro could see her sweating now from the effort of holding their magic shield in place. Based on the last time he saw her use magic in the Church of Solana in Graeton, this type of magic seemed very draining on the caster's energy, and couldn't be maintained for extended periods of time.

Nonetheless, the shield seemed to hold the snakes constricting coils back. The raft began to creak and snap on the fringes, but Lena's shield was holding it back enough that it couldn't completely consume them.

Lena began grunting from the effort and Faro knew she couldn't hold much longer. Tobi must have sensed it too, because it was he who spoke first.

"Are we able to leave this thing without getting hurt?" he yelled to her over the noise of the raft cracking and the crackling sounds of her magic shield.

"Ahh! Uhh... yes. But it's a one-way ticket. Once you leave... ahhh... you can't get back in!"

The dwarf had no hesitation in his decided action. "Gotta run then!" he yelled as he bolted out through the shield. The yellow light fizzled a bit as he slipped through, but then was placed back firmly around them.

Faro watched in amazement as the dwarf stepped to the edge of the raft and, without hesitation, jumped onto the back of the coiling snake and began running upwards like it was a ramp to the top of a tower. The broadness of the massive snake gave him plenty of room to move, but it wasn't long before the creature realized what was happening and writhed, trying to shake the intruder from its back.

Tobi wobbled and swerved this way and that, but the serpent couldn't seem to shake him without losing its grip on the raft. Frustrated, it loosened its grip and then and flicked its body furiously around.

This time Tobi lost his footing, but instead of falling he did what he did best and sunk his axe down hard into the surface beneath him. He wasn't anywhere near the beast's head, which is where Faro assumed his friend was aiming for, but the blow still caught the beast off guard, and red blood began raining down all around them, splashing off of Lena's shield and splashing down into the surrounding water. The mixture of the red blood with the green water turned some spots into rust brown colors.

As the snake reeled from the embedded axe, it shot higher into the air, and now Tobi was sliding down its back, dragging his axe along with him, and slicing the beast open even wider as he fell. The hydralisk was thrashing madly about, trying to whip its head around and strike down its attacker.

Tobi had slid so far down now that he was almost back down to the raft. The serpent wheeled it's head around and moved to strike at the young dwarf. Seizing his chance, Faro stepped out of the shield and met the snake's strike, stopping it mere feet from attacking Tobi. He drove the sharp end of his war hammer into the serpent's head, right between its eyes.

The head came crashing down into the raft as Tobi slid off into the murky green water. The impact from the snake plowing into them sent the raft flying backwards on an enormous wave. Lena's shield dissipated, and they all dropped down and grabbed splinters of raft boards to keep themselves from flying overboard. Faro held onto the handle of his hammer for dear life, dragging the entire snake along with them, until the raft came off the end of the wave to a slow, sloshing stop.

When he regained his footing, he pulled his hammer from the serpent's head. The light had gone from its eyes and the purple magic had disappeared. Pulling up his paw foot from the ground, Faro placed it squarely on the serpent's slitted nose and gave it a kick off the raft. The snake coiled backwards and fell down into the murky deep.

Mathias and Thora stood and tried to regain their footing to join Faro. Lena lay on the deck of the raft, almost completely spent from the effort of protecting them, her chest heaving up and down with large, deep breaths. Thora ran to the edge of the raft and looked out into the green and brown waters in search of her father, the dwarf.

Mathias joined her and placed a hand on her back for comfort. "He saved us all," he said, hoping that she would realize that his sacrifice was worth it.

"And he'd like some help up!" yelled a voice from the side of the raft. Faro spotted a small hand grasping to the far side and grabbed it, pulling Tobi back up onto the raft.

Thora's face grew brighter than Faro had ever seen it, and she ran to hug the dwarf she called a father. She almost knocked him back into the water with the force of her hug. Tobi chuckled and hugged her back. "You'll never get rid of me, darlin'," he said to her lovingly, patting her on the back.

Faro saw Mathias wipe a tear from his eye, moved by the relationship of the pair, and the fact that their friend was safe. He was sure Mathias couldn't stand to lose another friend in such a brief span of time.

He almost missed it, but he felt his ear twitch. The light sound of sloshing water caught his ear without him realizing, and he turned his head instinctively towards the sounds at the edge of their partially destroyed ferry raft.

Cold, greenish hands were again pawing at the edge. He turned and looked at the other side, and they were there as well. They were surrounded by the undead once again.

"Lena!" Faro screamed. "What do we do?"

Undead elves were making their way up onto the deck again. A scream so loud that Faro had to cover his ears pierced the air. Faro watched as Lena rolled over to the edge of the raft, spoke something in tongues, and thrust her hand down into the water. Bright blue fire erupted from her hands and cut through all the undead elves that surrounded them.

With another scream she thrust her other hand into the water, and strong magical currents shot out. The blast from the magic sent them all stumbling as the raft took off like a torpedo fish towards the opposite bank of the lake, propelled by the magic of the screaming elf.

CHAPTER FIFTEEN

ECHOES OF HOME

T he darkness and mist pressed in on them as they ventured their way through the wasteland towards Umbra's Veil. Spires of rock reaching up to the sky, the hard, rock ground, and the occasional snake was all they had seen for the past day, and Faro was tired of it.

He adjusted Lena on his shoulder and pressed on with the others. His paws were sore from walking on the hard ground with the extra weight, and his back wasn't feeling great either. He'd been carrying her since the lake, slowing down their progress forward, but not having a better way to carry her with them.

After the raft sped across the lake, it had smashed hard into the opposite shore, sending them all flying off the ferry and onto the muddy, black shore on the other side. Faro, Mathias,

Tobi, and Thora had all gotten up, covered in muck and a little battered, but no worse for the wear. Lena, however, had spent her last bit of strength to get them across the lake, and had just laid face down in the mud until Faro rushed over and picked her up. She had been breathing, but unresponsive, and had remained as such ever since.

Now, they all padded slowly through the wasteland, still covered in the dark mud from head to toe. They didn't dare venture back out into the lake to try to wash off, so it was their only choice to move onward, covered in muck, and hoping their friend would revive before they got to Umbra's Veil.

The conversation had been very light, with long stretches of silence in between. They had talked briefly about the encounter, wondered whether Lena had known any of the elves they had fought, and what type of horrors likely awaited them ahead. All the talk of what lay ahead brought their mood way down, so they had fallen into silence for the latest leg of the journey.

Faro had no idea what time of day it was, or night for that matter. They seemed to be stuck in a perpetual cycle of dusk-type lighting and mist, and it drove him mad. He was tired and needed a break, and heaved a sigh of relief when Tobi's voice cut the silence first.

"We've gotta stop," he said. "My feet are killing me. I'm starting to blister. There's no way you're doing any better there with the added weight, eh?" he added to Faro.

"Right," said Faro, pulling Lena down slowly off his shoulder and setting her gently down on the ground. "We'll stop here for, err, the night?" he asked, questioning his sanity. "Maybe let's just get some sleep in shifts and then head out after that?"

They all agreed, setting down their packs and weapons, grateful for the reprieve. Faro agreed to take the first watch as he felt he was to the point of exhaustion where he would just lay awake and not be able to sleep quite yet. He wasn't sure what he was keeping watch from in the barren wasteland, but it just seemed like a good idea to have someone available in case they were beset by elves from Umbra's Veil, a surprise from Jarl, or other lost travelers who meant them harm.

They had nothing to start a fire with, so Faro just sat in the dreary mist, grabbing rocks from the ground and tossing them at a nearby stone spire that stretched up to the sky. The spires amazed him. They were like nothing he remembered seeing before. It was almost as if they had been ripped straight up out of the ground and stood in the air, like a sword sticking out of the ground after being embedded there.

Picking up a larger rock, he felt its weight in both of his paws, and then spun around in a quick circle and heaved it at one of the spires. It knocked off of it with a loud bang, and he looked guiltily at his party, hoping he hadn't woken anyone up. Instead, what he got was a pleasant surprise. Lena was stirring on the ground.

She groaned as her eyes slowly fluttered open, and Faro rushed over to help her into a sitting position. "The lake..." were her first words as she sat up and looked around.

"The lake is a day or so back, by my estimate," he said, but then he gestured around them, "though it's hard to tell exactly in this endless dusk."

Lena just nodded. "It takes powerful magic to mess with space and time," said Lena, using a hand to rub the opposite shoulder. "My father must be more dark and powerful than I imagined. Obviously," she added, "my powers are nowhere near that strong, as I can barely hold a shield for five minutes."

Faro dismissed the thought. "You saved our lives more times than any of us could count in that situation, Lena. Amazadan alone could have done us in, let alone the hoards of other elves you protected us from."

A sad look fell upon the elder elf's face. "Amazadan," she said, sorrowfully trailing off, shaking her head.

"You knew him?" asked Faro.

Lena nodded. "He was my father's highest general and most respected friend. They had studied The Way of the Light together for centuries." Now she looked at Faro. "If my father has fallen so far as to doom his best friend to that fate, I hate to think what horrors he has prepared for us."

Faro's mouth drew tight. It would not be easy once they made it to Umbra's Veil. Not only did they have to contend with the mad wolverine who wanted to kill him, but a mad Elven sorcerer who was so twisted that he'd doomed his best friend to a watery death and a life of the undead.

"Do you have any ideas for what strategy we should take once we get there?" he asked her, fearing he already knew the answer.

"Do we have a strategy for anything?" she asked, smiling. "We just kind of amble into fights and somehow work as a team to get through them."

"Right," he said, smiling back on the outside, but inside feeling a sense of dread. It was true that they were good at teamwork in the moment, but it felt awful never going into anything with a plan. He resolved himself in knowing that they were walking into everything blind, and it wasn't like they had a second chance to do things over and make a different strategy if they failed the first time.

Thora stirred behind him, and he turned to greet her. "Good, uh, whatever time of day this is! Lena's awake!"

A huge smile broke out on Thora's face and she immediately stopped rubbing her tired eyes and raced over, stooping down to hug the old elf. Faro allowed them their reunion and dismissed himself to take his rest. He felt like Lena coming back to them had taken the edge off his exhaustion just enough that his body would let him get to sleep quickly. Faro curled up on the cold, hard ground and just as he'd hoped, he was off to sleep in almost an instant.

When he awoke and they pressed on it was more of the same, and the party was becoming irritable. Faro was in a slightly better mood because he'd gotten some sleep and didn't have the extra weight to carry, but the rest of the party were really feeling the strain of the hard trek. Tobi could be heard cursing the fact that they'd lost the horses, only to be shushed by Thora who was feeling sorry for the poor beasts' fate, lamenting how awful it must have been to be devoured by the lake's undead inhabitants.

Mathias and Tobi were arguing over the morality of using poisons on an enemy, when Faro saw it. A dark ruin of a castle stood in the distant shady mist, a very dim light showing from one of the towers.

"There!" he roared, pointing out into the distance with his big, furry finger. "There's a shimmering light in the distance." The others followed the direction his finger was pointing, and they could just see the light and the castle ruins making their way out through the mist before them.

"Oh, thank Solana!" Tobi yelled into the empty abyss. "There's something here after all!"

Mathias pulled out a notebook from his pack and started making notes, and Faro could see he was also making a quick sketch.

"Are you... taking notes?" Faro asked him, bemused.

"Of course I'm taking notes, good man. Good lion. Whatever you are," he said hurriedly. "We are on a one-of-a-kind adventure of a lifetime. We're seeing things people have never seen before, or at least seen and lived to tell. A scholar never stops being a scholar."

Faro looked sideways at Lena, who shrugged, looking amused as well. "I just live through it all and have an excellent memory," she said. "I guess notes are important if you only live sixty or eighty years."

Mathias scoffed at her and kept scribbling frantically in the book. "Notes are important no matter how long you live. Details are easily forgotten later. Plus, how do you share your discovery with the world?"

Lena tilted her head as though she kind of agreed, and then her face lit up. "Speaking of forgotten," Lena said to Faro, rummaging through her pack. "We haven't tried the cloak out yet!" From her pack she pulled a giant, white cloak. She had told Faro earlier in their quest that it would disguise him and make him appear human to everyone who saw him. She unrolled it and tossed it around his broad shoulders. "I don't think my father will take kindly to a lion beast in his new kingdom."

Faro felt silly, like he was wearing a bedsheet, and he could see Tobi stifling a chuckle.

"How do I look?" he asked them, not sure he wanted the answer.

"Like a cuddly little lion about to be tucked in for his wittle nap!" Tobi hollered at him, letting his laugh loose and slapping his legs.

Faro looked at Lena questioningly. "You have to put the hood on!" she barked at him, as if that was obvious. At her request, Faro slipped the hood on, and the other four gasped. He wished he could see himself. He pulled his paw up in front of his face, but it was still a paw.

"You won't see any difference," Lena told him. "We see jet black hair, a full face, big scruffy black beard," she looked closer, "blue eyes, and peach skin. Is this what you looked like before?"

Faro thought back. Even in his vision in the grove he hadn't glimpsed himself in any mirror or reflection. He didn't have any memory of how he'd looked as a human. "I imagine it's something like this... or I don't really know. If the spell on the cloak is more of a mask, I would think I look different than this. Lena?"

The elf thought for a second. "I don't know how to reverse your affliction or I would have done it already. All the cloak is doing is removing the visual facade of any enchantment of the wearer. I think this is how you would normally look."

Faro wished he could see himself, but decided it was really irrelevant at the moment. As it stood, he had a disguise to look normal when they got to Umbra's Veil. It was time to finish the last leg of their journey and face whatever evil lay before them.

They were very close to the castle now. The dark mist still covered the ruin, but they saw it all in greater detail now. From the crumbling towers down to the rubble around the base. Up ahead they could see a border wall. It looked like it was once a taller wall, but was now cut in half. The top looked very rough and uneven. Still, it looked fairly easy for them to scale.

When they approached it, Faro offered to climb up and help Tobi and Mathias up to the top first, since they were shorter and would likely need the most help. They both happily agreed. Faro took a rope and was able to lasso a rough-cut stone on the top. He climbed the wall part way and reached back down to help the two men up. Once they were up on the wall, Faro quickly had to duck as both men came flying backwards past his head and sprawled out on the ground below him.

"Daylight!" Mathias screamed, getting up.

"Daylight and a castle," said Tobi, shocked. His hair was sticking up from the force of the blow-back, and it was all Faro could do not to laugh at his new look.

"What are you two talking about?" asked Lena. Faro dropped back down off the wall to join them in their conversation.

"The other side of that wall. This is an illusion it seems. When you're on the wall, the entire area was daylight, and the castle..."

"The castle was whole! Intact!" Mathias cut him off. "It looked welcoming after all this dreariness. We've been played the fool to think that this place is in ruins."

Lena scaled the wall and looked over, still hanging on the side, but judging by the look on her face she could still only see the ruins. "Some kind of force field?" She asked. "Is that what knocked you back?"

Tobi shrugged. "Dunno. Got up there and the air felt thick, like it was vibrating. And an insanely strong wind kicked us back off the wall."

"Right," said Thora, sizing up the wall. "What if Faro goes first, braces himself, and pulls the rest of us up? We can all latch together, anchor off him, and become a bigger weight. Do you think Faro is big enough to stay up there against the wind?"

Mathias nodded, and Faro moved up to the wall, pulling himself up again.

The instant he was on top of the wall, Faro could feel what they were talking about. The air moved around him like it was pulsing, a wind trying to push him back off the wall. He glimpsed the magnificent, towering castle. It was no longer a ruin, but a full and beautiful kingdom in the middle of a lush, green grass field full of white flowers.

Holding steady to the wall, he braced himself and reached down for Thora. She pulled herself most of the way up the rope, and after taking Faro's hand to get to the top, clung tight to Faro to anchor herself down. Her added weight helped stabilize them, and they both worked to help the others up. After they were all on top, Faro took the lead to move slowly forward and dragged everyone through the invisible barrier. Once they repelled down the other side of the wall, the heavy wind immediately stopped, and was replaced by a gentle breeze. The soft grass below them was a welcome feeling after the barren, rock wasteland. There was even a sweet smell in the air.

"Gardenias! Just smell them!" exclaimed Mathias as he bent to pick one of the plentiful white flowers from the ground. He gave it a sniff and his face lit up.

Thora followed his lead and picked one up and smelled it. "They smell so sweet!" she said happily.

The others also picked the flowers to smell, except for Lena who was just staring at the brilliant white castle before them. Faro worked his way over to her and placed a hand on her shoulder, trying to hand her one of the white flowers to break her trance. "Nervous to see your father again?" he asked her, concerned.

"No," she said, barely above a whisper and ignoring his kind gesture of the flower. "It's not that."

"Then what's wrong?" he asked.

"This place," she said, pointing at the castle, "this entire kingdom. It looks exactly like Zelira."

Chapter Sixteen

The Gathering at Mireholm

The welcoming party for the new visitors was grand, and Jarl wasn't sure how it was all put together in such a short order. A dozen elves lined each side of the gate, and a small quartet of stringed instruments was situated in the back, ready to welcome the guests with festive song. Umbra himself stood in the middle of the street. If Jarl didn't know any better, he'd say the elf king looked nervous. His mouth was drawn tight, and it seemed like he was shaking a bit. Based on his calm composure since they'd met, it was odd seeing such a grand figure so put off.

The air was so still and silent they could hear bees buzzing around some flowers set outside a nearby shop. That was, until they saw five tiny figures in the distance, and Umbra took a weary step backwards. He turned to the band and gave a signal, and they all started strumming their instruments. A chipper melody filled the air to welcome their new guests.

Umbra stood there, wringing his hands together until the party made it to the other side of the bridge, halting hesitantly. Jarl could see they all had their weapons drawn. Just like him, they weren't sure what to expect when they got here. He knew they weren't expecting green pastures and music.

The party cautiously crossed the bridge, the old elf maid was at the front. Minutes before, on their way down to the gate, Umbra told him that the reunion with his daughter was centuries overdue. Jarl assumed the five of them were putting Lena out in front to show Umbra his daughter was with them, and that they should be granted a peaceful welcome instead of a fight. They obviously weren't aware of the elf king's penchant for foresight.

When they got closer, Jarl squinted and saw a sight he wasn't sure he'd ever see again. There was Faro, walking towards the back, fully formed as a human. For some reason he was the only one that looked clean in the group. All the other's looked haggard and dirty from their journey. Was the prince making the others do his dirty work? It didn't seem in character for the do-gooder that Faro was, but maybe the transformation had changed him.

Jarl suddenly felt like he was on the wrong side. How did Faro change back to a human so quickly? Would he be willing to help him get back to his own normal dwarf form? Maybe Faro had some use left after all. He had instructions to kill the lion, but it may not be in his best interest at the moment.

The party stood in the gateway looking very unsure of themselves, and the music grew softer at a signal from Umbra. He threw his arms wide in welcome, a tear running down his cheek. "Welcome, my good friends! My daughter has come back to me!"

The elves lined on the sides began to clap and cheer and the old elf maid looked back at her party who all gave her a nod. She walked quickly and with purpose until she was standing right before Umbra. After an awkward pause, the old elf king leaned in and embraced his long-lost daughter. The rest of her friends came in closer to the pair, still holding their weapons. Audible crying could be heard from the reunited father and daughter, but Jarl's focus was all on Faro, jealous that he wasn't still stuck in the same animal prison that he was.

After the long embrace between Lena and Umbra ended, Umbra sized up the rest of the visitors who had accompanied her to his kingdom. "Thank you, friends, for bringing my Lena back to me. I understand there was some trouble along the way, and she would be dead if it weren't for your heroic actions on the lake."

They all nodded, but Lena looked confused. "I didn't tell you about the lake," she said.

Umbra pursed his lips and nodded. "In my pursuits of the darkness my visions have gone from being random and sporadic to being totally under my control. Virmorphia allows you greater control of your powers. I've gained the ability of foresight, almost at will. That's how I knew you all were coming. Also, how I know that this man," he pointed at Faro, "isn't a man."

Faro looked shocked, still holding his war hammer in front of him in an aggressive stance. Jarl noticed his position said attack, but his eyes said run away. Either way, the wolverine didn't think he'd get very far. Umbra had the power of foresight and magic. It would be impossible to go up against a sorcerer who knew your next move. At the moment, Jarl was happy that he was mostly on Umbra's good side.

"We won't be needing that," said Umbra, flicking his fingers upward. The white cloak flew off of Faro's head and up into the air. The surrounding elves gasped, and the musicians stopped playing and stared. There stood a lion where the man had been, clad in a blue tunic, fury toes sticking out the ends of too-small boots. The cloak flew over to Umbra and he caught it neatly on his arm. Jarl watched it land and had to blink twice to clear his vision. For a second he could see up the arm of Umbra's sleeve, and it looked like his arm changed to a ghostly white. After he blinked, Umbra adjusted the cloak and he couldn't see it anymore. He wasn't sure what was going on in Mireholm, but a lot of things seemed to play tricks on his vision.

Jarl looked back at Faro and let out a sigh of disappointment. It was just some kind of masking spell. There stood the lion. The stupid, moronic lion. The lion that he had failed to kill in Graeton. The lion... *kill the lion!* The voice in his head was sharp and dripping with acid.

No, he couldn't. Umbra would kill him before he had the chance. *Kill him now!* The voice demanded, and he realized the thoughts were not his own anymore. He felt his hands twitch, wanting to reach for his dagger. His ears twitched too, and he could feel his legs move without his consent. Something inside him was urging him forward, making him draw his dagger and lunge into the air. He could see Faro notice him, and draw his war hammer back to strike, but it was too late.

"None of that either!" came the loud voice of Umbra over the crowd. He raised his hand and made a motion as if he were trying to grip the air, only it wasn't just air he was grabbing. Even though he was ten feet behind him, Jarl could feel Umbra grip the scruff of his neck and pull him backwards, like a mother cat lifting her baby kitten. Hovering in the air, Jarl was yanked over to the elf king.

"Interesting," said Umbra, looking at him as if he were the most rare and interesting weapon ever forged; something to be studied.

Jarl gnashed his teeth at the elf and tried to turn around to attack Faro. "I have to kill him! Let me kill him! Die!" he screamed at Faro over his shoulder.

Another motion from the elf king made Jarl stop talking. "Let's just see if we can..." Umbra said as he kept his grip with his left hand, and spun his right in continuous circles, chanting under his breath.

Jarl wasn't sure what he was trying to do until he felt it. It felt as if something was stuck to the inside of his head, to his brain, and was being ripped violently away. *No! Stop him! Kill the elf!* The voice screamed inside his head, and Jarl writhed and gnashed his jaws, trying to reach for his other dagger and kill his assailant.

Umbra looked unfazed as he continued his work.

The ripping sensation grew to a fever pitch and Jarl let out a scream of pain. He could hear the ripping inside his head, the voice growing so loud his brain ached. Then, in an instant, the sensation and the voice were gone. Umbra released his grip, and Jarl fell into a heap in front of him. The old elf bent over to physically pick him up, and brushed off his shirt.

"There!" said Umbra happily. "Now we can all be cordial and get along!"

Jarl, panting in pain, looked back at Faro who still hadn't dropped his attack stance. He knew he still had orders from his masters to kill Faro, but the instantaneous urge to do so had faded to nothing. Exhausted from the experience, Jarl nodded at the lion-man, who glanced at Lena. A slight nod from the old elf maid was all Faro needed to agree to be cordial and holster his hammer.

"Great!" said Umbra. "Today is a day of celebration! My daughter is here at last! Let's all head to the courtyard! We have quite the festivities set up just for the occasion!"

The walk to the courtyard was awkward as Jarl joined right alongside the party on the way up to the keep. They didn't say a word to each other, even though Faro had a million questions about his past that Jarl could fill him in on. Instead, they marveled at the vastness of the city and the intricacies of the Elven architecture.

When they reached the keep, they all stepped through the archway into the courtyard, and were greeted with another burst of stringed instrument music.

They all smiled as elves poured out from the open doors on all sides of the courtyard, dancing around in wonderful choreography, every step perfectly taken. The music picked up pace, and so did the dancers. They moved so fast that Faro wasn't sure how they didn't trip, not being anywhere near as graceful himself. They all moved intricately around the giant fountain statue of Solana in the middle of the courtyard.

Thora was laughing and clapping beside him. Faro smiled and clapped along to the music with her, but soon he felt an elbow in his hip. He looked down and saw Tobi. The dwarf with starring over to the back of the courtyard by the main door.

"Look there!" he said, nodding in that direction, and Faro followed his gaze. Standing in the back by the large double doors to the keep was Veronica. She was dressed in a flowing white gown with golden frills, twirling so fast that the bottom of the gown billowed out into a whirling umbrella shape. She was throwing her hands into the air and whooping loudly. Her face wore the biggest smile as she danced to her own groove.

On one particularly graceful twirl, Veronica caught sight of them watching her and twirled over toward them. "Hey!" she said, stopping her spin, but still dancing in place. "You're the folks I saw back in Graeton! What are you doing here? You're all really dirty," she giggled. "Did my grandfather send you?"

Mathias scoffed at the idea of being a lackey for Mayor Thornvale. "Kind of. We would have come anyway. We couldn't let a little kid be kidnapped and taken away by a little..." he trailed off as he saw Jarl was nearby staring at him.

Veronica chuckled. "I really appreciate you guys coming all this way! Isn't this place great? You can just dance and have fun. I can forget about my studies back home. It's amazing and free!"

Thora stepped closer to her, looking a bit concerned. "You haven't been hurt at all, have you? I mean you were dragged all this way here." The look on Thora's face showed her disbelief that their kidnapped query was doing so fine once they found her.

"It was a little rough at first," Veronica said, still dancing. "Been fine since we arrived here, though. Hope you all didn't have a hard time getting here to find me!"

Tobi's mouth fell open as Veronica twirled away and joined a line of dancing elves, falling perfectly in with their step as if she'd rehearsed the dance. "Oh, no trouble at all! Sorry for being dirty!" he shouted after her, though he knew she couldn't hear him. He turned to Faro to finish his thought. "Just climbed a damn water snake and almost became lunch to some Dark Humans."

Faro laughed. It wasn't just his own dark thinking about what the Dark Humans ate then. The thought sent a chill down his spine, but he quickly brought his mind back to the festivities. The elves had stopped moving about and had formed lines as the song changed to another upbeat jig, and they all began doing high kicks and singing. Before long, Faro felt a hand on his shoulder. It was Umbra.

"You all must be hungry. Please, all of you, join me in the great hall!"

Faro, Thora, Mathias, Tobi, Lena, and Jarl all made their way through the dancing elves. Everyone smiled at them as they passed by. No one broke their smile or their pace as their visitors made their way past. It unnerved Faro a bit, but he just smiled politely back and followed the others into the keep.

The great hall was just as magnificent as the rest of the palace. A head table was arranged towards the back, set high above the others. This was where the king and queen would sit, if there was a queen, to preside over whatever feasts and festivities the hall held for them. From the ceiling hung golden chandeliers, inset with countless subfluore crystals. The ceiling above them was painted to look like a sunny sky, so real to the eye that Faro could scarce tell it wasn't just a window to the world outside.

The hall itself was huge, but for this occasion only one smaller table was out on the main floor. Faro imagined that bigger tables were brought out for larger parties, and then possibly cleared away after meals to make room for dancing and entertainment.

They all sat around the small, rectangular table set for seven as elf servants brought out dish after dish and set it before them. Faro was starving after their long journey, but he was also interested in the conversation that was going on between Lena and her father just a few seats down. He grabbed a large turkey leg from his plate and ripped a huge chunk off with his sharp teeth. Since becoming a lion his appetite seemed to be insatiable, and he had a particular taste for meat. The turkey leg was so juicy that it dripped down his mane. He wiped it off with his paw and took another big bite, savoring the hot food. It sure beat dried meat and bread.

"It is good to be back, but I wouldn't say that I'm back, Father," Faro heard Lena telling Umbra. "What is this place? Why does it look exactly like Zelira?"

Umbra was sitting at the head of the table, an untouched plate of food sitting before him. He was obviously troubled and knew this subject would come up. "Mireholm is the kingdom I created when your mother and I had our falling out. I couldn't bear to leave her behind, but she demanded that I leave, that my dark ways were no longer welcome in Zelira. Mireholm looks like home because I want to be reminded of home."

Lena didn't seem to want to show him any sympathy. "Then why didn't you just cast aside your dark ways and *stay home?*"

Umbra shook his head. "You know I couldn't do that. My visions of the darkness that was going to befall this land grew stronger and stronger over the centuries, and I knew the day of reckoning was getting closer and closer." Umbra looked ashamed. "The light wasn't strong enough to beat the dark. My visions showed me that much. Unfortunately, I wasn't strong enough in the dark ways to stop all that has happened."

Shaking her head, Lena looked away from her father. Faro wasn't sure what had happened between them, but this reunion didn't seem to make anything better.

A belch rang out across the table, and everyone turned to stare. Tobi the dwarf sat at the other head of the table, slurping down a goblet of red wine.

He looked up from the goblet and shrugged his shoulders. "You know how long it's been since I've had a drink that wasn't made from a damned potato?"

Everyone laughed and dug back into the food. Lena looked very put off by her salty reunion with her father, but appeared hungry, and dug into the food none-the-less.

Given the break in the conversation between the elves, Faro decided to voice something that had been on his mind since he'd learned about Umbra being an elf with foresight.

"So, King Umbra," he started, "you know a lot about visions, what they mean and all that?"

The king took a drink of his own wine and nodded. "Yes, Faro. I'd say that I do. Even those of highly devout study and prayer may not get visions. I used to get them at random. A gift from Solana, as my wife used to say." Mentioning his wife seemed to make him sad as his face fell for a moment, but he pressed on. "When I devoted myself to Virmorphia, dark magic, I realized that with a clear mind I could urge the visions to come to me. Ask them questions. Really see in the places I wanted to look, instead of having places shown to me at random."

Faro could see the allure of wanting to control such a power, but also realized how scary it would be to see terrible things you had no control to stop. "A few days back, in a tree grove..."

This sentence seemed to set Jarl off, and he slammed his fork down on the table. "A few days ago! How the hell did you all get here so fast?" he snarled.

Faro was taken aback. "We didn't get here fast, we..."

Umbra cut him off. "No need to worry about what happened before you got here. The tree grove, you were saying?"

Faro wasn't sure if he should continue to tell Jarl that they had feared they were desperately behind and would be too late to save Veronica, but then he decided he didn't owe the nasty little beast anything. "Anyway, in the grove, we all ate some apples, and fell into a kind of trance. We all had visions.

Different visions. Visions we all remember happening in our real lives."

Umbra nodded. "Someone must have cast a spell on that fruit. Something powerful to make you all recall such things," he said.

"That's what I told them," Lena cut in.

"Right," said Faro, "but the weird thing is, in our visions we all saw the same man. A man with a large gash across his nose. He talked to us about the fate of Evania and a lost heir. The only thing was, all our visions were an impossibly long time-span apart. There's no way this same man lived that long to have talked to all of us."

Umbra burst out in raucous laughter that shocked Faro and made him scoot back a bit in his chair. When the elf king finally calmed down enough to talk he said, "Friend, I'm over three thousand years old. Lena here is over two thousand. Don't judge everyone by your extremely, and sadly, short human lifespan."

"Okay, fair enough," said Faro, a little depressed now.

"As for this heir," said Umbra, an air of mystery about his voice. "The hidden heir is something that has been talked about throughout the land since the great massacre of the Evania family. People have dedicated their entire lives to finding the heir, hoping to restore some peace to our magnificent land."

"So it's true," chimed in Thora from across the table. "The heir is out there?"

Umbra was in deep thought for a moment before he answered. "There has been no proof that such an heir exists." Everyone was staring at him with bated breath. "I for one like to hold out hope that they're out there, biding their time, waiting for the right moment to return to us and save us. Unfortunately, we've recently traded one tyrant for another, and still no heir has appeared."

"Still," Umbra continued, "the fact that you all remember this man is an odd situation indeed. Maybe you can each tell me the details of your visions?"

At that they went around the room and shared what they had seen. Umbra still didn't touch his food through the entire storytelling process, and instead listened intently, taking mental notes of what was said by all.

When they had all finished telling their version of meeting the mysterious man, Umbra sat with his fingers laced together in front of his face, deep in thought.

"Interesting indeed," he said. "The strings of destiny appear to have bound you all together." He paused and thought some more. "I will need some time to dwell on this and seek a vision that will provide clarity. I insist that you all stay here in Mireholm in the meantime."

Lena stood up from the table. "We cannot stay, Father. We've come for the girl. They will be expecting her. We must take her and go."

Faro thought he saw a flash of anger in Umbra's eyes for a moment, but then he calmed himself and simply waved her off. "I've only just gotten you back, Daughter. I know we don't see eye-to-eye on everything, but my kingdom is your kingdom. I insist you stay until proper answers can be found. I will send a crow to Graeton and tell them all is well."

Lena sat back down in a huff. It was almost comical to Faro that such an old elf could still be flustered by her parents.

Umbra stood from the table and threw his arms wide, as he often did. "I will go to my study now and dwell on answers. My servants will show you to your rooms. You all look weary from your travels and must be desperate for a proper bath." He took a step back and bowed to them all. "I truly hope you enjoy your stay in Mireholm. It is such a lovely place to be, after all."

CHAPTER SEVENTEEN

FEAST AND BEAST

Three days had passed since they'd first arrived in Mireholm, and so far, everything had been very uneventful. They had barely even seen Umbra. Every time they would run across him in the hall or at meals, he seemed distracted and too busy to talk. He would quickly greet them and then quickly make up an excuse to leave. Faro was enjoying the leisurely stay in the keep, but it was a bit frustrating that they kept being brushed off.

Lena didn't even try to be around her father. She barely spoke to anyone, and all they could gather from her was that she was still dealing with the surreal feeling of being in her childhood home without actually being there. The fact that Mireholm was an exact copy of Zelira gave her a weird feeling that she just couldn't describe to them.

As the first few days were spent resting, the third day brought a bit more excitement. The elves invited them all to a private arena at the back of the keep. They were told it was where the Elven soldiers sparred and ran training drills. It was also where elves could earn their stripes by fighting a bog troll.

"A bog troll?" asked Faro, searching his broken memory to no avail. "What in all of Evania is a bog troll?"

He, Tobi, and Mathias were standing on the perimeter of the arena, leaning on a low stone wall that served as the out of bounds for any sparring that took place in the arena. They were accompanied by a young-looking elf named Skye who had summoned them from their rooms for some excitement. Lena and Thora had declined the invite. Lena was still tired from her magical exploits, and Thora didn't want to partake in something so senseless and violent against an innocent creature.

"A bog troll is a big, fearsome beast. Not fat and dumb like a normal troll, but tall, muscular, a beast unlike any other. The best part is, though, you can't kill this beast. He has regenerative powers. We've been fighting this one for decades. Umbra retrieved him from the swamps south of Dracaryn," Skye told them happily.

Faro looked at him oddly, and Skye realized Faro didn't know the lay of the land. "Dracaryn? Way up north? Land of dragons? No? Well, anyway, this old boy is the best practice we have in training. Not many who can best him!"

At the other end of the arena there was a large, iron gate that led to a small stone room. An elf pulled on a lever that wound up a chain, and the gate started opening. "They're letting him out now?" Faro asked, a bit concerned.

"Well yeah," said Skye, "how else are you going to fight him?"

Faro and the others were taken aback. "Fight the bog troll?" asked Mathias. "Why would we want to do that? I thought we were here to watch a fight?"

Skye just smiled his wide elf smile at them. "Why do males do anything we do? We've got time to kill, and we want to make a sport of it! There's no watching here!"

"Aye!" yelled Tobi. The dwarf always seemed to relish any chance he got to fight. Faro felt the need to only fight when necessary. Looking over at Mathias, he saw he was the other extreme and seemed extremely timid. All the color had gone from his face, and he clutched his sword with white knuckles.

"Looks like we have our first volunteer!" smiled Skye happily. He slapped Tobi on the back and the dwarf grinned ear to ear.

"Snakes, bog trolls, what's the difference?" Tobi boomed as he went around and walked through the gate to the arena. He pulled his axe from his back strap and waited. The troll's gate was now all the way open, but it wasn't coming out. Tobi looked over at Skye expectantly, but the elf just shrugged.

"Give him a minute," he said. "Maybe he's fixing his hair."

This made Tobi laugh out loud. That was until the ground started shaking. He got into a fighting stance with one leg back, planted firmly on the ground, both hands gripping his axe. Out of the gate a figure emerged. It was a tall beast, nine or ten feet tall. Standing in front of Tobi, it looked like an absolute giant. Its greenish-gray skin stretched over gigantic muscles. Metal bracers were on its arms, as well as a metal belt around his waist with a skull engraved where a buckle would normally be, holding up a giant pair of brown leather pants. Huge tusks protruded up out of its bottom jaw, up and outward giving the troll a permanent, menacing scowl.

The large teeth weren't its only weapon though. In its right hand was a giant, curved club that came to a point on the end. The point wasn't sharp enough to pierce, but sharp enough to do damage. As menacing as the creature looked, Tobi still managed to let out a laugh.

"You weren't kidding about the hair!" he called over to Skye. Faro had to stifle a laugh too. As big and ferocious as the beast was, its long, black mane of hair was tied up on top of his head with some kind of rope, meant to keep its hair out of its face during the fight. Juxtaposed against the wild, fanged look, it was a comical sight.

The bog troll let out a roar, its mouth opening wide, spittle flying through the air. It smashed its club into the ground, and as it hunched over it lunged forward like an ape, ready to smash Tobi into the ground.

Tobi's laugh quickly left him as he panicked and jumped out of the way to avoid the beast's charge.

"Woah!" yelled Tobi, regaining his feet to swing around and meet his opponent. His axe smashed hard against the club of the troll, and the clang reverberated throughout the arena.

Skye whooped and slapped his hand on the boundary wall. "Now it's getting good!" he yelled as the troll pulled the club back with both hands over his head and brought it down hard on the dwarf.

Tobi blocked the blow again, but the force of the swing knocked him backwards and off balance. He went tumbling and landed sprawled out on the ground. The troll pursued and repeated the move, trying to bring the club down on Tobi and smash him into the ground. The dwarf evaded by rolling back and forth to avoid each blow.

"He needs help!" Mathias exclaimed as he hopped the wall and pulled his sword in one movement. Faro was shocked at Mathias' sudden boost of bravery. So far on their journey the healer had been hesitant to fight. Apparently, deep down, there was more bravery than he'd let on so far, or maybe that was just the healer in him wanting to help those in need.

Faro turned to Skye and raised his own war hammer, gesturing towards the fight inside the ring. "So I guess we're... uh..."

Skye just smiled and gestured for him to join his friends in the fight. Faro didn't even wait for the elf's hand to fall back down before he lunged over the wall with cat-like agility.

In the arena, Mathias knew that his little sword wouldn't do much against the big club and the force of the hulking bog troll, so he ran his sword into the beast's leg, slicing upwards and creating a big gash.

The troll reeled back, roaring in pain, and in its fury tried to swing the club to bat Mathias away. Faro came in swiftly and blocked the blow with his war hammer. The force behind the swing was unsurprisingly strong, but the shock waves that ran up his arm weren't something he was prepared for. Neither was the kick that the troll aimed his way, catching him in the chest and sending him flying backwards.

As Faro regained his stance and quickly helped Tobi to his feet, Mathias joined them, the three of them squaring off and waiting for the troll's next move.

Faro stared in awe at the large gash that was bleeding on the troll's leg where Mathias had stabbed it. One second blood was flowing freely from the wound, the next it abruptly stopped. They all watched in amazement as the gash glowed a bright red, and closed back up before their eyes.

"That's amazing!" Faro yelled over at Skye on the side of the arena who looked like he was having the time of his life.

"I told you!" he called back. "King Umbra brought us this ol' boy a long time ago! We've been sparring with him for ages! Not a scratch stays on him!"

Fully healed again, the bog troll turned its attention back to its three assailants. He appeared to grin at the fear on their faces as he took a few taunting steps forward, tossing his club from hand to hand. "You die!" the troll roared at them.

"Fuck! It talks!" Tobi yelled at his friends.

"We need a new strategy!" called Mathias as he took a step back to stand behind Faro and Tobi.

"Open to suggestions!" Faro yelled as he stepped forward to meet a wide, sweeping blow the troll made to knock all three of them down at once. Faro braced himself and stopped the club mid-swing.

Tobi seized the opportunity to swing his axe at the club, trying to cleave it in half. Instead, the axe stuck into the club, but didn't break through. "Fuck!" Tobi yelled as the troll pulled his club back towards him, Tobi and his axe flying up in the air with it.

Faro watched as Tobi was flung around like he weighed nothing. "Let go!" he yelled at the dwarf who was holding onto his axe for dear life.

Faro was surprised Tobi heard him over his own screams as he was flung around. Tobi let go and went rolling across the field back towards Mathias and Faro. Mathias hadn't even been paying attention to Tobi's plight, as he was concocting a plan and was now ready to go.

"We can't kill this thing!" Mathias told them, eying the troll as he was moving to advance again. "We have to beat it back and close the gate."

"How the fuck do we do that? This thing is as strong as ten oxen!" Tobi yelled at Mathias. They watched as the troll pulled Tobi's axe out of his club and tossed it back towards the dwarf. Apparently he had been taught to keep the combat going for training purposes and honored a fair fight in the ring.

"Take the attack to him!" Mathias snapped back at Tobi. "I'll move around him while he's distracted and get to the gate control."

Faro nodded and sized up their opponent. "Right. Tobi, you wanna go low, and I'll go high?" Faro asked.

Tobi picked up his axe and looked at Faro, his head tilted, eyebrow raised. "You really think I could go high on a ten-foot beast?" he asked the lion, sounding a little annoyed.

Faro smiled. "Right," he answered, stepping forward to block a swing from the bog troll. Tobi came in low to bury his axe in the beast's foot. It roared in pain and staggered backwards. Faro pushed in harder, bringing the blunt end of his war hammer in hard on the beast's chest. He felt bone crack under the weight of his swing and knew he'd broken some ribs on the poor troll.

A look of pain and terror crossed the troll's face, and it brought its club around in a fury to try to beat back the onslaught. The club caught Tobi in the face, sending him sprawling backward and crumpling to the ground in a heap.

Faro didn't have time to see if his friend was okay. Instead, he took the opening to drive the spike end of his hammer into the troll's leg. This was met with a spurt of blood and a loud roar. Faro quickly pulled it back out and brought the blunt end around again in one swift movement, catching the troll across the face.

This caused the bog troll to drop his club and stagger the last few steps backwards into his cage. Mathias was on cue, quickly dropping the gate back into place. The beast roared in pain as they watched the red lights flashing in the semi-darkness of the cage as the wounds of the bog troll automatically healed themselves.

When the healing lights blinked out, they all heard applause behind them. Looking back at the perimeter wall, Faro saw Umbra had joined Skye on the sidelines, and was now applauding their efforts against the troll, Skye next to him whooping and hollering loudly.

Mathias and Faro rushed over and helped Tobi to his feet. His face appeared to be instantly bruised from the impact, his jaw slightly out of line, broken. The dwarf grunted in pain as they all made their way over to Skye and Umbra.

"An excellent show, men! Good job!" Umbra exclaimed with joy. He took one look at Tobi and waved his hand, muttering a quick incantation. Tobi screamed as his jaw audibly snapped back into place. Faro winced in sympathy pain, imaging what it would feel like to have your jaw magically reset. "Good to go," Umbra said, "though you'll have the bruising for a while, unfortunately. All good though! It adds character!" he exclaimed, laughing.

"Yeah. Great. Character," Tobi grunted back, feeling his jaw with his hand.

Umbra just kept smiling. "Not many can go up against my bog troll with such ferocity! I truly commend you all for such a good show of strength and teamwork! Now if you all would like, I'll have the kitchens prepare a celebration for the occasion. A feast! Two days from today. I suggest you all go and clean up and try to recover before then."

The trio didn't argue. They hadn't been expecting to be in a fight today, and the bog troll had certainly taken the energy out of them. They all gave a small bow to King Umbra and headed back to their rooms in the keep.

Umbra and Skye were left alone, looking at the empty pitch, Umbra eying the bog troll through its gate. It was sitting slumped over, elbows on its knees, resting. "Thank you for the demonstration, Captain," said Umbra with a small smile to Skye. "Now we really know what they can do."

True to his word, Umbra held a feast in their honor a few days later. It was in the great hall where they'd had their first dinner in Mireholm, only this time the room was filled with tables and more elves than they'd seen since they arrived, combined.

Faro and the party were seated at the raised head table above all the others. It was surreal to be in such a place of honor. Faro was sure that he was used to it in his old life, being a prince of Incarta, but he had no memories of such extravagancies.

Much to Faro's chagrin, Umbra had allowed Jarl to sit at the head table with them. The little wolverine was seated right next to him, but was currently ignoring him and the festivities, slurping wine and wolfing down a prime cut of steak that was served to them. Faro ignored his annoyingly loud eating and scanned the room again, hoping to see the one person he couldn't seem to find.

"Have you seen Veronica since the courtyard dance?" Faro asked Lena who was sitting on his other side.

The old elf looked concerned, her eyes scanning the room. "I was just about to ask you the same thing," she said.

While it was a fairly big keep, it felt odd that they hadn't seen a trace of Veronica since the dance. So far Umbra had been stonewalling them on any information about their vision visitor, but as soon as they got the information they wanted, Faro planned to grab Veronica and get out of this place. He still wasn't sure what it was, but there was something unnerving about it.

"My father says she's taken up studying the materials he has on Solana. Apparently he kept the old texts from the Academy of Solana's Light," said Lena, though she didn't sound convinced.

Jarl's ears perked up at the sound of old texts, and he swallowed the food that was in his mouth and leaned forward to talk around Faro.

"Old texts, you say? Where's that at?" he said, barely masking his longing.

Lena looked at him suspiciously, sipping some wine to give her time to decide if she should answer him or not. She set down her goblet and said, "In Zelira, the library of texts was on the lower levels, down by the dungeons. Given that Mireholm is a mirror image of my old home, I would wager it would be down there. Why?" she added, narrowing her eyes at him.

Jarl shrugged. "Always open to a good read, you know?" he said.

"Yeah, the dwarf from war-hungry Underoth loves to read," said Lena, her voice dripping with sarcasm.

Jarl just shrugged again and went back to his food. Faro hated that people kept mentioning these places and kingdoms and he still didn't know what they were, though he was sure he'd been to most of them before. The frustration was biting at him enough that he decided it was time to talk to Jarl.

"So," he started, slowly. "You and I... we both traveled with Eli, then?"

Jarl didn't seem like he was going to answer, but then spoke after a pause. "Yeah. You both came to Underoth straight from Incarta. I was the third to join your little posse on its world tour. I didn't really want to go, but my father decided it was a worthy cause." After another beat, he finished, "We fought a lot of Dark Humans together. You were sure a force to be reckoned with."

Faro felt his face go flush, though he knew it didn't show beneath his fur. He was glad that the fighting instinct was something he had kept, even after losing his memory. "Do you know what went wrong on Mt. Fluore?" he asked, hesitantly. Did he really want to know that answer?

"Nope," said Jarl simply. "We were all given orders we were to defeat Cosimir so that your father could rule Evania in his stead. My old man was sure pissed," he added with a chuckle. "He still agreed to sharing his forces to help get the job done, none-the-less."

The mystery as to why Eli had betrayed them was gnawing at him. No one seemed to know what had happened on the mountain that night. No one knew why Eli had gone from reluctant savior to new dark king.

Jarl leaned forward and called past Faro again. "Hey! Down there! Dwarf! Mind passing me the bowl of salt? Steak needs a little flavor."

Tobi set down his goblet and wiped red wine from his mustache. "You burnt down my bar and my home, you little fucker. Get your own damn salt!"

Faro backed his chair up a bit. He wasn't sure if there was about to be a fight between the dwarf and former dwarf, but he didn't want to be in the way if one broke out. Jarl pushed his chair away from the table as if he was about to get up, but Lena grabbed the salt bowl and passed it down instead. "Not right now, boys. You can have it out later. This is a fancy occasion after all. Can't be spilling blood across the fine dishes." Faro could tell by her continued sarcastic tone that she was not enjoying their stay here with her father at all.

Faro looked down the table at Tobi, who appeared to be fuming, but Thora and Mathias were sitting by him, trying to talk with him and calm him down. They all went quiet and dug back into their food. A short time later, King Umbra stood from the center of the head table to address the room.

"Thank you! Thank you all for coming!" his voice boomed, deep and regal. An instant hush fell over the room. Umbra smiled and continued. "I know it doesn't seem like a grand occasion for such a feast, but I wanted to honor our guests for their ferocity in their fight against Rork, the bog troll!"

Applause erupted around the room. "And," Umbra continued, "an official welcome feast for my daughter Lena, who has graced me with her presence after all these years." A tear ran down Umbra's cheek as he looked sadly at his daughter. Lena just looked straight ahead, stone-faced.

"Lena has been missed more than she could ever know, and I wish her mother were here with us for an even more grand reunion." Umbra was looking over at Lena, but she was still trying to ignore him, instead staring down at her food.

"Our visitors have brought sad news of the new dark regime on the mountain," Umbra continued, "but I have faith in the future of Evania. Our great country is in the best hands with our brave warriors here," he said, gesturing at Faro, Mathias, and Tobi. "Bravery such as theirs will be almost as vital as using whatever means necessary to combat the dark magic that still envelopes this land."

At this, Lena finally turned to look at her father. She was glaring at him, and if looks could kill, Faro believed Umbra would be dead on the spot.

Umbra stared back at her with a fierce intensity. "I've done unspeakable things to get this far. Together we can finish what I started and use the means necessary to defeat evil once and for all. With your power, it's possible."

It seemed the celebration had taken an awkward turn. Faro wasn't sure what the elf king's angle was. Was this Umbra's plan all along? Call out and embarrass Lena in front of a crowd of people? Was that supposed to get her to agree to help him?

"Virmorphia cannot beat Virmorphia, Father," Lena said coolly. "Only the light can beat the dark. You will see."

"It's not that simple..." Umbra started, but Lena wouldn't hear it.

With that she stood up and walked out of the room. The absolute silence was painful as her footsteps were the only noise in the room. The guest stared after her, varying degrees of shock on their faces. Umbra didn't look fazed in the least. He kept up his grand smile and addressed the room again.

"Everyone finish with your food and drink, for soon we dance to celebrate our heroes!" he said thunderously.

There was some clapping, and then the noise picked back up as the elves began eating and conversing again.

Umbra left his place and moved over to Faro. "You will talk to her for me? I know you of all people do not trust dark magic, given your current...uh... state," said Umbra, gesturing in a circle at Faro's mane that surrounded his lion face. "The fact is, I tried everything using Solana's magic to stop the Scourge and the Virmorphia magic. Only dark has worked against dark." Umbra's expression looked off, but Faro wasn't sure why. He was looking down at the table as he spoke.

"What was it that pulled the darkness from my mind, then?" Jarl, who'd been eavesdropping, asked.

"Virmorphia," said Umbra simply. "It's the only magic I possess. It's a rare vessel that can hold both types of magic."

Faro wasn't sure what to think. Lena obviously wanted nothing to do with her father and his dark ways, and he sure wasn't a fan as Umbra had said. Virmorphia had done him no favors so far. "I can talk to her, but I'm not going to press her," he said, looking up at the tall elf king from his sitting position in the chair. He wasn't even sure what he wanted from Lena, exactly. Was he trying to convert her to dark magic? Did he need her light magic for something? Right now he was too afraid to ask.

Umbra nodded. "That's all I ask. No one else here is powerful enough to take on the new High King with me. Lena has centuries of experience, and by combining our powers we will be formidable to all."

The sound of a new, formidable dark magic entity didn't sound very appealing to Faro, but he also knew nothing about magic. All he knew was that something was off balance and causing havoc across the land. Eli had betrayed all of Evania, and if Faro could, he would put an end to Virmorphia magic for good.

When Faro didn't answer, Umbra placed a bony hand on his shoulder and said, "It really was an honor seeing you fight today. Reminds me of the ferocity of your father, James."

Faro stood from his chair to look Umbra in the eyes. The quick move made the table buck a little, and Tobi grumbled as his wine spilled. "You know my father?" Faro asked.

Umbra nodded. "We fought a few times as allies against Cosimir's forces. He was young and ambitious then. We left the second war to you who were young."

"Were you at the council for the Dungeon Lords, then?" asked Faro, recalling his vision in the apple grove.

"Yes," said Umbra. "I gave quite the speech to convince people to elect James as the new High King. Cosimir started it all from the mines of Incarta, it only made sense that a proper king from Incarta rise and do the job right. You would have made the perfect king of Incarta, and heir to the throne of Evania. Definitely much better than your *friend*," Umbra added, grabbing Faro's paw and clapping his other hand on top in an affectionate pat.

Faro wasn't sure he understood the king's logic, but there were a lot of things about Umbra that remained an enigma. Instead of arguing the point that he didn't feel like he would be the right ruler for the country, he simply smiled at the old elf king, putting his other paw on top of Umbra's hand, politely removing it from his grasp.

"Thank you," said Faro, a bit put off. "I'll be sure to talk to Lena for you. See what I can do."

Umbra took the hint that he'd made Faro uncomfortable, smiled, and said "I will meditate and see if I can find out anything about this mysterious man from everyone's visions. Please, sit and enjoy your feast." At that, he motioned for Faro to sit back down and left the room.

Faro sat and picked up his steak, biting half of it off in one bite, chewing it with his long, sharp teeth. It seemed like the air had been sucked out of the party. He hoped Umbra had answers for them soon, because he knew the talk with Lena wouldn't go well, and he wasn't sure what it was, but his sense of unease about Mireholm, and Umbra, was growing by the day.

CHAPTER EIGHTEEN

A KING'S GAMBIT

A few nights after the feast, Faro lay tossing and turning in the bed they had provided for him. He hadn't ever been fully comfortable in Mireholm, despite the cozy room with the roaring fireplace and comfortable canopy bed. It was a room fit for royalty and likely housed royalty when they visited. Of course Faro thought that Mireholm itself probably had few visitors, and the actual visitors stayed in the sister kingdom of Zelira.

On this night, Faro had gotten to sleep late. After the promise from Umbra that he would seek answers for them, there was another frustrating gap of no response. The last few days had left them waiting in angst. Now he was tossing and turning. He needed rest, but his dreams didn't seem to want to let him get any quality sleep.

In his dream he was in a dark stone room. The walls seemed to be made of solid rock, hewn from the existing earth. He could hear dripping water, and a musty smell filled the air. It was just him inside the large chamber. A feeling of loneliness and foreboding crept over him. He held his war hammer aloft, waiting for something to jump out at him in the darkness and attack.

Then there was a bright flash of light. The empty room was replaced with an eerie, glowing yellow light, and Faro was no longer alone. The light took the form of a bright sun, surrounded by three smaller suns. From the symbol's light he could now see in front of him was a dais atop which sat a throne. The throne was impossibly large for a normal human to sit on. So large he could barely hoist himself onto the seat if he tried. Surrounding the throne were a dozen specters, ghostly wisps that floated in lines on either side.

Floating above the throne, the symbol of the suns had turned into a full-bodied specter. A long, gnarled, transparent finger raised through the air and pointed directly at Faro. The figure opened its mouth and let out a ghastly noise before it spoke.

"Heir of Evania!" It called out in a loud voice.

Faro shook his head in denial. "No! I barely even know who I am," he said in a panic.

The specter swooped down through the air from the throne and brought its ghostly face right in front of Faro's.

"You were chosen," it wheezed.

He took a step back away from the terrifying form, but it pressed even closer.

"My father was chosen. I'm not the heir!" Faro roared back.

The specter backed off, and its face fell in disappointment. "Then you doom the fate of Evania to darkness." The ghost faded away to nothing, and the other specters went with it. He now stood alone in the dark room again.

Faro felt something tug at his arm. He looked, but there was nothing there. Something was clearly pulling on his arm, but his sleeve wasn't moving. Something...something somewhere else? A dream. This was a dream. Something kept pulling.

With a jolt, Faro sat up out of bed and opened his eyes. It did little good because the fire had gone out in his room and he was greeted with pressing darkness. And then a voice spoke out from the darkness, smooth and coaxing.

"Welcome to Mireholm. Such a lovely place to be!" said the voice.

Faro swiped his paw through the darkness, and connected with something solid.

"Gah!" the voice called as its owner flew backwards onto the stone floor. Faro lunged out of bed towards the intruder.

"Stop!" it yelled at him. "It's just me! Jarl!"

The confirmation of the intruder didn't make him feel less like attacking.

"Why are you here?" Faro roared, trying to get his bearings in the darkness. "Think you can kill me in the middle of the night?"

A dark purple light emanated near the floor in the darkness and shot across the room. Faro braced himself for the worst, but then saw the ball of fire hit the fireplace, and the room lit up. The purple fire lit the room, and then slowly turned into normal yellow and orange flame. Jarl stood up from the floor and moved over to the fireplace, tossing on a few more logs that were kept nearby to make sure it stayed lit.

"Don't be crazy, you fool," Jarl hissed at him. "If I wanted to kill you, you'd be dead." Faro nodded slightly, realizing that the wolverine wouldn't have broken his element of surprise if he had the intention to kill him in his sleep. "I was just mocking that tall oaf, Umbra. He's pretty smitten on what he's built here, eh?"

Faro still wasn't sure what to make of Umbra. He was nice and hospitable enough, but he also seemed like he was stalling to keep them here. Something about the elf didn't sit right with Faro.

"So what are you doing here, waking me up?" Faro asked, rubbing sleep from his eyes.

Jarl turned away from the fire to face Faro, the backlighting from the fireplace giving him an eerie, silhouetted look. "I'm tired of waiting around for High King Happy to give us any answers we need. He's stonewalling you on the visions, and I'm not getting anywhere with him on the location of any dark magic secrets I can take back to my... *masters*," Jarl seemed to balk at this last word. "Plus, that annoying girl still seems to be missing. Should have kept her on the rope," he finished, smiling.

It was true. Veronica still hadn't been seen since the day they arrived. "So you want me to go with you to steal Umbra's secrets?" he asked, raising a big eyebrow at the short creature.

Jarl just shrugged. "Seems we could be on the same side here. We both need to go around and look for answers. I don't trust old Umbra to not have another bog troll or something protecting his secrets." Jarl looked up at his old friend, and his face softened a bit. "We made a pretty good team, not so long ago. Not really our fault we were betrayed."

"Kind of your fault that you tried to kill me. Plus, you burnt down my friend's tavern," Faro said, matter-of-factly.

Jarl raised a finger in objection. "The Virmorphia was controlling me. Umbra removed it," said Jarl, defending himself. "You saw how I changed when he worked his magic."

"Right. So," said Faro, throwing on his tunic and grabbing his war hammer, "at the feast, Lena said your information is likely down by the dungeons. If I help you find the library, are you going to go into the dungeons with me and help search for Veronica?"

Jarl looked like he didn't like the idea, but said, "I really doubt there is information on the type of dark magic Eli and Eldryn are looking for just sitting in the library. I'm thinking I'll have to venture down into the dungeons with you. That's why I need backup."

"Because you're afraid of bog trolls?" Faro laughed.

"That Mathias guy told me it was really, really huge!" exclaimed Jarl, looking only half like he was joking.

At that, the two beasts set off from Faro's room. Being on the third floor of the keep, they had several flights of stairs to get down without being seen by Umbra or any of his castle staff. The halls were mostly dark, only lit by a subfluore torch on the wall every ten feet. The carpets under their feet were gold colored like much of the rest of the Mireholm keep, and Faro was getting a little tired of the lavish feel.

Both beasts quickly ran down the staircase at the end of the hall. It was tall and twisting, but they found themselves on the second floor in short order. They slowed down and implemented more caution here, as the stairs down to the first floor were the lavish arched stairs that led down to the entry room to the keep. It was here that Faro was afraid they would run into the king or his helpers, but he heaved a sigh of relief as he saw the area was empty. Apparently it was late enough in the night that everyone had gone to sleep.

Even though it was deserted, Faro still felt exposed. All the subfluore chandelier lighting overhead made this the brightest room they had encountered so far. Not only that, but they didn't know their way down to the lower levels from here, and without someone like Lena who would know the way, they'd have to do a bit of poking around to find more stairs leading downwards.

"You think we have to go into the throne room to find the next stairs?" Jarl asked, looking at the different route options. "Maybe through the great hall?"

Faro thought for a moment. It didn't make much sense for the stairs to the lower levels to be off any room other than this one. Then again, he couldn't remember being in a castle before, so he could be way off base. Maybe off the kitchens? Where were those even located? He knew if he'd designed the keep it would make the most sense for them to be...

"There!" he said in a loud whisper, pointing under the stairs they had just come down. Tucked away underneath the left set of stairs was a big, wooden door. The shadow of the stairs above obscured it, but Faro had a good feeling it was what they were looking for.

They made their way over, and Jarl reached for the handle. He gave it a hard pull, but the door didn't budge. "Locked!" he yelled, and Faro had to shush him.

"Well, it's definitely what we're looking for then. Why else would it be locked?" Faro sized up the door, wondering if he could break it down. It looked to be solid oak, and likely wouldn't budge. Besides the difficulty, it would make a loud noise if he knocked it down, possibly drawing unwanted attention.

"We can take care of this, easy," said Jarl. He lifted his hand and purple flames ignited. Arching his fingers he controlled it to a small area and burnt a hole around the door handle and locking mechanism. The surrounding wood burned clean through, and Faro reached in and broke the mechanism from the door. It easily swung inward, and they slipped through.

"What does the magic feel like?" Faro asked him.

Jarl thought for a moment as they walked down a hallway that was on the other side of the door. "It's weird, for sure. You just think about what you want to do, and just kind of command it. Sometimes you have to mutter incantations. Other times it just comes to you. Depends on how strong you need it to be, I think. I'm honestly surprised I still have it. When Umbra ripped the voice out of my head, I assumed the magic would go with it."

They reached the stairwell they were hoping to find and started heading downwards. The decor and luxury of the main hall ended abruptly, and they were left with plain stone walls and stairs. They were whispering in hurried breaths now as they picked up their pace.

"Did we all get magic?" Faro asked, the thought just dawning on him.

Jarl shrugged. "All the other disciples had varying forms of magic after the transformation." He looked up at Faro and saw his curious face. "You probably can do something with it. Unless your tumble down the mountain knocked it out of you."

Faro's jaw fell open. "You were there when I was injured?" he asked.

"Yup," said Jarl. "It happened within a few minutes of Cosimir being murdered. We didn't know Eli was going to do that. The plan was to kill him and install your father as High King. The prophesy said Eli was destined to kill Cosimir, but was to die in the process. Instead, what we got was a murdered Cosimir and Eli taking the dais as the new ruler."

"And we all got transformed into animals... how?" Faro asked, trying to piece everything together.

"No idea," Jarl shot back. "That dark mage Eldryn put some kind of spell on the spear Eli had, I think. As soon as it dropped Cosimir, the room turned purple. We were all knocked down and stood up as animals."

"And that knocked me down the mountain?" Faro asked.

Jarl laughed at him. "No. We all stood up in shock. For some reason Eldryn immediately killed Renn. Being the do-gooder you are you roared a loud lion roar and charged at Eli. Next thing we all know Eldryn lowered his staff and blasted you with green light. We all thought you'd died. There's no way a normal person could have survived that fall. Eli sent a few assassins after you to make sure you were dead. When they failed, they sent me."

More pieces were falling into place for Faro, but it was still frustratingly not enough. Why had Eli betrayed the plan? What was he planning now? Who was Renn? It also hurt Faro a little that his friend had send killers after him. It hurt, even though his only memory of being friends with Eli was the vision he'd had in the apple grove.

They reached the bottom of the staircase and came out into a big, dark room. Long, wooden bookcases lined the walls and stood running down the middle of the room. The library held an uncountable number of tomes. They picked a row and started walking down it. Faro's sensitive nose picked up the scent of dust and old leather.

"You sure what you're looking for won't be in here? There's thousands upon thousands of books and scrolls here," Faro said.

"Yeah, we have to keep going. We need to look for the girl anyways. If we don't find what I'm looking for down in the dungeons, I'll come back and scope out the library," said Jarl, not even glancing at the surrounding shelves.

Faro was surprised that Jarl was willing to go further with him, but he was thankful for the help none-the-less. They continued to make their way through the library until they came to another flight of stairs downwards. This flight was much shorter than the rest had been and led them down into a stone room with metal bars. They had reached the original dungeons of Mireholm, but Faro could tell this wasn't the deeper dungeons that had likely been built during the Scourge.

Sure enough, towards the back of the passageway, a hole that was roughly as tall as a man had been blasted into the stone. Jarl reached out a paw and felt the rough edges of the perimeter. "Blast magic," he said. "Everyone had to dig underground. The only life we ever knew was underground. Blasted and hewn by sorcerers and stone smiths. Desperate, quick work to escape the death that took so many above."

Sure that he had known this at some point, Faro just nodded in agreement. So many kingdoms living underground. So many mighty kings turned into Dungeon Lords, forced to hide and pay tribute to Cosimir the Eternal. A beloved family, rulers of Evania, wiped from the face of the land. That was, unless the rumors of a continued lineage proved true.

Walking through the blast hole, they found themselves in a rough, narrow tunnel. Any fineries that had existed in the upper levels, and even the basic roughness of the library, was totally and completely gone from this place. Instead, it was replaced with a hurriedly blasted tunnel that led them steeply downwards into the ground. The worst part was that it was completely pitch black, and they carefully felt their way through, hoping they didn't fall into a dark abyss.

After moving this way for several minutes, Faro getting extremely uncomfortable with the increasingly tight space, they saw a yellow light ahead. Faro urged Jarl along as fast as he could. When they finally reached the light, they stepped out into a wider corridor, and Faro breathed a deep sigh of relief.

"Woo!" he said, hunched over with his paws on his knees. "Being a big fella doesn't work so well in tight spaces."

"Seemed like plenty of room to me!" Jarl shot back with a grin.

Faro just rolled his eyes and started walking down the new corridor they had found. The walls were lined with brackets that held subfluore crystals. The rock appeared to be a bit more finely hewn out, as if whoever made this room had gotten to safety and taken a little more time to put craftsmanship into this new area.

They weren't really sure what they were looking for, so they simply crept along the abandoned corridor until they heard something up ahead.

"That's breathing," said Jarl, his tiny ears twitching.

"Heavy breathing," Faro added, his animal hearing picking up the sound as well. They saw a brighter light up ahead coming from the wall, and Faro assumed they were coming up on the first room. As they got closer, they saw that the room was more of a giant archway covered in metal bars.

They approached with caution, not sure what they would find. Faro was hoping it was Veronica so they could bust her out and get out of here before they were found. Instead, what he saw shocked him.

"The bog troll," he said, approaching the bars. Sure enough, on the other side of the bars sat the bog troll they had faced off against. He sat slumped against the wall, arms resting on his knees, staring intently at Faro and Jarl as they approached. Behind the troll Faro saw a small room with hay and what looked like the remains of several bitro carcasses. Beyond the room was a smooth, curved ramp that spiraled upwards around a corner to where they couldn't see.

"This must be the bottom part of his cage," said Faro. "Easy feeding and care down here, and then they release it for fighting up there in the training arena." So wherever they were, they must be right under the arena where they had fought the beast a few days prior.

"Kind of an ugly fellow," said Jarl. "What's up with its hair?" he asked, noticing it was tied up out of his face.

"*It* talks," said the bog troll mockingly.

"Woah! What the fuck?" said Jarl, surprised.

"Yeah," said Faro, tilting his head knowingly. "He told us we were going to die during the fight."

"Three on one, no fair," said the troll. "Want to come and do one-on-one?" Rork the bog troll finished with a big, toothy smile.

"No, no, no. All good out here on this side of the bars," said Faro. And then he had an idea. "Have you seen a little girl come through here in the last several days? She was wearing all white last we saw her. Little blonde girl."

The bog troll pointed his thumb over his shoulder. "Took her that way many days ago. And the rock monster. Lots of screams. Keeps me awake."

Jarl and Faro exchanged a look. "Screams?" Faro asked, getting worried.

As if on cue, a scream echoed down the corridor. Only, it wasn't the high-pitched scream of a little girl he was expecting. It was a deep, guttural sound that made them all shudder. The bog troll covered his ears as if the screams had been boring into his brain and driving him mad for some time now.

Faro and Jarl exchanged looks and then took off running towards the source of the sound. A short way down the corridor was another opening, but this one opened up into what looked like a makeshift mess hall. It was nowhere near as grand as the one up in the main keep, but it looked like it was suitable during the Scourge.

All the tables in the cavernous room were pushed to the side, and chained in the middle of the room was a beast that Faro had hoped he would never see again, the Vorath Shadruul that had kidnapped Veronica in Graeton. It wasn't alone, either. He was surrounded by five elves, all of which looked like they were carefully studying the creature. One elf sat in the corner, hunched over a table, taking notes.

"What are they doing to your buddy here?" Faro asked, nudging Jarl's shin with his foot. They both pulled back to one side of the entryway and peeked around the corner so they wouldn't be spotted.

"Pshh. Hardly my buddy," spat Jarl. "I was assigned to travel with a group of those things to kill you, which I haven't done by the way. You're welcome."

Faro silently laughed at this. "Such a great favor. Thank you. Wait. Who's that?"

A figure emerged from a doorway on the other side of the room. It was clad in a golden robe, a hood covering its head. The cloak swished fluidly across the ground as the figure seemed to glide forward until it stopped in front of the Shadruul. Faro's first thought was Umbra, but the only problem was that this figure was way too short.

The person lifted their hands and threw their hood back. Faro gasped as Veronica's face appeared before them. Jarl threw an elbow into Faro's knee and whispered, "This must be how they're going to fix Rotung. Umbra said they were going to try to free him from his rock prison."

Faro watched in fascination. Something good was finally going to happen. He watched as Veronica raised her hand towards Rotung. Yellow light formed in her palm, and she slowly extended it outwards towards the Shadruul. Rotung calmed down and seemed to be comforted, staring at Veronica in awe.

Then, in one abrupt movement, Veronica tightened her grip on the light and ripped the Shadruul's arm off its body. There was a deafening roar of pain from Rotung, and blood began to pour from where the human elements of the Shadruul remained.

"Oh, fuck!" screamed Jarl. His voice was luckily covered by the sound of Rotung screaming.

Veronica kept moving her hands. She quickly made several duplicates of the arm and fused the original back onto the Shadruul. Rotung's screams turned to more of a whimper as Veronica pulled one of the unsuspecting elves towards her, bringing one of the monster's arms close as well. In one swift move she brought her arms high, and then back down hard. The rock arm slammed into the unsuspecting elf, and there was another loud scream.

The entire room erupted in blinding light, and Faro and Jarl had to look away. When the light faded, they looked back in, afraid of what they might see. Standing where the elf once stood was a new creature. It was hunched over, with unusually long arms that ended in long, spindly fingers. The long, slender body was topped with a small head that had a small mouth and long pointed face. A fire was lit inside it, emanating from the chest and the spot where eyes should have been.

Faro's mouth hung open. They had just made a completely new creature from the Vorath Shadruul. The long, gangly form made it look like it would be much faster and agile than its predecessor.

"Gorrik Shadruul," said a voice from the corner of the room. Umbra appeared as if from nowhere, clapping his hands and smiling. "Our new High King can make as many Vorath as he wishes. We have a superior warrior to take him on. Do it again!" he loudly commanded Veronica. "We need an entire army!"

"No!" yelled Faro before he could help himself.

Both Veronica and Umbra turned quickly towards them. Veronica looked guilty, like a child caught stealing candy.

Umbra threw his arms wide in typical fashion. "Welcome, friends," he said, giving them his usual, off-putting smile.

CHAPTER NINETEEN

BOUND BY ILLUSION

The next morning Lena found herself in the great hall looking for some breakfast. She was having weird dreams about ghosts and the Shadruul the night before, and she was glad that daylight had finally come to restore some normality to her mindset. Or at least whatever normality she could get from the weird kingdom her father had created.

Breakfast in Mireholm had been the least eventful meal of the day since they'd arrived, but it was still quite a spread that was offered. One table was set out along the wall, and on it was all manner of fruit, baked pastries, and oats. Her favorite was the Sunrise Stew, or so the chef had called it. It was a mix of oats, eggs, honey, leeks, and carrots. It seemed like an odd dish at first, but after their bland travel rations the stew tasted amazing and kept her full most of the day.

She grabbed a bowl and started ladling some up when a sudden voice made her jump. She spilled some soup onto the table and made a mental note to apologize to the staff later.

"Good morning, Dear," said Umbra from behind her. She turned to see her father smiling at her. He was wearing his usual golden robe with droopy sleeves.

"Hello, Father," she said back, turning to finish ladling her soup. "To what do I owe the pleasure? Found anything out for us?"

Umbra's smile faltered a bit. "No. Unfortunately, every time I try to seek a vision of the man you all saw, it's cloudy. I'm working through it and will likely have something for you within a week."

"A week?" asked Lena. "We definitely weren't planning on staying that long. We have to get Veronica back to her grandfather in Graeton. I have to get back to my business. Graeton needs its healer back. Poor Tobi needs to rebuild his tavern."

Her father threw his arms wide and nodded as if he understood her plight. "I know, Dear. I've had so much more control over my visions. It's surprising to me that something is blocking them. It's not intentional, I assure you."

"Really?" Lena snapped back. "You're not keeping me here longer to wear me down to join you in your dark quest?"

Umbra looked offended at this. "Dark quest? I have spent a thousand years trying to prevent the very thing that has happened to this land. It has taken a lot of study of both Solana's and Baladan's magic, and I'm sorry to inform you, but The Light isn't sufficient in fighting the dark. I just wish I would have realized how to control it all before..." Umbra trailed off, realizing he was saying too much.

Lena narrowed her gaze at her father, turning from the table, her Sunrise Stew set down and forgotten. "Before *what*, Father?" she asked him, a hint of acid in her voice. "You couldn't control the dark magic? What did you do?"

For the first time in her life, Lena saw her father's face turn flush with embarrassment. "I... it was before I was even forced to turn to dark magic. I manipulated life and created the Scourge to try and run tests. Solana's magic had no effect on..."

Lena felt her hand clench into a fist. "You created *what*?" she yelled at him. She wanted to grab a knife from the breakfast table and attack her father, but thought better of it. She needed to hear more of what he had to say.

Umbra just hung his head. "It's true," he said shamefully. "I had visions for decades about the terrible Scourge that was to come and wipe out the land. I had to stop it. It drove me mad, what the world would come to unless I could save it. I worked tirelessly to create the Scourge in a controlled environment.

I spent all my time trying to use Solana's Light to cure the disease. My endless work drove your mother mad. We didn't hardly talk for years."

"And that's why you left?" said Lena, trying to understand.

"No," said Umbra. "It wasn't until she'd found out what I'd done that she'd finally had enough. She threatened to tell all the kingdoms what I had done. I had to stop her."

Lena's face fell. She grabbed him hard by both of his shoulders. "Did you *kill* my mother?" she asked him.

"No!" he yelled in panic. "No! But in my rage to stop her I... I don't even know exactly how it happened. The entire kingdom. It just kind of... ripped apart and relocated. In an effort to get away from her and complete my work..."

"And you ripped off an entire copy of the kingdom? An exact copy of Zelira?" Lena asked, shocked that such a feat could be possible.

"Somehow... yes," said Umbra. "We landed here. Just the buildings though. The people... somehow I just took half of them with me. Luckily it missed your mother, and I got Amazadan."

Lena looked sorrowful at the mention of her father's friend and top general. "That's a whole other story, yeah? We fought Amazadan at Mournfall Lake. He didn't meet a good fate, and that was before we even got there."

Umbra slowly shook his head. "My acceptance of Virmorphia and study of the Scourge continued here in my accidental kingdom. My dark island of mistake. Mireholm. Amazadan stood by me through all the...tests."

Lena gave him an odd look, and then her eyes went wide. "Tests? All those dead elves in the lake? They died of the Scourge? You exposed them and then failed to cure them? And you just... dumped them there?"

Umbra nodded. "I've done so much damage, Lena. I didn't mean for the disease to get loose. And the timing was awful," he said.

Lena pressed her fingers into her eyes. "You created the Scourge, *and* let it loose? Are you fucking kidding me? All this time you set out to stop it and you... you're the one who invented the damn thing. You created this mess. You created the need for dungeon kingdoms! Turned yourself and the other rulers into Dungeon Lords!"

A tear rolled down Umbra's face, his voice now sounding desperate. "That's why I have to set all this right, Lena. No matter what the cost. I've learned to control the Virmorphia. I've learned how to hone my visions. I was the one who found out how to stop the Scourge," he told her desperately, as if this made all of his actions right. "I know I've messed up, but it's time to right that wrong. In studying dark magic, I've come to another realization. Virmorphia isn't strong enough alone. It takes a combination of that and Solana's Light to do what we need to do."

Lena's face contorted in rage. "You've studied the way of Solana's Light for millennia! You don't need me!"

Umbra shook his head. "On my path, I've sacrificed things to... my new ways. I'm no longer able to wield The Light." He raised his hand and purple magic ignited from it. The veins in his face started pulsing with the same purple glow, as if the dark magic was running through his blood. "You must die to The Light to embrace the dark. The Virmorphia has consumed me."

"Stand down, Elf!" came a yell from across the room. They both turned to look, and Tobi stood at the entryway to the hall, Mathias and Thora standing behind him. The dwarf's mouth was curled into a snarl, and Lena knew what he was thinking. Seeing Umbra appear to be wielding the dark purple magic against Lena, the same magic that burnt down his bar, set something off inside him. It had become a vendetta against anyone who wielded the dark art form. "You back away from Lena!" he roared, grabbing his axe from his back.

Umbra dropped his hand and extinguished the magical light. "Calm down, Young Dwarf. I've no intention of harming my daughter. I'm simply trying to get her to see the way forward. I need her light magic to..."

"How do you think I'd ever help you?" Lena screamed at her father. Tobi backed down, realizing that Lena could handle herself, even against her powerful father. "After everything you've done? You released the Scourge on Evania! You allowed Cosimir to rise to dominance! You... yah!" Everyone stared in shock as the normally composed Lena dissolved into a screaming rage.

"Did you just say that *Umbra* released the Scourge?" asked Mathias as he and Thora moved closer.

"Yes!" yelled Lena. "He had a vision and set out to destroy the Scourge, but he invented the damn thing in the process! It was a self-fulfilling prophecy. Amazing that someone who can foresee the future couldn't foresee the destruction he'd cause."

Now Umbra's face was the one to contort in rage. It was clear that his daughter had touched a nerve with him. "Don't you dare accuse me!" his voice boomed. Tobi raised his axe again, becoming alert. "Everything I've done," Umbra lamented, his face emanating purple again, "everything I've sacrificed, was all for the good of Evania! I was tricked into causing destruction, and now I've found a way to fix it. You *will* help me whether you want to or not!"

Lena scoffed at this. "We're leaving, Father. Now." She walked away from the table, secretly wishing she would have grabbed her Sunrise Stew first because the smell was making her stomach rumble.

She reached her friends, and they all turned to leave when a mad cackle sounded behind them. "You can leave the kingdom," said Umbra, still chuckling wildly, "but you can never leave The Veil."

The words hit them slowly, and then they turned around to stare at the mad king. "I control who stays and who goes. You forced your way in, now you're my guests until I say it's okay for you to leave."

"You mean *if* you let us leave," said Lena, her heart sinking.

Umbra sighed. "I love you, Lena. I'm sorry that you think so little of me now." A silent stare between the two elves followed for an uncomfortably long pause before Umbra spoke again. "I will still get you the information you want on your visions, but I will also get your compliance to help me save Evania from what has happened, and what's coming."

Lena's nose twitched in disgust. "Enough is enough. We're leaving." At that she ushered her party along with her hands and they all left the room.

Umbra was left alone by the table of food. He stepped up and examined the table, seeing his daughters untouched bowl of stew. He grabbed a spoon and ladled some into his mouth. "Well," he said to himself, sighing, "I've come this far. No sense stopping what I need to do."

"Don't you think we should find Faro and Veronica first?" Thora asked timidly, afraid to interrupt Lena in the mood that she was in. They had marched straight from the keep, through the deserted streets of Mireholm, and right out the front gates. This time the green fields and gardenias didn't seem as welcoming, though the smell was still nice.

Now, standing at the barrier wall where they had come through The Veil, Lena stood before it, determined. The others stood back in fear of what might happen if they tried to cross it.

"No," she said sternly to Thora. "We see if we can get out, and then we will go back for them."

Thora, Mathias, and Tobi all looked at the wall with deep concern. From where they stood, beyond the wall looked like more of the same green pastures and flowers. They knew, of course, that this was an illusion as they had been in the deserted wasteland on the other side just a little over a week before.

Lena pulled the bow from her back and quickly strung an arrow she had made during their downtime in Mireholm. She aimed it high in the air and let it fly. The arrow whisked forward through the air. They all watched as it continued in its intended arc until it halted in the air above the wall and fell straight down. The odd thing was, it also looked like the arrow kept going on its intended path.

Thora gasped. "You saw that fall, right?"

Lena re-slung her bow on her back and slowly walked towards the wall. "Yes…" she said, her voice trailing off as she approached the wall. Without hesitation, she pulled herself up the wall and stood up.

Nothing happened. She could hear a loud humming coming from right in front of her, though could see nothing that would stop her from leaving. Cautiously, she stepped forward. To the others down below it looked like she walked smack dab into a solid wall. Lena stepped back and rubbed her forehead, watching as an image of herself was created by the veil. She stared in awe as her copy fell straight down to the ground and walked off into the green pastures beyond the wall.

The old elf turned on the wall and looked down at her friends. "We're definitely trapped here," she said, still rubbing her face, "and this whole damn place is one big illusion."

Chapter Twenty

DARK VISION

After failing to leave The Veil, the party somberly made their way back to the keep in Mireholm. None of them had any idea what the mirror image leaving The Veil meant. Even Mathias, who had read every book he'd ever come across, didn't know what it meant. Was there an arrow and another Lena beyond the veil? Was it just showing them their desire for escape? They had talked about it all the way back to the castle, and they couldn't agree. What they knew was that they needed to find Faro and Veronica and come up with a plan to get Umbra to release them from this prison.

They didn't even have to get beyond the courtyard before Faro found them and greeted them. "Hey! Where have you all been? I've been looking all over the keep for you. Thought you'd taken Veronica and left without me!" he called to them, smiling and laughing.

He met them in the middle of the courtyard by the statue of Solana. "We didn't leave you, Friend," said Mathias. "We've just been testing what Umbra told us about us being trapped here!"

"And?" asked Faro, looking concerned.

"We are," chimed in Tobi. "Some weird spell over the whole damn place. We're stuck until our gracious host lets us leave. Or maybe," he added as he picked up his axe and made a quick swinging motion with it through the air.

Lena rolled her eyes at him. "We've already tried getting through. Your axe won't break it down."

"What do you take me for?" yelled Tobi. "I meant kill Umbra!"

"We're definitely not going to kill my father," Lena retorted. "End of story."

"Just saying. It would likely break the spell!" Tobi answered back. "No? Fine. What's your plan then?"

Lena thought for a moment. "We have to wait a bit longer. Play his game. He cares about me too much to hurt me or any of you. He'll give us the answers we need and let us go in due time."

The others didn't look so sure about that. All except for Faro who just smiled at her. "Always so patient, Lena. I like that plan," he said, clapping his paw together. "That said, I need to get some rest. I haven't been feeling the best lately, and my big, comfortable bed is calling my name. I hope you all understand."

With that he turned from them and disappeared into the keep. Tobi pointed his thumb after Faro and raised an eyebrow at Thora, who shrugged. "Maybe he ate some bad fish. The food has been tasting a little weirder to me lately, too."

It was four days later when Umbra sent Skye to get them from their rooms and invite them down to dinner with the promise of the news they'd been waiting for. It had been a long, angst-filled wait, and Lena was glad it was finally over. Now she paced back and forth by the dining table, too anxious to sit and eat anything.

Tobi sat down at the table, also unable to touch any of the food. Instead, he had a steak knife in his hand and was whittling away at the grand wooden table, trying to calm his nerves. Thora sat next to him, enjoying an apple, while Mathias worked his way through a large slice of rhubarb pie.

Faro was ravenously devouring any meat at the table he could get his hands on, which was currently a large chicken breast. He had hidden in his room for the past four days, calling out to them how he still wasn't feeling well. Now he appeared to be a lot better and finally ready to eat again, his appetite back in full force after being sick.

Lena was eager to see her father. They still had seen no trace of Veronica since they got here, and it was unnerving her to still be in a replica of her childhood home. She was still pacing when she heard the grating voice of her father enter the room behind her. She flinched at the sound, no longer feeling the safe warmth and comfort in hearing it she once felt as a child.

"Greetings, my friends," he said as he glided into the room to stand by them. "I apologize for all the theatrics. You were going to leave, and I feel like the answers you seek are important, as is my mission to right what I've done wrong and help free Evania from its fate."

Lena scoffed. "We don't care about your mission. We just want whatever information you have about our visions, and for you to let us take Veronica and go home. Where has she been, by the way? We haven't seen her in almost two weeks now." She saw Faro nodding adamant agreement, his mouth too full to talk.

Umbra raised his hands, trying to gesture for his daughter to be calm, but she was anything but calm right now. "Veronica is fine. I told you, she's been studying. Not much else for a kid to do here, truth be told."

"Ok," Thora chimed in. She and Mathias had just split another piece of pie as Thora only wanted half and Mathias couldn't get enough. "She'll be ready to go then as soon as you've told us about our visions?"

Umbra ignored her question and heaved a sigh, his face turning into a frown. Lena braced herself for getting no news at all again. She was surprised as her father told them what he knew.

"I finally had a vision that connected with the man that you all saw in your vision," he said with dramatic flair. He paused for dramatic effect and they all stared at him intently.

"And?" asked Tobi, angrily driving the steak knife further into the table.

"And," Umbra continued, "I saw him in a time long, long ago. He was inside Mt. Fluore, surrounded by all manner of soldiers and royals. Constantine Evania was on the throne, offering this man a golden scepter embedded with a subfluore crystal on top. Constantine ruled over a thousand years ago, and from what I can tell this was a ceremony of great honor."

"Honor? What kind of honor?" Mathias asked around a mouthful of rhubarb pie. "Doesn't quite sound like a knighting ceremony."

"Quite right," said Umbra. "From my studies I've gathered that these Scepters of Solana were given only to the highest paladins in the land. Only those trusted with the highest secrets and powers of Solana's Light were tasked with protecting it as such."

"What kind of powers?" asked Lena, intrigued.

Umbra thought for a moment as if he wasn't sure if he should say what he was about to say. When he spoke, it was almost a whisper. They all had to lean in to hear him properly. "They say that those who wield these scepters have power over space and time."

"Like, they can travel through time and teleport around Evania?" asked Thora in awe.

The old elf king nodded his head. "Yes. That is the rumor anyway. And seeing as you all had a vision of this man, hundreds of years apart in Lena's case, it only makes sense that the rumor is true. I've only dreamed of such power. Nothing I could ever attain. It is only given to a select few."

They all waited for there to be more to the story, but Umbra didn't continue. Finally, getting impatient, Tobi broke the silence. "What else is there? What else did you see?"

"Well, not much I'm afraid," said Umbra. "Only that Constantine called him Therik."

Lena raised her eyebrows at her father. "That's all you've got?" she asked incredulously.

"I'm afraid so, Dear. It was the damnedest thing. There I was," Umbra said, picking up his dramatic flair again, "watching Therik's ceremony like I was there in attendance. Constantine gives him his staff, pronounces him a 'Great Gift of Solana', and then Therik turned to look at me."

"How could he look at you?" Thora blurted. "It was a long time ago, and it was just a vision."

Umbra shrugged. "No idea. Never experienced anything like it. He looked at me, smiled, and then the vision went blurry. I snapped back to the present, and no matter how hard I tried, I couldn't get back to the vision of the ceremony. It was like he had kicked me out."

They all stared at each other in confusion. "What does it mean?" Lena asked.

"It means," said Umbra, looking concerned, "this man has great power and has brought you all together for reasons unknown. I don't trust someone with this much power. I must continue with my own preparations. Lena..."

"If this is another pitch to get me on board with whatever dark plot you have going on, it won't work, Father," said Lena with a look of disgust on her face.

Umbra sighed. "This is the last time I'm *asking*," he said to her pointedly.

Lena shrugged. "We're going to spend a few days packing rations and preparing for our departure, and then we're leaving. I hope you right whatever wrongs are troubling you, Father, but we're not going to be here for it. I hope you have the decency to lower The Veil and let us out when we leave this time."

All Umbra could do is watch in silence as his daughter beckoned her friends to get up and follow her out of the room. Tobi embedded his knife into the table with a thunk, twisting it for good measure, and the others set down the food they were eating. They all fell in line behind her and left the king without another word.

Umbra heaved a sigh and walked around the table to where Tobi had been sitting. He pulled the knife out of his ornate table. He looked down at what the dwarf had been carving there. It said 'Fuck You'.

He ran a finger over the jagged letters, marveling at the crudeness of mortal defiance. "How quaint," said Umbra with a smile, tossing the knife back onto the table and turning to leave the room.

The dark chamber was lit by a single subfluore crystal. Umbra knelt down on the floor in the middle of a circle he had etched in the ground with blood many years before. Within the circle were many runes that Umbra had learned about in ancient texts that were filled with ways to worship the dark God Baladan.

Umbra had discovered the dark magic while he was still living in Zelira. When his wife had found out what he had done and who he was planning on working with, that had been their final falling out. The falling out that had caused him to fall into a rage and rip a copy of the kingdom out and away into the first place his mind was thinking of, the grand pastures of the Academy of Solana's Light. It was here that his new dark kingdom had planted itself with such force that the very ground rose to the sky. It was better this way. Zelira would never understand his lifelong frustration of being denied the highest ranks of Solana's Light. Succumbing to dark magic was his only option to gain the power he needed.

His fingers traced the runes on the floor as he said the enchantment. He remembered being so nervous the first time he had done this, not sure what was going to happen, or what was going to come through. Now it was a habit, as he had taken and enacted the guidance of the being from beyond numerous times. It was this dark being that had saved them all from the Scourge by blocking the sun for thirty-nine days, cutting off the Scourge's power. Umbra had learned the ways of Baladan when Cosimir had befriended his son Eldryn all those years ago. He learned the true power that could be harnessed if you drove the traditional ideas of good and evil from your mind. It was more of a mindset of power versus weakness. Taking things as they were, versus enacting the change you wanted to see in the world. He just wished his daughter could think like that as well.

After tracing the last rune and uttering the final words of the incantation, Umbra changed his position from kneeling on both knees to one, and rested his arm on his raised knee. It was the submissive form he had to take, or else face the wrath of those that he was contacting.

The runes on the ground glowed purple. The air in front of him began to hum and vibrate as a small purple ring of light appeared in the air. Umbra glanced up, only daring to move his eyes, to see it. Through the growing circle he could see a different chamber, a different world even. It looked to be some kind of study, a place of learning and reflection, but everything was very dark and metallic. The purple energy circle grew into a full, tall oval, and Umbra averted his gaze.

Within seconds, a tall and ominous figure appeared on the other side. It was a slender humanoid figure, except something was terribly wrong with its image. Where a human head would normally be was the long, drawn out face of a dark horse. The same face that perched above his throne up in the main keep, always looking down on him and his rule in Mireholm. Always watching. His patron. His Virtrodan.

"You have summoned Sydon," the horse-man said in a low, hushed whisper that still seemed to echo throughout the chamber. "What is it you need, *King* Umbra?" it asked, putting an emphasis on the word 'king' that suggested it thought the title a little bit funny. It folded its black, robed arms across its chest, staring judgment down on Umbra.

"Great Sydon!" Umbra called up to his patron. Umbra hated being subservient to anything, but this was the only way he'd figured out how to access the dark ways of Virmorphia at this level. In his desperation, it was also the only way he had found to stop the Scourge he had created. "My daughter isn't willing to comply with our needs. The little girl, Veronica, isn't strong enough for what we need. I'm out of options."

Sydon glared down at Umbra with his black eyes. "You are not out of options. You know what you have to do now. If you want to defeat this new, weak, King Eli, you have to wield the ultimate power of Solana's Light and Virmorphia. Get Solana's Light by any means necessary so you can create your army."

Umbra knew what Sydon wanted him to do, but he couldn't bring himself to do it. "Yes, but..."

"Do you question your Virtrodan?" Sydon raised his voice at him.

"No! No, my lord," Umbra stammered back, not daring to leave his kneeling position. He dipped his head a little lower to the ground.

"Good," Sydon whispered. "Then capture her and drain her of Solana's Light. You cannot charge the Charred Scepter to work for you if you don't have equal parts of both types of magic. The little girl's power isn't enough."

Umbra nodded, still bowed. The Charred Scepter was a magical item that he had recovered to prove his worth to Sydon and gain his Virmorphia magic. It was held within the depths of Dracaryn, the land of dragons. He'd even come back with a bonus, a bog troll he'd faced in the swamps South of the Dragon Kingdom.

"Yes, My Lord," Umbra said, though he wasn't feeling happy about what had to be done.

Sydon clenched a fist and looked upwards as if looking into the future. "Once you have the scepter and the means to wield light and dark, nothing will stand in your way. You will be the new ruler of Evania, and a proper reign will finally begin. A reign backed by me, instead of Glaryn." Umbra winced at the sound of the name of the other patron that backed his son on top of Mt. Fluore. "Eldryn and Glaryn will die along with the false king."

A gasping sound could be heard behind Umbra. He twisted to see what it was. Sydon starred at the spot the sound was coming from as well. There was nothing there, but having just been kicked out of a vision himself, he knew that someone was watching them from afar.

Umbra heard Sydon whisper something from behind him, and purple light flew over Umbra's shoulder and into the darkness.

Lena sat up in bed, gasping, her forehead wet with a cool sweat she had worked up while sleeping. What she had seen was unbelievable. Her father working with a demon, doing its bidding. She knew he had ventured into dark magic, but this was a whole other level. And her brother Eldryn was apparently heading down a similar path.

She threw the blankets off of herself and dressed. If the vision was real, it meant that her father was talking to his patron right now. Throwing on her lavender cloak, she slung her bow and sheathed her swords.

It was time to confront her father and get out of Mireholm once and for all. If he wanted to drain her of her magic and kill her, it was time to strike first. It was time to wake the others.

CHAPTER TWENTY-ONE

SHATTERED ILLUSIONS

L ena didn't even bother knocking on doors. Instead, she just walked right into each room of Thora, Mathias, and Tobi, waking them up and telling them to get ready to take the fight to her father. She briefly explained the vision she had of her father's patron, and what they had planned, and then she was off to the next room.

Overall, she was happy with how fast Thora and Mathias had gotten ready and were in the hall ready to go. When she went to Tobi's room, she was in for a bit of a surprise.

"Nice pajamas," she said with a smirk. The dwarf answered the door wearing a full baby blue nightshirt that went all the way down to his ankles.

"Can't a dwarf sleep in a bit of comfort while in a castle?" he asked, looking unphased at her jest. Lena told him the story of her vision, and within a few minutes Tobi was ready, axe in hand. The last person they had to get was Faro and they would be ready to head down to the dungeons and confront Umbra.

Lena walked with the others trailing behind her. When they reached Faro's room, she shoved the door inward with force. The door clanged against the wall, and instead of barging in and waking him up like she had the other members of the party, she just stood in the hall, shocked.

Faro stood a few feet back from the door, fully dressed, war hammer in hand. Lena wasn't sure what to make of it. Her hand instinctively went to her swords, but she hesitated. "What's going on, Faro?"

"You're going to see Umbra," he said, taking a step forward.

"Yes, we're heading there now. How did you know we were going?" Lena asked. She felt Tobi and Thora press in behind her, hands on their weapons. They must have sensed something was off too. Mathias was somewhere behind her, presumably doing the same.

Faro walked forward, and they backed up. He wasn't speaking anymore, a look of menace was in his bloodshot eyes. Mathias came out of nowhere and stood in front of the other three. More and more Lena was surprised at the healer's courage. "Faro, it's us. We're your friends. We're here for you," Mathias said, his voice unwavering.

Faro's gaze looked angry, and yet somehow dead. "No one's going down to attack Umbra!" Faro yelled at them, and then he let out a loud lion roar, bringing his war hammer overhead. Mathias raised his sword just in time to block the blunt end of the hammer coming down on him. The force from the mighty lion made him stumble backwards into his companions and they all fell over in a heap.

Faro pressed his advantage and stepped in, bringing his hammer down hard again. Lena threw her hands out and blasted Faro backwards with a jolt of yellow magic. The lion slammed into the wall next to the doorway of his room and crumpled to the ground. This gave the other four a chance to stand up.

Tobi didn't waste any time barreling forward towards Faro. The dwarf got to him before he could stand and took his axe handle and pushed it hard against Faro's throat, pinning him to the wall.

"We're your friends, dammit!" the dwarf yelled in his face. "You're not right in the head! Umbra has some kind of spell on you!"

Faro was struggling to breathe with the weight Tobi was putting on his axe handle against his neck. His arms were flailing, trying to get a grip on the handle to pull it away.

"Stop!" Thora yelled from behind Tobi. "You're going to kill him!"

"He's trying to kill *us*!" Tobi yelled back, keeping the pressure on the handle.

Thora leaned in and tried to pull Tobi back, succeeding just enough to accidentally let Faro get a good grip and push the axe and its owner away. Tobi stumbled back and Faro jumped to his feet in one quick move, bringing his war hammer around, aimed right at an unsuspecting Tobi's head.

This was met with a parry from Thora and her mace. The force of the blow didn't even move her. Faro was caught so off guard by her strength that he didn't move in time as she brought the spiked mace around and sunk it into his skull. The spikes embedded deep and Faro dropped to his knees.

Thora let out a wail, letting go of her mace, her face the picture of horror. "I didn't mean to! He was going to kill Tobi!" she yelled desperately to the others.

Faro's body fell forward, but as it hit the ground, the image of his body faded in and out. Lena wasn't sure what they were looking at. Then she noticed as the body flickered, the walls and ornate decorations around them did too. The golden hallway quickly flickered to dark, eroded stone and back a few times before settling back on gold. Faro's body, however, flickered and disappeared completely. Thora's mace clattered to the ground.

"What is the world?" said Mathias as Thora walked over to pick up her mace. "Where did he go?"

Lena's eyes were narrowed as she looked around. "A full-bodied apparition. Here in physical form. And the castle..."

"It was flickering," said Thora. "Why did it do that? How?"

Lena thought for a moment. "No one in all of Evania has magic strong enough to make an illusion of an entire castle. It seems what we saw from the distance before coming to Mireholm was the actual castle. Whatever is causing this illusion can only do so within a close range. You broke part of the illusion for a moment, so everything flickered in and out as the magic wavered."

Tobi patted Thora on the back. "Thanks for saving me, Dear. Even though you thought it meant putting down our friend."

Thora shrugged. "It was just a knee jerk reaction. And honestly, it would never be a choice even if he was real. You're my *Andre*."

A tear rolled from Tobi's eyes, and he quickly wiped it away. "Uh, ahem," he said, clearing his throat, then turned to Lena, "If no one can do this kind of magic, what are we dealing with here? And where is the real Faro?"

Lena walked down the hall towards the stairs and motioned for all of them to follow her. "We need to get to the dungeons. If Faro is still alive, that's likely where my father is keeping him.

As for the magic, my father must have obtained an Orb of Olasis."

Mathias shot her a sideways look of confusion, and she realized no one knew what that was, not even the book-smart healer. "Olasis was a famed oracle and illusionist. Toured many kingdoms with her circus troupe, putting on grand performances for all the kingdoms. Only problem was, there was no circus troupe. Just Olasis, her orbs, and a big distracting circus that performed for the royalty while Olasis cleared out their coffers."

Tobi chuckled at this, but Lena ignored it. They'd reached the stairs and headed down to the second floor. "Rumor has it the trickster made a deal with Baladan for the orbs. Others say she just spent years pouring as much of her own magic into the orb as she could, harnessing the combined power of her magic over time. Either way, she was caught and killed in Underoth eventually, but the orbs remained."

"And you think that's what we're dealing with here? This whole place is an illusion projected by this, this orb?" stammered Mathias. He didn't look happy that Lena knew so much that he didn't, but to be fair, magic and enchanted items weren't his specialty.

"Yes," answered Lena as they reached the curved stairs that led down to the first floor. They were surrounded by gold and the most ornate decorations in the whole keep, but now

Lena knew it was all fake. It wasn't a gold-plated version of her childhood home. It was a veil of illusions to hide her father's shame. "The orb was strong enough to project circuses, and now this circus that we're in as well. It holds the massive illusion, so he doesn't have to. No one has that amount of magical stamina."

At the bottom of the stairs Lena pointed to a door under the left set of stairs. "Dungeons are this way," she said, examining and pushing open the broken door. "I used to go down to the library to get away from my brothers and sister when we were younger. Dungeons are down past that."

The musty smell of the underground castle floor greeted them. Inside they were all grateful that they lived in Graeton and not the musty underground dungeon kingdoms, though Tobi still had memories of life in the mountain mines.

The group quickly made their way through the books to another set of stairs, this one rougher than the last. They bolted quickly down them, in a hurry to reach their destination, but also afraid of what they would find once they got there.

Walking into the small room they were greeted with a friendly sight, though not in the shape they wanted to see him in. Faro was slumped over in one of the cells. He looked dirty, and was skinnier than when they'd last seen him. Even though he looked rough, they were just happy that he was alive.

"Faro!" cried Thora, running up to the bars and gripping them as if she wished she could rip them apart and give Faro a hug.

"Eh?" grumbled Faro, wearily raising his head. He squinted his eyes, looking out through the bars and his face cracked into a weak smile at the sight of them all. "Welcome to my new home," he said with a weak chuckle.

"How did you get in here?" asked Tobi. As he spoke he walked over to the bars and grabbed them, testing them for durability, trying to decide whether they could break them down.

Faro slowly got to his feet and worked his way over to the bars. "Jarl and I saw Umbra use Veronica in some dark ritual. They took part of the Shadruul and made some other creature that looked strong, but also very agile. He was planning to make an army of them."

Lena looked very concerned. "So you saw Veronica, and she's okay?"

Faro nodded. "As of last time I was free. Not sure how long ago that was," he said, fishing for them to answer for him.

"We haven't seen the real you in four days," Mathias chimed in.

"Real me? What?" asked Faro. He grabbed Thora's caring hands that were extended through the bars and breathed a sigh of comfort.

"My father sent some kind of clone of you to cover your disappearance. Thora killed it," said Lena with a half smile.

Faro tilted his head at Thora and released her hands. "You killed it?" he asked incredulously. "You killed *me!*"

Thora looked hurt. "It was a clone, and it was trying to hurt Tobi!"

"You didn't know it was a clone, did you? Maybe I was just possessed," said Faro.

"Never hurt my *Andre*," said Thora, shrugging. Faro gave a weak chuckle in reply. It was clear where the lines were drawn in their friendship. It was a line he never intended to cross.

Mathias was examining the bars as well, seeing if there was a more practical way to remove the bars than force. "And what happened to our little wolverine friend if he was with you?" asked Mathias, looking around quickly at the other cells.

"He escaped," said Faro, looking disappointed. "He scurried off and Umbra and his elves took me down. I woke up here, and he was gone. Probably found his information and went back to Eli by now.

"Not possible," said Lena, taking her turn to examine the bars. "My father has us trapped here."

"That's why we're going to find him and kill him!" exclaimed Tobi. He went silent as Lena glared at him.

"We're not going to *kill* him, Tobi," she said, looking disgusted at the thought. "We just have to force him to let us go. Anything less than a show of force won't get through to him, or his patron." At that Lena gestured for everyone to back away from the bars. Once clear, she grabbed two of them with her hands and began muttering in tongues. They all watched in awe as the middle section of the bars all melted away and curled away from the center to give Faro enough of a gap to bend down and get out.

Once he was out, Thora ran over and hugged him. He grunted a little from the force of her hug as he was still weak.

"Thanks for your concern," said Faro, "but I could really use food if you've got it. They've fed me nothing the whole time I was in here."

"Oh!" exclaimed Thora. "I've got some dried meat here in my satchel. Just wait a..."

"No time," said Lena. She stepped forward and placed both of her hands over Faro's heart. Again she was muttering in tongues, and he could feel warmth emanate from her hands and fill his body. He could feel his strength returning quickly. Even his aching stomach stopped its pang of hunger.

"I prefer the taste of chicken," he said, squeezing his paws into fists and feeling his returned strength, "but this works too. What did you do?"

"Energy transfer," Lena said, panting a little. "All living things are made of energy. I moved some from me to you."

The look on Faro's face suggested he was horrified at the thought of this. "Not a good time to be weakening yourself, going to face your father and all."

Lena shrugged. "I think having a big brute like yourself in full force will come in handy. We'll get in there and you'll pounce on him and pin him down." At first he wasn't sure what to make of the comment, and then Lena's face broke into a smile.

Faro smiled back. "Cat jokes. Great. Don't happen to have my hammer, do you?"

"No," Lena answered while pulling one of her two swords out of its sheath. "But you can make do with this for now," she said, handing him her sword.

The lion nodded, his big fluffy mane bouncing up and down as he did. "I prefer blunt objects, but this will work for now," he said, examining the weapon. "Alright. Veronica was down in the lower dungeons when we saw her," he said, pointing at the blasted doorway at the back of the dungeon hallway they were standing in. "My guess is your father will be down there as well. With his... patron?" he added, a bit confused.

They all took off through the dungeon and out the door in the back. It was a rather quick jogging pace, though it slowed to a walk when they hit the pitch black stairs, which Faro assured them led to the dungeon kingdom below. Lena explained her vision to Faro in a hushed whisper on the way down the dark stairway. He listened intently, the darkness pressing in around them making the revelation seem even more dark and foreboding.

The group made it through quicker than Faro and Jarl had the first time since Faro knew there was actually something ahead besides a drop into an endless pit. At the bottom of the stairs they saw the subfluore light brackets on the walls, and Faro pointed down the hall.

"Up that way is a dining hall," said Faro as they made their way down the new hallway. "Not sure what's beyond that. We just saw the mess hall with the Shadruul in it. That and the…"

"The bog troll," grumbled a voice from up ahead.

Lena put up a hand for them all to stop, but Faro waved them all forward. "It's okay. He's locked up. He can't hurt us."

They all moved forward up to the bog troll's cage. It was standing, gripping the bars, and casually looking down and watching them approach. "Could still spit on you," the bog troll said casually.

Faro just smiled at the creature. "Rork, is it?" The bog troll nodded. "Do you know where Umbra is?" he asked, wondering if the troll would even give him an answer. Surprisingly, Rork pointed down the hall.

"End. Down there. That's where he talks to his demon," said Rork.

"Thank you, Rork!" said Faro, and they all turned to leave, but before they could, Rork yelled after them.

"Wait! Free Rork," he said, almost pleading them.

Faro looked at Lena, who shook her head no. Thora looked sad and gazed in at the captive creature. Tobi raised his axe as if ready to fight Rork again. Mathias was stroking his chin, thinking.

"I don't think we can, Rork," said Faro. "We have to go face Umbra and... well... honestly, you're kind of a wild card here. Especially after what we did to you in the arena."

Rork slammed his fist loudly against the bars. "You regret," he said in a low, somber tone.

"I'm sorry," Faro answered him. "We'll see what happens after we talk with Umbra."

Faro turned to leave down the hall, and the rest of the party followed him. Thora gave one look back at the poor beast before following the others. Rork connected with her gaze, and he ran a hand slowly and desperately down the bar, watching his chance at freedom run away.

A few steps down the hall and they were at the old mess hall. Faro peered inside and did not find what he expected. He expected the Shadruul to be tied up there, but the room was empty, the chains left unattended on the floor. He heaved a sigh of relief, and motioned for them all to follow him to the large archway at the end of the hall.

Before they could get there, though, the ground rumbled. They all looked at each other in a panic, pulling their weapons to the ready. In the next second the doorway filled with rock, and then a growl pierced the air. They all flinched from the sound, and then the stone archway exploded.

They all ducked for cover as rock and debris flew their way. A big piece of stone caught Faro in the foot and he roared in pain as the Shadruul pushed through the dust, only it wasn't the same Vorath Shadruul they knew before. This one was three times the size of the other. Its hulking frame filled most of the giant hallway as it advanced forward to attack them.

Before the party could think how to confront it, the air filled with dozens of high-pitched shrieks. Spindly creatures poured out of the gaps around the Vorath's legs. Faro raised his sword and called to the others. "These are the new Shadruul they had Veronica create! Band together and we'll take them!"

Before the others could even reach Faro, the Vorath lunged forward and gave Faro a hard backhand. He went flying back down the hallway. Thora and Lena led the charge against the new Shadruul.

"We have to free the bog troll!" Thora yelled as her mace connected with a lanky creature, turning its head to rock dust.

"You *cannot* be serious!" Lena called back as one of them jumped on her, swung around, and gripped her neck in a chokehold. Lena gasped and struggled for air, trying to reach up to rip the creature from her back.

Thora brought her mace hard into its back, freeing Lena. "Do it! Go! I'll cover for you!"

Lena caught her breath and gave Thora a stare that told her this was a really bad idea and then bolted back down the hall towards the caged beast. She prayed silently to Solana that her friend was making the right choice.

CHAPTER TWENTY-TWO

RORK

Faro was only halfway back to his feet when Lena reached him and helped him up. The chaos of the battle raged behind them. They could hear the shrieking Gorrik Shadruul, and felt the vibrations from the movement of the giant Vorath.

"Thanks!" yelled Faro over the din. "Let's get back in there and help them!"

Lena didn't move. "I'm freeing the bog troll first!"

"Right!" Faro yelled as he took off, but then paused. "You're what?" he yelled at her. "Are you insane?"

"Thora thinks it's the best move. Just go help the others!" Lena yelled back, turning from Faro and facing the bars. Faro didn't have time to move before they were surrounded by Gorrik Shadruul. The nasty creatures were gnashing their needle-like teeth at him and swiping their spindly arms and sharp claws towards him, as if daring him to move.

"Do what you gotta do and make it quick," he told her, swinging the sword and getting a feel for its weight in his grip. "We've got company." Faro knew with his smashed foot he wouldn't be able to move very quickly, so he planted himself between the Gorrik and Lena to protect her while she did what she needed to do to free the bog troll.

The bog troll stared down at the old elf as she approached his cage. He still didn't look happy about them leaving him before, but Lena trusted Thora's judgement. "Hey, Rork," she said as she approached the bars and put her hands on them. "Let's get you out of here, and then you can help us out, yeah?" she said, sounding uncertain.

Rork just glared at her. "Right," she said, and then started speaking in her tongues. Rork was a bigger beast than Faro, so she couldn't just dissolve a small middle section. She would have to completely dissolve the bars to free the troll.

Behind her she could hear Faro panting as he fought off the smaller Shadruul. "Really wish I had my hammer!" he yelled between sword thrusts. "Much easier to smash these damn rock monsters to bits with blunt objects!" he yelled as he thrust his sword into the glowing orange eye of one, pulling it out and swinging it around to lop off the head of another.

It was hard for Lena to focus on her incantation with all the noise around, but she closed her eyes and spoke the smooth, rhythmic language. Feeling the light emanate from her hands, she focused the energy onto the metal bars, and they began heating up. She spoke louder and quickened the pace, bringing more power to the magic. She could feel herself weaken as the bars glowed brighter. Behind her Faro was making a choking sound, and she assumed he was being choked by the creatures like she had been moments before. She was yelling loudly over the din by the time the bars finally dissolved.

Now only a pile of dust stood between her and Rork. The bog troll looked down at her, and she looked up at him expectantly, trying to judge what he was going to do, ready to pull her sword if it didn't go how she hoped.

"Thanks," Rork grunted before he stepped over her and grabbed Faro from amongst his assailants. He brought his other fist down hard on the ball of Gorrik, killing them all. He set Faro down gently next to Lena, and took off down the hall, swiping at other Gorrik along the way.

Lena faltered, and Faro caught her. She pushed him away. "I'm fine," she said, though didn't sound it. "I just need to meditate and regain my strength. You need to go help the others."

At this, Faro helped her sit down in Rork's cage and then limped off into the fray. Lena sat with her legs crossed, trying to block out the noise of the battle, focusing on regaining her strength. She'd always had magical stamina issues, though she was never sure where the issues stemmed from. She hated now more than ever that she wasn't as resilient as other magic users, and now sat helpless to help her friends.

Down the hall, Rork had dispatched several small groups of the Gorrik, and now had his sights set on the giant Vorath. Even though he was around ten feet tall, the Vorath still towered over him. This didn't seem to faze Rork, who just smiled and charged the bigger beast head on.

Mathias and Tobi, who had both been attacking the Vorath's legs and dodging its swipes, barely got out of the way as the beasts clashed. The bog troll jumped up and grabbed the Shadruul's shoulders, planting his feet on the beast's knees. Then with one fist he started beating it in the head. This barely seemed to bother the rock monster who reached up and grabbed Rork, pulling him off and slamming him hard into the ground.

The wind was knocked out of him, but Rork quickly sprung to his feet, landing a kick square in the Vorath's chest. That sent it stumbling backwards into the archway that was already in tatters. More rock rained to the ground, smashing the Gorrik Shadruul and was barely dodged by Thora, Mathias, and Tobi who were having a hard time battling off the smaller creatures without being crushed by the larger.

Rork pressed his advantage and charged forward, grabbing the Shaduul by its giant head and repeatedly smashing it back into the wall. The party retreated down the hall to avoid getting hit with the falling rock as the wide hallway continued to crumble around them.

The Shadruul flailed its arms desperately, finally connecting with Rork's side, slicing it open with its sharp claws. Rork roared in pain, but within a few seconds the bright red light flashed from his side, and the wound healed itself. Having not seen it before, Thora stared in awe at the quick, self-healing of the bog troll.

Now the Shadruul was back on its feet and bearing down on Rork. He got his hands up under the Shadruul's underarms and felt the rock hands gripping his shoulders. The bigger beast squeezed, crushing Rork's arms under its mighty, forceful grip. They were pushing hard against each other and roaring their fiercest roars, but Thora could tell that Rork was losing out, being the smaller of the two.

Smashing another Gorrik in the face, she glanced around the room for anything that may help their oversized ally. Her gaze landed on the subfluore bracket on the wall. The crystal was set into a sharp metal spike. It almost looked like a torch, except where fire would go, a crystal was inset with its natural glowing light. She ran over and pried on the fixture, trying to get it to break from the wall.

Behind her, Rork ducked down and laid flat on the ground, using the momentum to drive his feet into the Shadruul's stomach and send him flying down the hall. Rork hopped up and charged after the Vorath, grabbing its head and twisting back and forth, trying to rip it from its body and kill it. The Shadruul's head didn't budge, and the Vorath grabbed Rork off its back and slammed him down to the ground. Rolling on top of him, it was its turn to grab Rork by the face and try to smash his skull.

"Rork! The eyes!" yelled Thora. The bog troll, head smashed down into the ground, turned under the Shadruul's grip enough to see the subfluore torch whipping at him through the air. He reached out his hand and caught it. Using his shoulder to knock the tight grip loose a little, he twisted enough to free his face from the Shadruul's grip long enough to locate his glowing blue eye.

Bringing the torch over his head, Rork grabbed it with both hands and drove the bottom point of it upward as hard as he could. The point drove deep into the giant Shadruul's eye socket. It stopped struggling and Rork kicked up with both his feet, sending the pile of rock back towards the archway. As the Vorath flew back, the subfluore crystal struck a fallen rock that was on the floor and cracked. The crystal pulsed with yellow light, and the power from it shot down through the handle of the torch and down through the Shadruul's lifeless body.

Thora's eyes widened. She'd seen this once before, and it didn't end well. "It's going to explode!" she yelled, grabbing Tobi and Mathias by their shirts and pulling them in the opposite direction of the pulsing crystal. Faro, who was still fighting a ways down the hall, saw them moving for cover and ran back to Rork's cage and dove inside by Lena, who was still there recovering.

The Shadruul's entire body was pulsing in yellow light from the subfluore crystal, and it started breaking at the seams between rocks. Thora and the others didn't get far when Rork jumped forward and threw himself over them. They were all smashed together as Rork pulled them close, smashed but safe from the blast as the Shadruul exploded with great force, sending rock and yellow energy through the entire room. Rork screamed a blood-curdling scream of pain and horror as the energy from the explosion cut through his clothes and melted the skin on his back.

After five seconds that seemed like several minutes, the energy explosion stopped. Thora pushed out from Rork's grip and the others followed. When they moved, the bog troll fell forward onto his face, his expression motionless.

"Is he...?" Thora asked, horrified.

"No, he's still breathing," Mathias answered. "He's just stunned from the blast." He walked around to examine the injury Rork had taken while protecting them. Mathias winced when he saw the damage. The flesh was red raw and bleeding. Bone from his rib cage could be seen sticking out in places.

Blood was everywhere. "Not sure if he'll recover as easily from this as other injuries though."

They all looked around the rest of the hall. There were no other beasts in sight. All the other Shadruul had turned to dust in the explosion. Faro and Lena emerged out of Rork's cage. Faro had his arm thrown around Lena's shoulder and was still limping. Lena looked ashen-faced.

"He protected us from the blast," Tobi told them when they approached. "Threw himself over us and took the damage."

They all watched as small, red tendrils of light began emanating from Rork's massacred back. It wasn't the normal blazing light that usually fired through him when he was healing, but a weak, light red spark that fired in different spots on his back. They stared in amazement.

"He's weak, so the healing is weak, but he's started repairing himself," said Mathias in awe.

"He's such a magnificent creature," said Thora, the sad look on her face feeling every bit of the sacrifice Rork had just made for them.

Lena put a hand on Thora's shoulder. "We can't wait here for him to heal. My father is either well prepared for us, or gone by now."

Thora nodded and looked around the group. Lena was weak and Faro's foot was still injured. "How can we go into a fight in this state?" she asked Lena.

Lena shrugged. "Hopefully it's not another fight. Hopefully, my father sees the error of his ways and lets us leave." She paused and thought for a moment. "Given my vision, and the fact that he serves a master, I'm guessing we will have a confrontation though. That's why I brought this on our journey," she said, reaching into her side satchel.

She pulled out a small vial of purple liquid. She held it between her thumb and forefinger for all of them to see. "Concentrated moonshade," Lena said, pulling the little topper out of the vial. "I turned it into an ultra-concentrated potion to hopefully amplify its effects and speed healing time."

"Hopefully?" asked Faro, eyeing the concoction wearily.

"Yes, hopefully," said Lena, tipping it up to her lips and drinking half the vial. "You and I are the dirgerats," she said, referring to the shelled rats that scientists and healers like Mathias often caught and experimented on to see how concoctions affected living beings. The dirgerats were easy to find and test on as they were slow to move, and made loud squeaking sounds that sounded like a sad song.

She handed the vial to Faro. "Here. It helps with vitality, and it should also help the damage done to your foot."

Faro grabbed the tiny vial in his large paws. The small glass cylinder looked almost comical in his large furry hand. It was so small he had to hold it delicately between two of his sharp claws. "Fine," he said, tipping the vial to his mouth and drinking it down. He immediately felt the familiar warm feeling that he felt when Lena had healed him with her energy transfer.

He handed the vial back to Lena and put his weight down on his foot. He felt the soreness go away even as he did it. Next to him, Lena looked like her color had returned to her face.

"Hope you have more of that packed away," he said, feeling like he could take on a full-grown dragon.

"Only a few vials," said Lena. "I'd love to say it would help our friend Rork here, but the potion could kill him. Never tested it on a bog troll before. Best to let him heal on his own. I'll need to make more potion when we get back home. Sooner, hopefully, rather than later," she added. It seemed she was getting homesick, and being in this reminder of her childhood home wasn't any help.

"Let's go face your father, and then we *can* go home," said Faro, ready to confront their captor. Lena nodded, and they all walked through the broken archway, across another large hall that ran perpendicular to the one they just came from, and into the antechamber.

The small room was more ornate than the hallway they just came from. There were torches and decorative vases throughout the room. On the other side was a large wooden door with gold trim. A bright, white light was shining from the crack underneath, piercing the muted tones of the antechamber. Faro thought the door looked very Umbra; flashy and over dramatic. Their muffled footsteps bounced off the walls, and the silence was almost deafening compared to the rage of battle that had just taken place.

Lena took the lead and grabbed both door handles, throwing it open wide. Inside was a grand throne room, almost a mirror image of the one on the upper levels, only this one was much darker, as no natural light could reach here. Huge stone pillars supported the ceiling somewhere up in the darkness where the light refused to go. Placed in the center of the room was a magnificent golden throne on a raised dais. Looming over the throne was the same horse figure as above, only this one was dark, and more lifelike. It was a grand place for Umbra to rule during the Scourge.

The elf king himself sat on the golden throne, awaiting them. He sat sideways on the throne, his feet kicked up on the arm, as if he'd grown bored waiting for them to get there. It was odd to see him in such a lax position, given his normal nature of pomp. A score of elves flanked him on each side. These elves were no longer the smiling elves they'd grown accustomed to. They all wore stern looks, and carried two sheathed swords each, along with magic staffs tight in their grips.

Faro noticed a podium beside the throne with a glowing orb on top. It was emanating a white energy in waves down the podium and into the floor, likely the source of the bright white light they'd seen under the door.

Umbra sat up at the sight of them and threw his arms wide in his typical fashion. "Welcome, friends!" he exclaimed with his typical smile. "I see you're all still alive!"

Chapter Twenty-Three

THE CHARRED SCEPTER

Umbra kept smiling at the party, a mad laugh escaping from his lips as if his greeting was normal, or somehow entertaining. Faro and the party all clasped onto their weapons, waiting at the ready for Umbra's next move. It was obvious by his statement that he wasn't looking to have a conversation. To Faro's surprise, Lena tried talking to him despite his ominous comment.

"Yes, we're all still alive, Father," she said with malice. "Thanks for sending your minions to kill us."

The elf king kept smiling, but instead of walking over to Lena to get close and comfort his daughter like he'd tried in the past, Faro noticed he didn't give up his prominent position on the dais. "I knew you would survive. You're my daughter! As for these others… I was really hoping we'd be alone right now so I could try one last time to convince you."

Lena scoffed at him. "We're beyond done talking about this. You've made your dark bed. Now you have to lie in it. Our stay here is done. Give us Veronica, and let us leave."

The smile fell from Umbra's face. Without his smile, he looked all of the thousands of years old that he was. "If you won't listen to reason, then I will have to kill your friends, and take your Light," he said, looking genuinely sad. He extended his right arm out, and from the side of the room flew a black scepter right into his outstretched hand. The staff looked as though it had been charred and burnt. The top was a twist of decorative metal encasing a glowing white gem.

A wicked laugh left the elf king's mouth, echoing through the chamber, and Faro's heart skipped a beat. Such a sound had not come from Umbra since their arrival, and hearing it was chilling. His eyes narrowed at them and his mouth curled into a grin. Not his usual, friendly smile, but an evil smirk that showed he'd been waiting for this moment since they arrived.

"I've been waiting too long to right my wrongs. Kill the others," said Umbra, "and bring my daughter to me!"

At his command, the rows of elves flanking either side of him raised their staffs and began muttering incantations. Their staffs ignited in magical purple light.

"We've got to move!" Lena yelled to the others, looking around for cover. They saw the support pillars that stretched up to the ceiling, and they all made a dive for the nearest one. Taking cover put Faro, Tobi, and Mathias on one side of the room, and Lena and Thora on the other. The magical blasts flew around them and struck the other side of the pillars, blasting large chunks out of the stone columns. They all knew their cover wouldn't protect them for long.

Lena looked around the room in desperation. They were outnumbered, and with her being the sole magic user in her party, they were largely outmatched. She chanced a peek around the column and saw the elves with their staffs lowered, taking turns casting their spells so there was no reprieve between volleys.

"They can't all be real!" Thora called to Lena over the noise of the blasting.

"What?" she called back, confused.

"Everything is an illusion, right?" said Thora, clinging tighter to the column as a magic blast whizzed by her. "That means that if we break the orb's spell, we'll have better odds. At least some of them have to disappear. If we're lucky, all!"

Lena thought about this logic, and then nodded. "You're right. Faro was fake and was still physically able to attack us. The orb is powerful. Didn't realize it was that powerful. That gives me an idea."

Over at the other column Faro, Mathias, and Tobi were all taking cover against the crumbling structure with no plan of action in sight. Faro was getting nervous because their cover was falling apart quickly, and his large frame couldn't hide behind it much longer. He looked up into the darkness where the ceiling was somewhere above and wondered whether they would get blasted by magic first, or buried by rock as the ceiling collapsed. He was about to tell the other two that he'd cover for them while they made a run for it when he saw Thora bolt out from behind the other column and around the side of the room.

Faro watched her in awe and horror as the magic blasts shifted from the column to target her. Even Umbra himself turned towards her, shocked at her audacity. He took several steps away from his throne and sent out a blast of magic after her. She did a rolling jump and dodged every spell they cast at her. Umbra cackled and struck again, impossibly fast, and this blast struck Thora down. She went sprawling down to the ground and Faro gasped, eyes wide in shock.

Just then, another figure of Thora ran out from behind the pillar, and Faro had to blink and do a double take. There were two of them, but the elves were focusing their attention on the first. It could only mean that Lena had copied her as a distraction. The decoy was at the back of the room lying on the ground, and the elves' attention was now turning back toward the rest of the party, but too late.

The second Thora ran straight for the dais, mace drawn back over her head. She lunged up the three curved steps of the dais and brought her mace crashing down hard on the glowing orb that sat beside Umbra's throne. Umbra turned just in time to see Thora strike, and his face changed to one that Faro had not seen before: his smug confidence had been replaced by sheer terror. His eyes were wide, his mouth agape in a silent scream.

The ball shattered, and the energy inside exploded, blowing Thora backward down the stairs, her body smashing hard into the stone floor below.

The elegant chamber and its Elven inhabitants flickered. "No!" yelled Umbra as he braced himself against the exploding energy. Once the ball's light flickered out, the chamber stood much darker. It was now drab, decaying rock instead of the elegant sheen it had before. The golden throne was now also gray and dilapidated. The valiant horse that towered above the throne was now jet black, with piercing dark eyes.

But it wasn't the change in the room that made them all stare in amazement. Faro's eyes grew wide. Half the elves were now gone, flickered out of existence. Those remaining, including Umbra, were shown for what they were. There stood the mighty elf king in his flowing, golden robe, but where his face had been was now just a skull with thin, gray-green skin stretched over it. The skin and cartilage was undecayed enough to still show his elf ears, but the rest of his body was a decaying mass. His eyes glowed purple as he stared down at the party. For the first time, they were seeing him for what he truly was.

The party made their way out from their hiding places behind the pillars, and Thora quickly scrambled to her feet to fall in line with the others. They all stared in wonder at their undead host. Lena came out from behind the pillar in a slow trudge, arms down by her sides, eyes wide in shock. "Father," Lena said, "what have you done?"

The skeletal figure of Umbra looked embarrassed, ashamed that she was seeing him this way. When he spoke, his voice was more raspy than before as it echoed hauntingly through the dark chamber. "The Scourge couldn't be controlled. We held out as long as we could. We dumped those who died early in the lake, but before long, it was just too much. The Scourge overtook us all. I had to seek out a patron to help me destroy the Scourge and learn dark magic to bring some of us back with necromancy, but many remained lost."

"This illusion was to hide your failure? The veil that you show the world?" asked Lena.

Umbra nodded sadly. "My life has been a failure since I abandoned The Light. I've been digging myself out of a hole that turned out to be a sinkhole," he said. Then he lowered his head and narrowed his eyes at his daughter. "A legacy I cannot let be my last! I was once the most respected king and Dungeon Lord in Evania!" he yelled as he swiftly lifted the Charred Scepter.

Before Lena could move, a blinding white light shot forth from the scepter and hit her square in the chest. She shrieked as the light consumed her entire body, lifting her slightly off the ground. Yellow threads of light made their way from her body and up the light beam and back to the scepter. At the same time a light shot back at Umbra, and consumed him as well, drawing out purple light from his skeletal form and into the gem atop the scepter. The tiny gem morphed slowly from white to a deep goldish-brown as their energy combined within it.

Faro and Tobi both sprinted forward to strike Umbra down, but the remaining elves that accompanied him all lowered their staffs and threw up a shield around themselves, Umbra and Lena, blocking the party out so Umbra could finish what he started. Faro roared and Tobi cursed as they smashed sword and axe against the magic shield to no avail.

Within a minute Lena had gone pale, collapsing to the ground as the white light withdrew. Umbra pulsed with the golden magic aura that the staff was now emitting. It was running through the burnt shaft and down through his entire body as he was absorbing its energy, basking in the glow of some new strength it was giving him. His skin was getting its color back as he regenerated himself.

Not even considering the danger, Thora rushed over to Lena who was crumpled on the ground. "Lena! Oh, Solana! Lena!" She threw herself over her friend and embraced her. Faro looked from the fallen Lena to Umbra and snarled. The smile never left Umbra's face.

"Lena made her choice," said Umbra. Though there was a smile on his face, Faro thought he could see sadness in the old elf's eyes. "And you've made yours as well, Lion," he continued, raising a hand and waving it. In an instant Veronica appeared from behind the dark throne. She was wearing the same dress she had several days earlier when she had created the Shadruul with her magic. Her eyes seemed dead, hollow, like there was no life there. It sent a chill down Faro's spine.

"You've come all this way to save her," Umbra said in his deep voice, "and now, she's going to kill you all!" At this, Veronica raised her hand, palm up, and ignited a yellow ball of magic within it, the same creepy smile as Umbra crossing her face.

"Shit!" said Tobi. "We can't kill her! What do we do?"

Faro's mind was reeling. They were still surrounded by Umbra, twelve of his undead elves, and now a possessed Veronica. Lena was down, possibly dying. They had no magic among them to fight back. They needed to kill Umbra, and then the other elves would either disappear, or at least flee if their master was dead. As for Veronica, killing Umbra should break the spell on her too if he was right about how the rest of the magic worked. He hated all he could do was guess. He felt very out of his league here.

"Thora, get Lena into that side chamber over there," said Faro, pointing to an entryway to another room near to them as the twelve elves and Umbra all lowered their staffs to point at them. "Boys," he said, quickly turning to Tobi and Mathias, "we've got to move fast. Same plan as when we fought Rork."

They both nodded at him, and Faro could see Tobi's hands wringing around his axe handle, relishing the chance to jump back into a fight instead of cowering behind a pillar.

"Now!" yelled Mathias. Tobi and Faro lunged forward before the magic started bombarding them again. Mathias ran back behind the pillar to take cover from the initial onslaught from the elves. Peering around, he saw Faro and Tobi dodging and rolling between blasts. A few of them were close, but they were evading. Even Veronica had joined in the magical barrage. He could see Thora had moved Lena safely into the side room as all fire was targeted on the two fighters. Mathias took that as his cue and bolted around the side of the room, hugging the wall. Instead of pulling a lever like he had with Rork, he planned to wait at the back of the dais, his sword at the ready.

All the elves were recharging for their next attack, and Faro and Tobi pressed their advantage. "Going low!" yelled Tobi happily, and Faro had just enough time to see the humor in this before making his move. Taking the three steps up to Umbra, Tobi swung his axe low at the Charred Scepter, trying to smash the weapon in half and rid Umbra of his new power.

The elf king stepped back and dodged the swing, cackling. Just then Faro came in high with an overhead swing with his sword. Umbra stepped backwards again, but brought the scepter up to parry the blow. Faro hoped they could overpower the spindly old mage, but he was drawing strength from the Charred Scepter. His plan to break the staff in two failed, and the king held fast as the staff did its job to block the blow. His elf underlings and Veronica just watched the battle with their hollow eyes, too afraid to fire magic at the fighting trio for fear of hitting their king.

Faro could see Mathias waiting, sword ready to impale Umbra once he fell backward off the dais. Bolstered by the sight of this, he broke into a furious rage-fighting mode and kept delivering blow after blow, pushing Umbra back further. Just one more step and he'd fall backwards. Faro held his breath. Tobi came in low again and tried to take out one of Umbra's legs, hoping to knock him off his balance.

Umbra cackled as he slammed down his staff, and the light ignited. Faro and Tobi froze mid-swing, unable to move. "I know your strategy, gentlemen. I am no dumb bog troll," he said as he thrust the staff backwards. Without touching him physically, the magic from the staff sent Mathias flying backwards, smashing against the back wall. He fell unconscious to the floor. "And now, Veronica, please come finish these two."

Faro and Tobi starred unbelievingly in horror as the little girl they had come all this way to save walked in front of them, her magic flaming in both hands, ready to kill her rescuers. Everyone in the room was staring at them, waiting to watch their master dispatch his enemies in gruesome form. "Too bad you didn't count on me knowing how you fight!" cackled Umbra.

Just then a spiked mace came whirling through the air and sunk deep into the elf king's head. His skull caved in and a silent scream hung on his gaping mouth. Trails of purple fluid ran down his face from the wounds the spikes had created in his skull. "Too bad you didn't count on me being here!" said Thora as she yanked her mace free from Umbra's head. Umbra collapsed to the ground in a heap, as did the other undead elves around them. Faro and Tobi could move again now that the magic holding them there was broken.

Veronica's magic faded in her hands, and she shook her head wildly. When she opened her eyes and looked at Faro, the innocence of a little girl had returned to her gaze, and Faro smiled. Veronica burst out into tears and she lunged forward to hug Faro. "You came for me!" she said, waking from the deep stupor she had been in since she got here. "You saved me!"

Faro didn't have time to answer as a clapping sound rang through the air. They all turned to look at who was applauding this moment, and a ghastly sight greeted them. Walking out of the room where Thora had taken Lena for shelter was a seven-foot-tall demon with a grossly elongated face resembling a black horse. His robe was black, with flames dancing along the fringes.

"Oh, brova!" the horse-demon whispered, and yet his voice somehow carried throughout the entire room in a demonic hiss. "You defeated the elderly and saved a talentless sorceress child by hiding. You all should be proud." His voice was rife with sarcasm.

The horse-man approached the dais and looked at them in contempt. "Such insignificant, pitiful beings defeated my champion." Now he looked down at Umbra, who was writhing on the ground, grasping to his last moments of life and breathing loud, raspy breaths. "I can't believe I devoted centuries of time on such a lost cause. Hundreds of years without purpose!" The demon smiled. "Although not all is lost."

The horse-demon held out his humanesque hand and made a motion through the air. The fallen Charred Scepter shook on the ground as the demon attempted to summon it. As it lifted and moved through the air Umbra used his waning strength to reach up and grab it before it moved out of reach.

"No!" Umbra croaked, his voice very weak. Veronica screamed as Umbra's other bony hand latched onto her ankle. Faro felt her body shock him and he jumped back as his hands that were still on her shoulders felt the jolt. He watched as Umbra, barely alive, latched onto the poor little girl and began siphoning the life from her.

Veronica's scream became shrill as the life left her body and went into Umbra. Faro could see it was some sort of reverse of what Lena had done for him by giving her life force earlier. Instead of giving, Umbra was rejuvenating himself by using his captive.

Tobi swung his axe at Umbra's arm, but was blasted back by the same electric jolt that had sent Faro reeling. Whatever the connection was, it was not meant to be broken until it was complete. The demon below the dais laughed menacingly, not attempting to break the bond either. He looked as though he was enjoying this turn of events.

Veronica dropped to the ground, too weak to stand now, her face pale white. Faro raised his sword, ready to strike Umbra down the second the connection was broken. The dent in Umbra's skull didn't seem to reform, but Faro could see that the elf king was still regaining his strength and ability to move. He wasn't sure how much the undead needed an intact skull, but the life he was draining from Veronica seemed to be what he needed to regain functionality.

Faro watched in awe as Umbra seemed to grow taller, bulging with more muscle than he had in the entire two weeks they had known him. When the magic finally broke, he was much wider than Faro, and taller by several feet. He was more of a beast than an elf now, and a hatred raged in his eyes as he stared down at the demon. The demon broke out into another cackle that sounded like a snake hissing as it slithered through the grass towards its unsuspecting prey.

"There he is!" the demon said, almost dancing a little jig at how much this amused him. "There's my champion. Too bad you're broken now."

Umbra's good eye narrowed at the demon. The other seemed to have been damaged by the mace, not following along. "You are breaking your laws by being here, Sydon," he said, looking down on the demon from the dais. "Virtrodan have no place here on this plane."

Sydon shrugged. "I've wasted hundreds of years at the bottom of the pecking order placing my bets on a powerful elf king. 'The Greatest Dungeon Lord' as he called himself. I thought that my bet would have paid off, but instead I just got failure after failure as your hubris drove you to ruin," the demon said as he paced along the steps, eyeing his prey at the top. "I'm taking the Charred Scepter with me so I can deliver it to someone more... capable," Sydon finished.

"That's not happening," said Umbra, raising the staff and pointing the golden gem at the demon. "No one else will use it to set things right. Everything I've done has been for the heir…"

"Everything you've done has been undone by a lowly girl with a mace," laughed Sydon. "Even as you persevered after your death and killed off most of Evania with the Scourge, you continued to fail with increasing magnitude. This charade of a kingdom you made… was all to hide your massive piles of failure. You are nothing, Umbra. I have no more use of you."

As this exchange went on, Faro picked Veronica up off the ground and into his arms, slowly backing down the stairs and away from the mad elf king. She was ghost white, but still breathing. Sydon and Umbra were still locking eyes, both too concerned with each other to worry about the others who were still conscious in the room. Faro moved quickly away from them and hid behind the shattered column with Tobi, Thora, and Veronica.

Up on the dais Umbra looked hurt for a moment at Sydon's comments, and then his one good eye blazed with rage. "I have done much that has hurt my family and Evania in my efforts to save it, but I'll be damned to Baladan myself if I let you take this staff and walk this plane."

Sydon chuckled. "Fine. Use it on me," he said, shrugging. "Virmorphia cannot hurt the Virtrodan, and that staff is now infused with it." The demon threw his arms out wide, conveying his general uncaring for anything that Umbra had to throw at him. There was a pause where no one moved. "Thought not. Now I'm going to take it," he finished, raising his hand to summon the staff.

Umbra slammed the staff into the ground, and it lit up. Only it wasn't the gem that lit up, but a force field around the staff. Sydon grunted from the effort of trying to summon the staff, but whatever Umbra had cast around it made it so he couldn't pull it towards himself. The demon screamed in rage, a high-pitched, shrill shriek, almost like a youngling who didn't get his way.

Umbra tossed the staff to the side, and it landed by the pillar. It was still covered in the shield, so Faro didn't dare pick it up, but he watched in awe as Umbra faced off against his master without the mighty weapon he'd just forged by sacrificing his daughter. Clapping his hands together and clasping them, Umbra muttered in the tongues that Faro had quickly become accustomed to hearing lately. The beast of an elf king's whole body glowed pure white.

Sydon laughed as he waved his arms, summoning purple light magic to his hands. "You stole Solana's Light from the girl? You think you have it in you to use it now, here at your end?"

Umbra ignored him and kept muttering the strange language of Solana's magic, taking steps down from the dais to approach his master. The light coursing through him was growing brighter and brighter until Faro had to squint just to see what was happening. Veronica gave a soft whimper in his arms and he tried to calm her.

"Shh...shh...shhh... it's okay," he told her, but as the white and purple magic surrounding the two adversaries met, he wasn't so sure they would be okay.

Umbra was so close to Sydon that their light clashed together, and the resulting noise was deafening. Neither stopped staring at each other the entire time, Umbra muttering in his tongues, and Sydon willing his magic to be stronger with some kind of nonverbal cues.

The light from the elf king reached pure white, and Umbra was gone within it, totally engulfed in his own spell. For the first time a look of terror crossed the horse-demon's face, and he took a step back, but it was too late. Umbra threw himself into the demon, whose light was extinguished.

Sydon whinnied in pain and agony as he was entangled in The Light, unable to free himself. The white light shrank in an instant, imploding upon itself, and for a brief second, as if time stood still, Faro could see Umbra had his arms fully wrapped around Sydon, the demon trying desperately to free himself. This sight only lasted a moment, and then the light that had withdrawn came bursting out of Umbra in full power.

Faro ducked back behind the column, throwing his body over Veronica, Thora, and Tobi. He said a quick prayer to Solana that Mathias and Lena were far enough away from the explosion not to get hurt as light rushed past the column and lit up the entire space so bright they all had to slam their eyes shut, though they could still see bright light through their eyelids.

The light lasted a few seconds before it blinked out, and then the room went pitch dark.

CHAPTER TWENTY-FOUR

BLESSINGS AND BURDENS

It was dark unlike anything Faro remembered experiencing before. Even after several moments of waiting for his eyes to adjust, nothing was coming into focus. He wondered if he was dead, when he heard a whimper from underneath him.

"Is... is it over?" said the small voice of Veronica. Faro's sense of touch came back to him, and he realized he was still sheltering everyone in a big, protective hug. Pulling back a bit, he allowed his three wards room to move again.

"It wasn't even this fucking dark in the mines!" Tobi exclaimed, somewhere from Faro's immediate left.

"Breathe, *Andre*," Thora said somewhere to the right. "We will find our friends and our way out soon enough."

Faro knew they could get out eventually, but he wasn't sure how long it would take in the pitch black that surrounded them. He reached forward and felt his way around the column. He felt the smooth stone surface quickly turn rough, and he knew he'd made his way around to the other side where the magic blasts had bombarded it minutes before. Turning around, he knew he was now facing the dais. He needed to find his way up and across. That would be the easiest way to Mathias to see if he was okay.

Before he took two steps, Faro froze. Ahead of him, a faint wisp glowed, and he could see the broken stone throne underneath it. Above it, the face of the horse had fallen off the statue, and now Faro could see it lying crumbled on the ground around the wrecked throne. The wisp glowed brighter, elongating itself to become taller, and slowly it took on the form of a human. No, not a human, but an elf.

Faro's jaw dropped as he stepped forward hesitantly. It was the form he had seen in his dream, and it was soon joined by a dozen other wisps forming behind it on either side of the throne. The larger form in the middle took its place on the throne, and the face fully formed into that of Umbra, though in this ethereal form he looked much younger, and his face was whole again, no longer bashed in by Thora's mace. He was shining so bright it was hard for Faro to keep eye contact in the otherwise dark room.

He could hear a gasp from Thora behind him as she, Tobi, and Veronica came hesitantly out from behind the crumbling pillar. The ghostly figure of the man who had just tried to kill them looked down at them, a sorrow in his eyes. He looked at the four of them and raised his right hand.

"It seems we are a few short," he said simply, motioning the light that represented a hand. There was a groan from behind the throne as they could hear Mathias come to life. Within moments he was slowly making his way around the throne, coming around from behind the back. He was covered in dust and soot, rubbing his head at the back where he'd struck the wall hard from Umbra's blast.

As Mathias joined them, a confused expression painted across his face, the ethereal Umbra raised his other hand and made another motion, this time Faro knew to revive and bring Lena to them. His heart sank as no one emerged from the side room. Umbra kept his calm expression, and this somehow comforted Faro.

After what felt like several long minutes, a tall, slender figure emerged slowly from the side chamber where Thora had taken Lena. Lena moved slowly, Faro's war hammer clutched tightly in both of her hands. She was having a bit of a hard time wielding the heavy weapon, but she still looked like she could swing it if need be. Faro had been wondering where his weapon had gone after he'd been captured. Apparently Umbra must have brought it to this side chamber for safekeeping back when he was still alive.

"What's happening?" Lena asked as she limped into the room to join the others and square off against the group of specters.

"Your father sacrificed himself to destroy his patron," Thora whispered to her. "And this is...uh... your father... I guess?"

The ghostly king nodded his head at this. "Unfortunately, it still wasn't for the right reasons," he spoke, and when he did, his voice seemed to echo throughout the chamber. It was a whisper like before, but somehow more comforting than when he was trying to blast them into dust. "I didn't kill Sydon to save you all, though I should have. Instead, he broke the rules of the Virtrodan and walked on this plane. He was a threat to Evania."

Tobi, the only other of the party who had his weapon drawn and ready to attack like Lena, spat on the ground. "What the fuck is a Virtrodan? Some sort of horse demon?"

Umbra looked at Tobi with a bit of disdain, but still answered him. "The Virtrodan take many animalistic forms. They are watchers from the fiery plane. Servants of Baladan. Since Solana won the celestial war, Baladan is forbidden to interfere with matters in the realm of the living, but that doesn't stop him from using his servants to manipulate those of us here to do his bidding. He's trying to find a way that he can break the barrier, and unleash his hell upon the world. His servants vie for his favor by trying to manipulate those of us here to bring back Virmorphia and free Baladan from his prison."

Faro could see Lena's eye twitch. "And you followed this demon to help bring back the God of Darkness and destroy Solana?" Lena asked. She had a look of complete and utter betrayal written on her face. She had spent her whole young life being taught by her father to follow Solana's Light, and here he was following demons.

Umbra just shook his head. "A means to an end. I spent a few hundred years trying to use The Light to fight Virmorphia. I made Amazadan learn Virmorphia, and I would try to combat him. Again and again The Light failed. By infiltrating their ranks and using their own power, I was hoping to destroy them from the inside with their own magic, but it was too much for me to take. Through all my failures I became more and more consumed by the darkness. Finally, I found the way to destroy Virmorphia was a mix of The Light and Virmorphia, but by then it was too late for me."

Lena lowered the war hammer and shook her head. "You wasted your life and almost killed me just now. What would mother say?"

Umbra's face fell. "My dear Zelira has been in my heart all these years, but I had work to do for the greater good. She never saw the bigger picture. And as for trying to kill you *just now...* let's just say that was quite some time ago for me.

Different places and different planes have a funny way of how time works," Umbra said.

"What does that mean?" Lena asked, not quite understanding.

"To you, our fight was but moments ago, but for me, it has been several years. I've been under the guidance of Solana himself, learning the path he has set forth for each of you, and I've been sent back to this moment to bestow his blessings upon you."

Tobi waved his hand. "Tell the Light God thanks for the 'job well done', but I think we'll be gettin' the hell out of this place now," he said, and he turned to leave.

Umbra watched him take a few steps and then spoke again. "Blessings, as in items and abilities you will need for your dangerous road ahead, Young Dwarf. Against my better judgement and frequent requests against it, Solana has included you as an important member of this party."

Tobi turned back to face the spectral Umbra, his face cracked into a smile. "Always happy to be of service," he said with a chuckle. Faro could tell that Tobi enjoyed getting under Umbra's skin, or at least what used to be his skin. Even in death the dwarf could still get to him. "I'm just glad we fought so well we're getting rewarded!" he finished with a triumphant fist pump. He pulled his hand back down slowly when he saw Umbra shaking his head.

"It's actually because of how poorly you fought," Umbra said. Tobi's face turned to a frown, and his eyes narrowed. Beside them, Veronica threw her hands up to her mouth to stifle a giggle. "You all have a destiny tied to you that is going to require great strength and courage. What you showed today was dumb luck mixed with very little skill. To move forward on the path laid before you, you will need to shed your previous selves and use these gifts that we bestow upon you."

Umbra floated up from the throne and hovered over them. He waved a hand and a yellow circle with runes appeared on the floor between him and the party. They all took a step back, not sure what it was, and not trusting what Umbra was doing.

"Tobi, please come forth to the Tetricle," Umbra said, gesturing for the dwarf to make his way forward.

"Did he just say...?" Tobi began.

"He said *Tetricle*," said Thora sharply, pressing her fingers into her eyes and shaking her head.

"Right," said Tobi, slowly moving forward and eying the circle. It glowed with a yellow light, and was marked with strange letters that drifted around the circle. Tobi looked down at it suspiciously, and then back at the party. "I'm not stepping in that fucking thing. No way. I'll get sucked into another dimension, or turned into an animal like our friend here," he finished, pointing a thumb at Faro. "No offense, Friend. You look great, really!"

Faro chuckled at this, and Thora stepped forward. "It seems alright, Andre. He's right. We barely made it through that fight alive, and if we're wrapped up in something bigger than ourselves, we need all the help we can get."

Tobi scrunched up his lips, as if unsure, and then turned and handed his axe to Faro. "Keep a good watch on her if this goes south," he told him. Faro didn't have time to ask whether he'd meant to keep an eye on the axe or on Thora before Tobi took a step forward into the glowing circle.

He gasped and let out a scream of pain causing the others lurched forward to pull him back out and save him, but he couldn't fool them long as he burst out into laughter. Thora reached forward and punched him in the arm. "That's not funny!" she chastised him.

"It was a little bit," said the dwarf, before turning to face Umbra.

The ghost shook his head. "I argued long and hard with Solana about including you in this," said Umbra in disdain. "He ascertains you are to play some important role yet, so here we are."

Tobi just smiled up at Umbra. "Deep down I know ya love me!" he said cheerfully.

Umbra scoffed. "Anyway. Solana has seen you in battle and has glimpsed battles that may yet come. Therefore, he wants to grant you The Power of Rage."

"Well, I've already got plenty of that," said Tobi, laughing.

"Yes..." Umbra replied, frustrated. "But since dwarves are not inherently magical creatures, we will have to instill the power into your weapon," said Umbra. He raised his bright white hand, and the axe went flying out of Faro's hands and into his ghostly grip. From there he dropped it down, and Tobi caught it in both hands. As soon as he touched the weapon, the coin that was embedded into the handle, the one with the Evanian crest that Thora had given him as a child, glowed bright red.

Tobi stared at it in amazement. "It's never done that before," he said simply.

Umbra nodded. "In the heat of battle when you are overwhelmed, you can bring out The Power of Rage and berserk against your enemies. Just touch the coin and say 'Solana help me', and you will be granted the strength of ten warriors in battle, as well as the ability to see an enemy's weak points."

"That's great!" exclaimed Tobi. "I'll be able to... wait," he paused, looking down at the coin on his axe confused, "that means we're going to be fighting in wars?"

The spectral image of Umbra just looked at him and remained silent.

"Oh," said Tobi, grasping the weight of their destiny and what was yet to come. He left the circle silently, his face fallen. They all remained silent until Umbra spoke again.

"Thora, please step into the Tetricle," said Umbra. Tobi's face lit up again, and he stifled a chuckle. Thora shushed him as she made her way forward. She stepped into the circle and knelt down before the elf king.

A smile crossed Umbra's ghostly face. "Always so humble. Always so caring. Solana has seen your courage, and how you deal kindly with others, especially with beasts like Rork."

Thora lifted her head a little, reacting to the fact that her actions were being watched and judged so closely. After a moment she put her head back down and Umbra continued. "Because you are such a master of caring and beasts, we wish to grant you the power to communicate and control beasts around you." The circle around Thora glowed green. She didn't flinch as the green light enveloped her.

When the light faded, Umbra raised both of his hands, and between them a small piece of wood appeared. "Rise and accept," said Umbra, as Thora stood and saw what had appeared there, "this whistle. Blow the whistle and nearby creatures will listen to you and obey your will."

Thora smiled and reached forward to grab the gift. "Keep in mind," Umbra added, "some beasts have a much stronger will than others. You will need to concentrate and work harder to control beasts of a stronger will, but as you practice over time, you will get better at it."

Smiling, Thora left the Tetricle and pulled a necklace chain from the pocket of her dress, fastening the whistle to it, and looping it around her neck. She cupped it in her palms, holding it like a precious jewel she never wanted to let go of.

"Mathias," Umbra said. "Please step forward into the circle."

Faro glanced sideways at Tobi as Mathias made his way up, and he could see the look of disappointment on the dwarf's face at the absence of the proper name for the circle.

Mathias stood within the circle and looked up at Umbra, still rubbing the back of his head where he had smashed into the wall earlier during the battle. "Not sure what you're going to offer me," he said, a bit put off. "There is already a healer in our group, and Lena has proven to be a much better healer than I."

Umbra shook his head. "There are other plans for Lena. Not only that, but healing wounds is not the only healing that our Evania needs. We must also work, sometimes, to heal minds." Mathias balked at this, not believing the phrase that was used. It was similar to the odd phrase that was said to him by the mysterious man with the gash on his nose all those years ago.

"Do not be hesitant in this task, Mathias. Your friends will need you to be a great healer in the journeys ahead. Mathias, do you accept the use of magical healing?"

The healer hesitated. His whole life had been about not using magic to heal, ever since the untimely death of his childhood friend that died because a magical cure went wrong. He shook his head, as if he were about to say no, but then the thought of his dying friend Osric crossed his thoughts, and he knew in that moment what he had to do.

"Yes," he said, his voice shaking.

"Good. Then please," said Umbra, waving a hand, making the circle glow yellow, "take these gauntlets of healing. Along with the power bestowed upon you now, these gauntlets will allow you the extra power and energy you need to heal even the deepest of wounds, whether body or soul."

Two gauntlets dyed red appeared in the circle before Mathias. He hesitantly reached down and picked them up. He slowly slid them onto his arms, flexing the fingers once they reached the tips of the gloved end. Without hesitation, he reached up to the back of his head and spoke in tongues that seemed to come naturally to him now. There was a bright yellow glow, and then it faded.

Mathias moved his head back and forth as he stepped out of the circle and made his way back to the others. "Glad I said yes," he said to them all. "That blow to the head was giving me a headache like no other." They all laughed at this as Mathias settled back in among them.

Umbra threw his arms wide. "Daughter," he said, and Lena froze. A look of sadness was in the eyes of the spectral king, and Faro suspected the elf father would cry if he had the ability. "Please, Lena, step forth into the Tetricle."

Tobi threw an elbow into Faro's hip, "Good thing there's not two circles," he snorted.

"Shh," said Faro, though he couldn't help but crack a smile at the dwarf's childish antics.

Lena handed the war hammer to Faro, and made her way into the circle, and as she did, it glowed a deep golden-brown. There was a long pause as they both stared each other down. Finally Umbra's face broke into a smile. "I'm so proud of who you have become, my dear Lena. You showed the most courage anyone could show in confronting your own father to do what was right. Unfortunately," he looked down at the ground, "I am not the only one of our family you are fated to face," he said.

She shook her head in disbelief, but Umbra nodded. "Your brothers and sister have all fallen in different ways. It is a dark time indeed. That's why Solana has called for you to be his official mage. Your powers will grow over time with practice, but I will restore your power to you, along with extra essence.

You will wield your powers better than before, and for a much longer time."

Before Lena could react, Tobi cut in, "Learn over time? You can't just give her the power she needs to trounce any enemy? We're talking power from Solana here!"

Lena shot a dirty look back at him, but Umbra acted like he expected nothing less from the dwarf. "You do not start someone at the top with all the power in the world. Part of being powerful is knowing how to use that power. If you know it all from the start, you have no experience in actually using it, and dangerous mistakes will be made." This statement seemed to shut Tobi up for the moment.

"Lena," Umbra continued, "I know you don't see eye-to-eye with me on Virmorphia, but I assure you, the Charred Scepter is the solution to destroy the dark magic for good. So first, let's get rid of this bow and arrow," he said, snapping his fingers. Lena's bow rose from her back and vanished. Her face looked angry, but Umbra looked unapologetic. "All elves use bows. It's a bit overdone. But the Charred Scepter... The mix of absolute light and absolute dark come together to bring balance to the scale of magic. You need to take it," he finished as he raised his hand and called the scepter to his hand from the ground where it had landed during the fight. He held it but for a second when it hit his hand, and then he dropped it down to his daughter below him.

Lena didn't move a muscle, and Faro was sure the scepter would drop to the ground. Instead, the base of the handle hit the stone floor, and it stood upright before her, refusing to fall. Lena just stared at it in disdain, not daring to move. It spun slowly in a magical beam of light before her. Umbra waited for her to take it, but she didn't. Instead, she turned and walked away from the circle and back to the others. Her father frowned at her.

"You will need that on your journey," he said, gesturing down at the glowing staff. Lena didn't move. "Fine," said Umbra. "If you want to pout, I'll give it to Thora for safekeeping in the meantime," said Umbra angrily, and he waved his hand. The staff disappeared and then almost instantly reappeared strapped to Thora's back.

"Woah," she said from the unexpected added weight. "I... don't really want to get involved here," she said awkwardly. However, she didn't dare touch it to remove it from her back.

Umbra ignored Thora and continued on, "Finally," he said, raising a long, ghostly white finger and pointing at Faro, "the Heir of Evania."

Faro took a hesitant step forward and then froze. This was exactly what had happened in his dream. "No," he whispered.

"What was that?" Umbra asked him.

"No," said Faro, much louder so all could hear this time. "I'm not the Heir of Evania."

Umbra nodded his head. "I was at the meeting of the Dungeon Lords. We all voted that your father, James Envato, was the rightful king to sit on the throne. That means that you were to be next in line. The fate of Evania rests on your shoulders, Young Lion."

Faro shook his head again. "I can't be. A king of Incarta, maybe. That was always my destiny. Not to lead the entire country. It has to be someone else. There has to be another heir. The one that the people speak of."

Umbra cocked his head sideways at Faro. "That is one option of many, though most likely not the best option," he said simply. "Whether or not you take the throne is a decision you will have to make if you are successful in your endeavors. For now, please step forward into the Tetricle.

Tobi couldn't take it this time, he ducked behind the nearby support pillar and burst out in a full bout of laughter. Thora hid her face in embarrassment. Faro smiled again, but tried to ignore him as he stepped forward into the circle. The light glowed bright blue, and Faro waited, wondering what his fate held.

"Solana has his new mage in my daughter, Lena," he said, "and she will use these powers to vanquish enemies of Solana," he said. "And now he needs a protector of all the good that this world has to offer. The Light needs someone to fight for it, and you have shown the greatest honor and integrity of all. That is why you are to be a Paladin of Solana," said Umbra.

Faro's war hammer glowed in his hands. Runes appeared on the head of the hammer, and he stared in amazement, feeling a new energy buzz within the weapon he had come to call his own. An indent appeared where the handle met the head of the hammer, and Faro felt it with his fuzzy finger, then looked up at Umbra, confused.

"That is where you can embed different types of crystals," said Umbra, "based on the path you decide to take, and the powers you chose to wield. Hopefully, someday that path will lead you to wielding a Scepter of Solana, but for now, much like Lena, you have to start at the bottom and learn to wield what you learn properly."

Faro nodded his head and made to leave the circle, but Umbra cleared his throat. Faro stopped. "A protector also needs something to protect himself and others," Umbra continued. "That is why we also grant you this shield." A slit of light appeared in the ground and a shield arose. It was in the shape of a heater shield, one with a point on the bottom and a point that sloped down to two other points on top. Emblazoned across the front where a crest would go was a yellow sun surrounded by three smaller suns, the sign of Solana and The Light. As soon as Faro touched the shield to pick it up, the suns turned blue, and the light faded.

"This shield will provide protection not only for you, but those around you. And the hammer will help Lena in taking down those enemies that oppose Solana's rule over Evania. Take them, practice with them often, use them to free those under oppression, and protect those in need."

Faro didn't know what to say. A few weeks ago he was bumbling down a mountainside into a town full of strangers, not knowing who he was or where he had come from. Now he had a magical weapon and shield, and a spokesman for the God Solana was calling him the heir of the entirety of Evania. He could feel tears of shear overwhelm building up behind his eyes, but forced himself to keep them in. It was all too much to handle in such a brief span of time. Instead of answering, all he could do was nod and return to the others. He joined them and stood behind Veronica where he had been before.

Tobi patted him on the lower back. "Powerful protector of Solana, eh? All I got was angry rage monster. Suits me, I guess," he finished. Faro was glad that Tobi was with him on this journey, if for nothing else but to keep him smiling through all this adversity.

"Veronica," Umbra said next. "While you will not continue on this quest, I feel it is time to restore your Light that I took from you."

At this, Veronica took a step back into Faro and hugged him around the waist. "No..." she said, shaking a bit. "I don't want anything to do with any of this anymore."

A look of sadness crossed the ghost's face at this. "I'm sorry to hear that, young Veronica. I know this all must be traumatizing for you. I deeply apologize for all that I've put you through." There was a pause as Umbra considered what to do next. Finally, he waved a hand and the circle of light glowed white. A small orb appeared at the center. "Please," he continued, "take this, and anytime you feel the need to come back to The Light, this orb will grant you what has been taken from you."

Veronica timidly moved forward, stuck the orb in her gown, and scurried back to the group and the protection of Faro. The lion wasn't sure if she would ever be confident enough to use the orb again after all this, but he was glad that she had the option to take back the life that was stolen from her. The Tetricle flickered out of existence before them.

Umbra stared at all of them gathered before him and smiled. "My goal was always to separate the dark rulers of this land from Virmorphia and destroy the vile magic. To combat that, I took on the dark magic myself, but it consumed me. Always remember to walk the fine line, my friends. Too far in either direction is a recipe for absolute disaster."

They all nodded and looked at each other. Faro wasn't sure how venturing too far into The Light could be a bad thing, but they all had set roles now, ready to move forward and help protect Evania from the evil that had plagued the land for so long.

Faro realized, though, that none of them really knew what the next step was. "So," he spoke into the spectral-lit darkness, "what are we supposed to do now?"

"That's always the question, yes?" asked Umbra candidly. "All that I can really say, is that after you return your young ward to her home, there may be some business that you have to tend to in Underoth."

"Underoth?" asked Lena. "What would we possibly want to do in that war-hungry kingdom of dwarves?"

Umbra just continued to smile his mystical smile at them. "I hear tale that there is an orb, and an oracle there that may aid our lion friend here in restoring his memories. Getting Faro back his memories will serve you well in guiding you on your journey forward."

"The oracle? She lives?" asked Lena.

"Well, there is only one way to find out," said Umbra, and he left it at that. "Now, my time on this plane has ended. The fate of this land now rests on the five of you."

None of them said anything. It was all too much to take in at the moment, and none of them knew what dangers lay ahead of them. Their adventure to save a little girl had led them to this life-changing event, and now the fate of an entire country seemed to rest on their shoulders.

Umbra's light flickered as he was being called back to the realm of Solana. "Please hurry," he said as he wavered. "I'm afraid much has changed outside Mireholm since you got here. Changed more than you know."

And with that, Umbra and the other spectral ghosts that had accompanied him flickered out of existence. Complete darkness ensued once again.

CHAPTER TWENTY-FIVE

THE DUNGEON LORD OF MIREHOLM

Lena conjured up a light to combat the pressing darkness, and they all worked their way out of the dungeon throne room. As they shuffled through the doorway, they'd originally come in through, they were greeted by a friendly sight.

Rork was sitting in a cross-legged position in the destroyed hallway. His eyes were closed, and he was loudly humming. Faro smiled at this. He could see the last of Rork's blast damage healing up, glowing red with whatever regenerative magic he was blessed with. Faro secretly wished he had that ability, but then again he wasn't even sure what abilities he had now with the blessing from Solana.

Another dark thought creeped into his mind. What about the dark magic that had overtaken Jarl? The wolverine's dark magic had been removed by Umbra, but Faro felt suspicious that something dark still lurked deep inside of himself. He pushed the thought from his mind, something he'd have to deal with later.

Thora ran over and gave Rork a big hug. Faro saw the whistle swinging around her neck, but apparently she didn't need it to have a good relationship with the sentient bog troll. "You saved us! I mean, it would have been good to have you in that other fight too, but you got us there!"

Rork just simply nodded. "Glad you live," he said, the last of his wounds healed. He stood up and looked at all of them. "We can go now?"

Thora's face broke out into the biggest smile. "Yes, Rork! We all can go now."

He seemed to think about this for a second, and then spoke again, "And...I must go with you?"

Thora seemed taken aback by the question. "You are as free as any of the rest of us now, Rork. You are welcome to stay with us on our journey, but it seems to have gotten a lot longer than returning Veronica home."

Rork thought for a moment. "I will stay with you...for now," he added.

"Great!" exclaimed Thora. "Let's get out of here. Lena, do you think we're safe to head back up through the castle?"

"Yes," she said, "but I think I have a better way."

A short walk down the hall and they were at Rork's old cage. They walked through the entry where the bars used to be, and up the ramp that led to the training arena where Mathias, Faro, and Tobi had fought Rork some days before. Upon reaching the top of the curved ramp they came upon the other set of bars that had kept the bog troll locked in the space between.

Seemingly without effort, Lena placed her hand on the bars, and without talking, a quick yellow light evaporated the bars to dust. Mathias shot a look at Faro, who nodded at the marked improvement in Lena's magical abilities.

The sight that greeted them when they stepped outside was jarring. Where the seemingly beautiful castle keep of Mireholm once stood, was now a crumbling, desolate ruin. The facade that had stood there mere hours before was now busted, and all that was left was the true Mireholm now that Umbra's Veil was gone. Not only that, but there was a massive chill in the air.

"So... cold," said Thora, using her hands to rub her opposite arms.

It was true, Faro could see his own breath. It was odd, given that the weather had been very temperate last they had been outside. Finally glad to be a lion covered in fur and likely warmer than the others, Faro wrote the cold off to the magic spell they had broken. Did magic produce cold when it shattered? He pulled Veronica close to him as he could see her shaking.

They all took a few steps into the arena, taking care to walk around Rork's blunt club he had dropped during his fight with Faro, Mathias, and Tobi. It was a grim sight to take in. They made their way past the arena wall and were about to cross through an archway that would lead them around to the front of the castle when Thora turned around and noticed that Rork wasn't with them. The bog troll now had his old club in hand, but had stopped at the outer wall of the arena.

He was staring at the wall, a single tear running down his cheek. "It's okay, buddy," Thora said to him, still shaking from the cold, and taking his gigantic hand and leading him past the wall. None of them knew how long Rork had been held prisoner inside Mireholm, but it was long enough for it to be overwhelming for him to finally be free of his captor.

"You are kind," he said to Thora when they caught up to the others.

She just smiled at him. "There's really no other way to be that is good for the world," she said, letting go of his hand and letting him walk on his own.

As they wandered the streets of the city on their way back to the front gates, the contrast of the beauty that had been there before was stark. Where they had recently seen shops and happy elves working within them, now stood the dilapidated ruins of those same shops. Even the bridge they had entered on was barely traversable, made up of crumbling rock and missing segments.

The lush, grass field that had been full of gardenias was now a burnt, barren field. There was no more life here, only death. They all remained quiet the entire walk, the sound of their footsteps now echoing strangely in the empty wasteland. Faro looked at Lena from time to time to judge her reaction to the nothingness, but her face remained blank, stern and unreadable.

When they were getting close to the border wall at the edge of The Veil, they were greeted with a peculiar sight. Short little Jarl was trying to scale the wall, but with no luck. Faro assumed the Shadruul had helped him over when they had entered the veil, and now he was having trouble getting out. Faro also noted the brown leather satchel that was slung over the wolverine's shoulder that wasn't there before. He knew Jarl had been sent to Mireholm to look for information. Faro was now curious if he had found what he was looking for during his days of absence.

Lena reached for her bow to knock an arrow and then realized it was no longer there. "Too many elf archers…" she muttered under her breath, looking angry. As a substitute for her bow and arrow she threw both hands out to the side and lit balls of yellow light with them. "Jarl!" she yelled at the wolverine. Startled, he wheeled around, flinching like he expected a punch to already be aimed at his face.

"Hello, friends!" he exclaimed, trying to look innocent. "Crazy what went on back there, huh? This whole place was an illusion! As I was running for the door, even the night elf was gone. All fake! That Umbra was insane. Such a..."

"Enough!" yelled Lena. "Why are you trying to get out in such a hurry?"

"What?" Jarl said, looking offended. "I'm in no hurry, really. Just trying to get out of here so I can go see my father in Underoth. Haven't been home since before the war started, you know?"

Lena stared at him a moment, not wanting to trust him, but she put out the balls of light and walked towards the wall, motioning for the others to proceed forward as well. They all gathered by the wall, and Faro took one last look back at the ruins of Mireholm. The kingdom now looked as it had from outside the veil, broken down ruins cast against a gloomy gray sky. The shimmering light was still lit in the top tower of the distant keep, but he had no idea what it was. He really didn't care. He was just glad to be rid of the place.

Looking back to the wall, he saw the others gathered there. They were all looking up at Rork, who had easily pulled his head above the wall to scope out the other side.

"What's happening here?" Faro asked, curiosity getting the best of him.

They all turned to look at him, but no one spoke.

Finally Rork broke the cold silence. "Snow," he said, though he looked as if he couldn't believe it.

Faro laughed. "I mean, I know it's cold, but snow? It's summer!"

Lena shook her head. "Somehow, it's not anymore."

"But..." he stammered, "we were only here for a fortnight at the most. There's no way it's winter."

"Let me up to see!" Thora called, coming over to Rork. Obediently the bog troll obliged, lifting her up to stand on the wall.

Jarl scurried over to Faro. "Time seems to work funny here. You arrived about an hour after I got here, and yet you all said you were at least four days behind. That doesn't add up. It's been gnawing at me since."

Faro crinkled his eyes in thought. He remembered Jarl had been surprised they had somehow caught up with him. He'd put it out of his mind because of his concern for finding Veronica, but now it seemed very odd. Did time work differently in the veil? Had they really missed the entire summer and autumn season while they were here? He dreaded the thought, as that would have given their enemies extra time and preparation to work against them.

His line of thought was cut off by Thora yelling from the wall. "Holy Solana above!" she exclaimed. "Snow! Snow everywhere!" She looked back down at the others. "How?"

Before they could answer, Thora spoke again. "Hey, everyone. You may want to see this."

Looking at each other in concern, they all rushed to Rork who threw them up onto the wall, and then easily hefted himself up in one swift move. Once up, they all stood along the wall staring out into the snow-covered scene before them, but it wasn't the snow she was talking about anymore. Coming out from behind a large rock formation in the distance were several dots. Beings on the horizon.

Before long, the dots had grown big enough to make out. "Vorath Shadruul," said Mathias, swallowing hard and sounding nervous. "At least an entire battalion of them. And..." he adjusted his glasses on his nose to make sure he was seeing clearly, "...and what appears to be... elephants?"

"Yes," Lena added quickly, using her keen elf eyes to see better at a distance. "Elephants fitted with a rider and large ballistas on top."

Tobi scoffed. "Great! More fuckin' Shadruul already. I mean, I enjoy having berserker powers, but I kinda wanted to sit on them awhile before having to use them."

Thora placed a hand down onto his shoulder. "We can slip down the wall and escape before they get here. My birth parents were weapons experts. There's no way that ballista can reach us yet. We're too far out of..."

"Move!" yelled Lena, sending a quick shield spell into Faro, and knocking him out of the way. He fell down hard onto the wall. A large bolt flew through the air where Faro had been standing a moment before.

"What the hell?" asked Thora, putting out her hand to help Faro up. "Weapons shouldn't be able to reach this far. Not unless they were powered by..." she trailed off, and her mouth fell open. "No..." she said. She looked horrified, as if she'd seen another undead elf pop out of a lake.

"What is it, Dear?" Tobi asked her, looking concerned, but also monitoring the approaching army in case they needed to take evasive action.

"The only way they could reach us that far away would be if they had subfluore-powered weapons. And the only way they have subfluore-powered weapons..." she looked like she was going to be sick. Tobi gave her an encouraging look and a nod to get her to finish. "They're using my parents' technology.

From the notes that Cosimir stole when I was a girl, the night my parents were murdered."

There was a moment of silence as they all stared at the ground, not knowing what to say to the girl who had lost so much. The chill wind whipped between them, and the army was in full view now.

"We need to move," said Faro, not happy about feeling so exposed on the wall. They all nodded and moved along, when a fell voice hit them through the air, almost a hiss.

"Don't move... or we'll fire another," hissed the voice.

"Fuck that!" said Tobi, looking back to the side of the wall on the Mireholm side. "I say we jump back down and run along the wall till we get somewhere safe.

Thora shook her head. "No, Andre. That weapon can pierce through the wall. We've got nowhere to run."

"Dammit!" roared Faro. Just when it seemed they were done with danger for the time being, they couldn't even make it out of Mireholm without more trouble. He grabbed Veronica and pulled her in close to himself. She was just a poor, defenseless little girl caught up in something she would have never been involved in. Especially without her magic, she was more vulnerable now than ever. Faro didn't remember having any children, but he was prepared to protect Veronica as if she was his own.

When the army of Shadruul were close enough, one figure stood out from among the others. It was a tall, sleek, black panther. They were wearing a dark green long vest and green trousers underneath. In the panther's hands was a longsword. As they got closer, the panther pounced to the front to make sure they were the first to confront the party on the wall.

"Sister! Everyone thought you were dead, or in hiding! You're not dead, so you must be in hiding," the panther said in a woman's voice.

The party all looked at one another in confusion, and then Faro noticed the look of disdain on Lena's face.

"Sable? Is that you?" she asked incredulously.

"In the fur!" she chuckled. "What have you been doing all this time?" The Shadruul were slowly falling into rank behind her as she spoke.

Lena looked confused. "We were on a short rescue mission to save this girl," said Lena, pointing to Veronica. "It appears we've somehow misplaced a few months, as it wasn't snowing when we entered."

Sable shook her head. "I was sent here to find and kill you all, and take over Umbra's Veil. I get to be a Dungeon Lord!" she exclaimed. "The thing is," she looked at them to judge their reactions and see if they were messing with her, "you left on your famed mission over three years ago."

Faro's eyes grew wide. Judging by the looks on the other's faces, they thought they were being played. "That's impossible," Faro spoke up for everyone. "We traveled for less than a week and we couldn't have been in The Veil for more than two weeks. You lie."

The panther laughed a booming laugh. "Lie! You think I wanted to be camped out here in this wasteland for three years? We were assigned to take Umbra's Veil and discover its secrets. That was three long, miserable years ago. This morning we heard a loud crashing sound, and lo-and-behold, the veil is finally down! You all and that little wolverine just waltzed right in. Nothing worked for us. It wouldn't let us pass through. Where is that little devil dog Jarl anyways?" she added, looking around the party standing on the wall.

Faro quickly looked among the group and realized that Jarl was no longer with them. The little coward must have taken off in all the commotion. He sighed. Would anything ever go right?

"We lost track of him several days ago," he said to the panther, unsure why he was lying. For some reason, he trusted Jarl more than this new enemy and her army.

She nodded. "Always a slippery little fella, that one. Anyways, once we realized the veil was broken, we broke camp and started this way."

Faro didn't know what to think or what to do. They were surrounded by the enemy. They had apparently lost over three years of time. There didn't seem to be any way to escape this situation without a confrontation, and they were vastly outnumbered.

"You look old, sister," Sable continued. "How was your visit with father?"

"He's dead," said Lena without missing a beat, or showing much sympathy. "You should have an easy march into the city. No one's there. All dead."

Sable simply nodded. "I assumed father was dead once the veil was down. No one to hold the magic spell anymore. Sad really. But after everything he did to our family, it's kind of a fitting end."

To Faro's horror, after all the Shadruul came out from behind the rock formation, another group of beings made their way forth. They were way off in the distance, but from the haunting experience they'd had with them, he would recognize them anywhere. Glowing an eerie green, undead elves came slowly out to join the ranks of the Shadruul. Since Sable and her army hadn't been able to get into Mireholm and the elves there, Faro assumed she had brought them out of Mournfall Lake.

"Quite an army you have here Sable," said Faro. "Why do you need this many fighters to take such a desolate kingdom? Eli doesn't want to take any of the better kingdoms out there?"

"Yeah…" Sable said slowly. "You don't know because you've been gone so long. Most of Evania is already under the control of Eli, Lion. With the exceptions of Underoth and Dracaryn, now that The Veil is about to be mine, there's little left that Eli and Eldryn don't already control."

Thora wept audibly. Mathias' jaw dropped open. Faro didn't want to believe it either. "The Dungeon Lords would never bow to another tyrant," he said defiantly.

"No," said Sable, sticking her sword into the snow and leaning on it, "they wouldn't. You're right. They are all either dead or captured. As I said, just a few holdouts left."

Faro felt sick to his stomach. This wasn't worth the powerful war hammer and new shield. It wasn't worth missing three years of life. Guiltily, he looked down at Veronica. Okay, maybe it was worth it for her, but they had already lost so much, and now the world was coming crashing down around them all at once.

Sable locked eyes with Lena, whose face was unreadable. "Sister, please come down from the wall. I don't want to kill you today. For the memory of our dear father and our life together, and for the sake of getting this girl back to what's left of her home." That phrase sent another pang of panic through

Faro's stomach, but it sounded like they were getting out of this alive, so he decided to unpack that with the others later.

"And what if we want to kill you?" asked Lena, and Faro closed his eyes. So close to escape.

The panther threw her arms wide, gesturing to the army surrounding her. "If you're as smart as I think you are, you will take your out, Dear Sister. It's a whole new world out there for you, and you're not going to like it. I don't want to kill you, not today. Today is about my victory in taking our father's kingdom."

Lena jumped down from the wall and walked slowly over to Sable. "We will meet again, *Dear Sister*. I will be more powerful, and you will be less fortunate in how this plays out."

Sable's mouth curled into a smirking half smile at this. "Looking forward to it, Lena," her voice dropped and the leaned in closer to Lena, "but getting the girl home safely isn't really why I'm letting you live today. Mother is trapped in the dungeons of Zelira. My business is here. I implore you to free her." Lena looked at her in shock, but before she could retort, Sable spoke again in her hushed tone.

"Say nothing now. My army cannot know our plan. It's taking every fiber of my being not to kill you right now. This magic is hard to control." Lena could see her sister's face twist and contort, and recognized the same struggle she had seen in Maggie and Jarl.

"Now go!" Sable yelled at Lena so all could hear.

Lena went back to the wall and helped the other's down to the ground. Rork hopped down and looked like he wanted to step on Sable and smash her flat into the ground. Lena shook her head no at him, and his expression eased. They all walked along the wall to skirt the army blocking their path.

When they'd left the army a ways behind, Veronica looked up at Faro with tears in her eyes. "What did she mean by 'what's left of home'?"

Faro wasn't sure how to answer her. "We've been away," he said finally, "for a very long time. None of us know what to expect anymore."

Veronica broke down into full, sobbing tears.

Chapter Twenty-Six

THE SPLINTERED PATH

On the road back to Graeton, their travels were mostly uneventful. The only issue they came across was Lena arguing avidly with Faro to stop by Zelira on the way home to try to rescue her mother. The others in the group averted their eyes from the pair as the argument heated up.

"My mother needs our help, and she can be a good ally," Lena said desperately to Faro, "especially if we can take back control of the kingdom. Having a home base near to Mt. Fluore will be a good advantage in the war."

"Our mission is not over yet!" Faro roared. "We have to get Veronica back to Graeton. How can you not see our mission through? I understand your mother needs you, but we don't know what's waiting for us back in Graeton. We may need your help to make sure she's safe when she gets home.

Finishing this mission will keep us in Solana's favor, and then in Underoth we can..."

Lena curled her fingers like she wanted to summon magic, but didn't. "Don't act like you know a damn thing about Solana compared to me just because you're his paladin now. You just care about going to Underoth and getting your memories back."

Faro nodded. "That's part of my mission that will be helpful to all, but it's also one of the last free kingdoms in the land. We can make our stand from there."

"No," Lena said, shaking her head. "The dwarfs of Underoth are vile, savage, unpredictable heathens. They can't be trusted."

In the end Faro had won the argument, Lena agreeing to see Veronica home, and then taking the time to discuss the next best action for everyone. Now as they walked into the fields outside of Graeton, Faro wasn't sure where their argument would lead them next. What he did know was that things were definitely not right here in Graeton.

Where potato fields used to be, stood rows and rows of brown, dead, short corn stalks. Seeing the wrong crop in the field was jarring, but what was more jarring was the patrol of Shadruul who wandered through the fields, monitoring the workers who appeared to be townsfolk. Likely not workers, Faro noted, but slaves.

The party snuck their way through the fields, staying out of sight of the Shadruul, and working their way towards town where they hoped Mayor Thornvale would still have an office in the Church of Solana. Instead, they found him much sooner.

Veronica was the first to spot her grandfather. Despite his advanced age, there he was, toiling away in the cold field. Without regard to the possibility of a Shadruul patrol wandering by, she took off through the snowy field and ran straight to her grandfather, throwing her arms around him. The others hurried quickly after her. When they got to the pair, they were still embracing, and a tear was in Thornvale's eye.

"My dear granddaughter! It's been so long... I thought you were dead!" he blustered out.

"It didn't seem so long to me grandfather," she said back, absolutely sobbing. "Why are you in the fields in winter?"

Thornvale looked around to see if any Shadruul were near, and then spoke. "We are growing the crop that feeds this army of mutant rock beasts. They eat corn meal and have droves of domesticated animals in the forest that they butcher. We've been charged with spreading manure on the winter soil to enrich it for spring. It's not natural how they're growing corn in such little light."

The ex-mayor of Graeton looked at all of Veronica's companions and smiled. "And all of you, you saved her?" They nodded, and Thornvale thanked them all, even giving Mathias a grateful handshake. After he thanked them, he stepped back and inspected Veronica. "How is it you haven't aged, child? It's been three years!"

Veronica explained the time change that had happened while they were in The Veil. Thornvale's mouth was open the entire time in shock. "I don't believe it. A place where time moves slower? Fascinating."

Faro knew they had little time to talk, so he tried to change the subject to leaving. "Mayor Thornvale, we need to get you out of Graeton to somewhere safe."

Thornvale shook his head. "Nowhere is safe anymore. I hear only Underoth hasn't fallen to the new Dungeon Lords, and they are a bunch of vile monsters that live there. Nowhere. Nowhere to go. Nowhere is safe."

Lena stepped in. "We're not staying, we have other pressing business to tend to. You and Veronica need to get to somewhere safe that isn't here. You can't think of anywhere you can go?"

The old man wrinkled his brow in thought for a moment. "The jungles of Mirasor may be safe, but the kingdom itself has fallen. The jungles are vast, though, so we may find a place untouched by Shadruul there," said Thornvale.

"Good," said Tobi, who had been hanging back with Mathias, Thora, and Rork. "We're heading to Underoth. You and Veronica can join us."

Lena threw a dirty look at Faro. "No one agreed we were going that way. We still have to discuss…"

"It's the only way that makes sense right now!" Faro hissed, tempering his voice to try not to attract attention. "We have to get moving, or Rork's giant size is going to give us away, and I say that we go to Underoth. It's the safest place for Veronica and Thornvale, and we can gain allies while we are there."

The old elf stomped her foot and dug it into the snow, showing she was sticking to her position. "I'm going to help my mother. She's the only reason my sister spared us. She's the ally we need. Once we take the city, these two can stay there."

"We can't take Veronica into another war zone!" said Faro. He was losing his patience with Lena. He knew that the both of them had assumed leadership roles over the group thus far, but now they were at an impasse, and no true leader was going to win over.

There was silence until Mathias stepped forward. "It may be in everyone's best interests if we part ways."

They all turned to stare at him. "No!" yelled Thora, and then clapped her hands over her mouth to stifle the noise. "We can't," she finished in a whisper.

Lena sighed. "It may be the only way here. I have to go and save my mother. Faro wants his memories back and seems to think Underoth can help us." She looked around at every person in the group who wasn't Faro. "Who of you would go with me?"

No one spoke. They all stared at the ground awkwardly, not sure what to do. Fate had seemed to bring them together, but now it also seemed to be tearing them apart just as abruptly.

"I like saving people and fighting," said Rork, who was ducked down as low as he could go. Given that the corn stocks were brown and dead, they didn't have much height for him to hide behind. "Would like to get going soon, or we will all be found."

"Well, I'm going with Faro," piped up Tobi, taking a step towards the lion. "I can be of use with the dwarfs of Underoth. They're all a bunch of crotchety bastards like me," he finished, smiling.

Thora looked as though she was about to throw up. She looked back and forth between her father and Rork and Lena. "We can't do this!" she said again, but she knew it was to no avail. "I can't do this," she admitted.

Tobi let out a big sigh and walked over to hug his daughter. "I love you, Thora," he said to her, "but I think you need to stick with Lena. Her and Rork can use your talents, new and old."

"No," said Thora, crying.

"Yeah, sweetheart. I think it's time," said Tobi, wiping away his own tears. For some reason the words 'stick by your little girl, and you can't go wrong' ran through his mind, but he pushed them aside. "But we will meet again when it's all over. As soon as Veronica is safe and Faro finds his memories, we'll come find you in Zelira."

Slowly, Thora nodded and walked over to stand by Rork and Lena. She had been with Tobi for almost as long as she could remember. It was the first time they would be separated for longer than a few days since she was a child. She moved behind the other two and broke down hard, wailing.

All eyes now moved to Mathias who was still yet to speak. He looked from one group to the other and then nodded his head.

"I will go to Underoth," he said. "Lena is great with magic and a fine healer. These four may need my new skills in magical healing along the way. It's only fair that I go with them."

They all stood apart in their new travel groups, not sure what else to say. When no one spoke, it was Veronica who broke the silence. "Thank you all for saving me, but we should really get moving out of here. The Shadruul will catch us before long."

They all nodded and started walking away in their separate directions. Tobi glanced back at his daughter walking in the opposite direction. "I trust in that girl's abilities one-hundred percent," he said to Faro, "but I pray to Solana that I see her again."

"You will," said Faro. "I stake my life on it. I will protect you with all my being. All of you."

"Aye," said Tobi. "You truly are a good friend, Leo," said Tobi with a wink, taking him back through how far they'd come on their journey together in such a short time.

Faro nodded, looking out to the northern sky and the snow-covered plains. "We've certainly come a long way from you stabbing me," Faro jested, and Tobi chuckled at this. "Besides, it seems like each other is the only thing we have left. So much of the world has fallen already."

Snow embedded deep into his fur, Jarl made his way into the extravagant throne room that sat at the top of Mt. Fluore. The walk up the mountain had been treacherous, given the snowstorm that was going on outside, but he was happy to be away from Faro and the others who had presumably met their end from the giant army that had faced them at Umbra's Veil.

As soon as the first shot was fired at such a distance, Jarl knew they were way outmatched and had ducked down on the safe side of the wall, taking off at full sprint. Several hours later he'd found a portion of the wall that was climbable and made his escape. The proceeding journey and the climb up Mt. Fluore were nothing compared to the fate that he'd escaped.

Now, as he slowly made his way into the throne room, he saw that not much had changed in his absence. He couldn't say the same for the whole of Evania, as on his journey back he'd questioned some strangers in a tavern and learned that much of the land had fallen, and that somehow his father's kingdom of Underoth had eluded the new rule so far. This gave him hope, hearing that his father was still alive. If his dealing with Eli today went south, he still had a place to call home.

As it stood now, though, he possessed a very valuable piece of information that Eli had tasked him in finding, and he knew it would fetch a handsome price from the high ruler of Evania who had impossibly deep pockets.

Two Shadruul guards allowed him to enter the main room, and there on the opposite end sat Eli. Jarl sized him up as he walked down the long, lavish red carpet. Eli was still his huge, hulking self, complete with ram's horns and an aura of purple magic about him, but he looked somehow different from the last time Jarl had seen him. When he saw him before he still looked like a scarred boy, not sure what to do with his new rule. Now the look in his eye was hard, his eyes no longer containing the gleam they once had. A twisted smile crept to his lips, but it didn't make him look one bit friendly.

The new High King called across the room in booming echoes, "Welcome back, Jarl my servant. We all thought you were dead."

Jarl slowed his pace, no longer sure he had made the right move coming back here. He nodded and did a slight bow, throwing his arms wide in humility while keeping his slow pace. "Yes, My Lord. Apparently there was some kind of time difference within Umbra's Veil and the outside world. I have been gone less than a month from my perspective."

Eli cocked his head to the side, confused. Jarl stopped cold in his tracks as another figure appeared from behind the golden throne. Eldryn, the dark mage came around the side and leaned casually against the high back of the throne. "My father had a lot of tricks up his sleeve," he said in his low, acidy voice, "but I hear that still didn't save him in the end."

Jarl nodded, picking up a very slow pace until he made it to the foot of the stairs that led up to the throne. He knew he wasn't allowed to step on them, so he stopped. From this close, still in his bow, he looked up at Eli and saw the truly deranged look on his face. His eye was twitching as he stared down at the wolverine.

"You...have something for us, I presume?" said Eldryn. "It wouldn't be wise to show up after all this time unless you did."

Jarl didn't care for the elf's tone, but he wasn't stupid enough to say so. "Yes, My Lord. While I was inside Umbra's Veil, I slipped away from the others long enough to procure what I think is some very important information..." he patted the satchel slung around his neck, "for a price," he added, but then immediately regretted doing so.

Eldryn narrowed his eyes and clutched his magical staff hard in his grip. "How dare you, you insolent little..."

Eli raised a hand up to silence Eldryn. "Let's hear what he has to say before you go off all half-cocked again like you usually do." Jarl could sense the tension between them, but had no way to play that to his advantage here. Instead, he threw open the flap of the bag and rustled through the folds until he found the book.

He pulled it from the bag and held it up for them to see. A red leather-bound book, the pages inside yellowing and mismatched in size, as though they were all added separately to the tome. "The personal journal of King Umbra of Mireholm," said Jarl triumphantly.

Eli sat forward on the throne, his interest peaked. Even Eldryn seemed to loosen the grip on his staff and lean forward in interest. "Notes about what?" Eli asked with bated breath.

Jarl shrugged. "Many things. An entire chronicle of his research in the dark arts. How he accidentally created Umbra's Veil. His dealings with summoning his Virtrodan..."

"None of this sounds like anything we can use!" Eldryn blurted, cutting him off.

Eli turned and shot the elf a nasty look. "You talk too much," he said angrily to his adviser. Turning back to Jarl he said, "Anything else we may find interesting in there?"

Jarl smiled. "Just instructions of how to create even more vile creatures than the slow, bulky army you've created thus far, courtesy of Umbra's Virtrodan..." This seemed to catch Eli's interest. "...and the tidbit about how he could raise all of his dead followers and reanimate them to fight for him..."

"I've done that thousands of times," Eldryn scoffed.

"...after having killed them with the Scourge... *he created*," Jarl finished, his smile now even wider.

Both men on the dais stared at each other. Jarl could tell it was the piece they had been waiting for. A piece that would bring any enemy to their knees.

"Well, gentlemen," said Jarl, feeling a bit more confident now. "I can see there is interest here. Can we discuss my payment now? It was a lot of dangerous and hard work to get this information."

Eli couldn't seem to take his eyes away from the book in Jarl's hands. "Yes, payment," he said slowly. "Eldryn, can we see that this creature is well taken care of?" With a quick flick of his wrist, purple magic sprung forth and attached itself to the book in Jarl's hands. It flew through the air and into Eli's hands before Jarl could stop it.

"Oh, absolutely, Your Highness," said Eldryn, a smile curling on his lips. He pulled up his staff and aimed it at Jarl. The wolverine's eyes widened, but he didn't have a chance to turn and run before Eldryn's magic blasted out from the staff and hit him square in the chest.

After that, everything faded to black.

ENJOYED DUNGEON LORDS? LEAVE A REVIEW!

YOUR FATE DEPENDS ON IT!

Okay, maybe your **actual** fate isn't at stake... but your review **does** help keep the story alive! Reviews tell the mystical forces of the algorithm that *Dungeon Lords* is worthy of being seen by more adventurers.

Whether you **loved it, laughed at it**, or **threw the book across the room in emotional distress**, I'd love to hear your thoughts!

Just a few words can help more readers (and maybe future Dungeon Lords) discover the journey.

Review on Amazon

dungeonlords.com/the-lost-disciple/

STAY UP-TO-DATE

WITH DUNGEON LORDS

Get exclusive behind-the-scenes content, early access to future launches, and special bonuses only for subscribers! As a member, you'll unlock sneak peeks, deleted scenes, exclusive lore, and even chances to win signed books, art, and other epic rewards. Don't miss out on contests, insider news, and surprises from the world of Dungeon Lords.

dungeonlords.com/newsletter/

About the Author

J.B. Coleman is a lifelong gamer and fantasy storyteller, with a love for **RPGs, medieval worlds, and immersive lore**. He's been writing since **Junior High** and has a background in **SEO and digital marketing**. Now, as the author of *Dungeon Lords: Fate of Evania*, he's excited to take the **Dungeon Lords legacy** to the next level. He lives with his **wife and four children**, balancing **family, writing, and gaming**—always ready for the next adventure.